Peter Fanning is author of two young adult books, *Nobody's Hero* and *Hear the Blackbirds Singing,* published by Dennis Dobson. He has also written a memoir, *The Divided Self* (Greenbank Press) and a biography of *Henry Beeching, Professor*, *Poet*, *Priest* (Sacristy).

"They fleet the time carelessly as they did in the Golden World."

– As You Like It

To the actors and musicians with whom we too have spent the golden time.

Peter Fanning

NOT EXACTLY FRIENDS

AUSTIN MACAULEY PUBLISHERS™

LONDON • CAMBRIDGE • NEW YORK • SHARJAH

A CIP catalogue record for this title is available from the British Library.

ISBN 9781398460010 (Paperback)
ISBN 9781398460027 (Hardback)
ISBN 9781398460034 (ePub e-book)

www.austinmacauley.com

First Published 2022
Austin Macauley Publishers Ltd®
1 Canada Square
Canary Wharf
London
E14 5AA

With grateful thanks to Michael Morrogh and to Heather Neil for their insight and comments on early drafts; to Jane for her tolerance and understanding and the actors and musicians, who have been The Good Companions of a lifetime.

Part One
Dayroom

Chapter One

The bomb explodes in a thunderclap. An orange curtain fills the sky and hot wind blows the beech trees black. Rhododendrons burst in all their bones and bleeding sinews. Gaunt skeletons of flame lick at the wings. And everywhere is burning light and yellow leaves and falling timber.

Scarlet mouths scream silently, as wood and forest blaze. Deaf amid the tumult, I am running, running helplessly through fir cones and the crackling of branches. Gasping, breathless, hopeless, knowing nothing can be done to stop the flames that pour across a shattered, blazing frame.

Sweat streams from my face and neck, my chest beats out a fierce tattoo. My foot is caught in roots and I am tripping, tumbling down a steep, wet bank, as darkness rushes up to greet me.

Dark as pitch, I lie there rigid, panting in the silence. Shivering and damp, I gaze to where the shutters ought to be. Someone knocks, a muffled cry; a crack of light – the door stands open. Millie in a wide ballooning gown.

'Millie, is that you?'

'Yes dear. Another dream?'

'The same one, yes. I wake up when I hit the root. What time is it?'

'It's nearly four. You'd better settle down again. It won't be light for hours.'

I stare into the dark. Another hour before the planes begin and traffic starts to prowl along the leaking lamp lit street.

'Perhaps a cup of tea?'

'Millie, I'm fine. Go back to bed. I'll read a book. Go back to sleep.'

'You're sure. Then drink some water, love.'

The light goes out and footsteps creak along the corridor. The orange flame is drifting out beyond the pale ceiling, where it will hide for weeks on end – then suddenly return, along with other orange flames which rise above the gardens.

How these bonfires play upon the buried life of midnight! While bodies sleep, the mind spins out unhappy far-off memories. Turning and returning

11

thoughts of all that we have left undone. The past within the present like a grinning boomerang.

More than ever now, it seems I think about the boy. The boys. For we are all still boys, stepping through the maze of life. For some, a journey to the core, for others, just a *cul de sac,* cut off before the journey ever started.

And I, for whom each journey seemed a special new beginning, starting from the same point, till I found I was returning and returning, like a moth to burn upon a flame.

Fragments from the fire hung in charred black twigs and broken branches, as a new day filtered slowly through. Later on, they shovelled bits of mangled flesh and scattered clothing; the sole of a boot, a piece of shirt, not a lot to recognise. A disk from the collar of a mongrel dog, a piece of broken crockery, while smoke still hung in wistful patches round the theatre's edge, like morning following the Blitz. Stubs of ash and silver birch pointed angry fingers at the sky.

That clarion to rouse the dead has come the night before. I totter down the well-worn stairs. Rain has deluged through the night, pounding all the dahlias. They lie spread eagled in the yard amid the scent of late September.

Now the River's tent is broken – those are pearls that were his eyes.

Memories are all we have. They rise at night like tidal waves, half-forgotten souvenirs; drying on an empty stage, missing deadlines; acting in a play whose title is unknown. Failed auditions, stage fright and the early signs of deafness. 'Was that a cue? Was that my cue?' Cold sweat gathering below the neckline.

Travelling on the Tube last week, invisible amongst the crowds speaking foreign tongues, a bright Australian stood up and offered me his seat. Rare indeed – but foreigners will often help the elderly. And grateful though I was to be amongst the pregnant mothers, the disabled and infirm, I realise there's little time before we lumber off into the nearby darkness of the wings. Marginal, of no productive use to man or womankind. A button missing from a shirt, a fraying collar, shuffling, sans breath, a zip at half-mast – God preserve us from indignity.

Steadying my legs, to sink before the open laptop – new ache in the knees, as if they're tethered by elastic bands – I find the emails stuffed with junk. (*Must ask Millie how to 'unsubscribe'*). Now, today, a strange, familiar message strikes the inbox. Reading – and re-reading – it, I blink against the autumn light. Black words on a pale screen, portents from another world.

Outside on the patio, Millie snips the dead black dahlias, stretching down her wide round rump and straining like a Millet peasant. Autumn. Green leaves curl and smoke winds into speedwell blue. They are stacking the punts on the river like coffins, waving off departing strangers. The parks will be curtained in cinnamon and blinds drawn down for tea.

Connaught Shakespeare Festival

Dear Charles,

After a search through the archives, we have discovered that you were one of the founders of the early Festival. As you are no doubt aware, the Connaught Festival is part of the annual calendar.

We warmly invite you to join us in a Gala performance of Shakespeare's much-loved comedy 'As You Like It'. Our cast will feature well-known actors and a special guest…

I look for Millie, who is busy rattling the dustbins. Here, the morning debris lies – the butter dish, the smears of ash, rings round cheap brown coffee mugs. Millie stands to rest her back, breathing in cold autumn air.

'*As You Like It.*' Rosalind, Orlando and an exiled duke, 'fleeting the time, as they did in the Golden World'. Love and Marriage – Hymen, romance, reconciliation. Connaught – ah, the word is tolling back, funereally tolling, to the final lines of Jacques' Seven Ages of Man.

Jonny Tait played Jacques. Rather nasally, I thought; clad in black, reciting the speech like a vicar whispering last rites.

'All the World's a Stage
'And all the men and women merely players…
'First the Infant… then the Schoolboy' –
Finally, '*Last Scene of All…sans teeth, sans everything….*'

An aged man… a tattered stick, unless soul clap its hands and sing.

I do not feel like singing, as I read the email again. But the Seven Ages running through that famous monologue – each is surely present in the other. Jacques speaks of mewling Infants and the 'Pantaloon'. But surely both are one

– the infant lives within the Pantaloon. Schoolboy, Lover and the Soldier play their part, but they are one.

And if I play a different role with every year that passes, am I not deep down the very self-same Schoolboy that I was, for all the lines that Time has carved, for all the ashen hair?

Yes, and I remember what the Whining Schoolboy did – as well as what the Lover thought and what the Lover did. The thread remains. The scene may shift – the actor is the same.

'Millie!'

Through the open window, there she goes, along the path. Heartsease, rosemary and rue – Life has not been kind to you, loving, childless wife of mine.

Nowadays we sleep apart. Millie is a restless sleeper – says that I disturb her in the night.

'Millie – look, an email. From Connaught Hall. Inviting me—'

To act? Hell no! I've done with that. I'm eighty-six if I'm a day. And yet – for all the misery, for all the bleak unhappiness which Connaught and its consequences handed out like booby prizes, something of the magic still remains. Connaught was – and is, perhaps – the place I visit in my dreams.

Peacocks on the lawns with turquoise tails outspread like emperors, echoing their cries across the leafy bamboo jungle. Rhododendron petals drifted like confetti from a wedding that no guest had ever seen.

'Charles, there's crumbs across your cheek; you're looking dreary. Come outside and help me with the dahlias.'

'Millie, darling, tell me what you think of this?'

'You're far too old – '

'But just suppose I could – '

'Go back and resurrect it all? Reconcile yourself to what occurred? Go digging through the past? It only makes you wretched, love.'

'But Mill – '

'Besides, it will have changed. I gather it's a posh hotel. For weddings. They do weddings there for brides from Haslemere.'

'I don't object to weddings. After all, we married, you and I.'

Millie shakes her wise old locks. 'You've seen her – haven't you?' she asks.

'Yes – yes, I saw her.'

In my dreams.

'Which must account for this malarkey. Charles, my darling, honestly!'

14

I should explain that Millie and me, we live a sort of open marriage. Not all that unusual here, although our lives are pure as driven snow. But Millie has her passions too. Dreams of unfulfilled desire. We like each other's company; we end each other's sentences; we cook, support, empty the bins; we dine together every day. We share the gossip, pay the council tax and greet each other's friends.

Our *menage* here is comfortable. We do not grudge each other's dreams.

She shrugs and pours the dead heads from a cardboard box. 'Look, Charles.' She used to call me 'Charlie', but she pauses, gives a weary look that is not all unfriendly. 'Charles, I don't mind, honestly. It's just I know it causes grief.' Millie's eyes are kinder than her words sometimes imply.

'Sometimes it's better not to see what isn't really there.'

And yes, I see her every day – in rustling leaves or crossing fields in the level light. I catch the half-glimpse of a face that fades into a hedgerow.

Her. And him. As much as her.

'We're both too old.' She rumbles to the scullery, removes her gloves and turns the tap on full to wash her hands.

Ah yes – but I remember the azaleas and rhododendrons, scattering their petals like confetti in the night; many coloured, pink and purple, some a pale tangerine, touching all the lawns and gardens in the dew of early morning.

Millie stops and shakes her finger. 'Charlie, it was mid-July – you don't get rhododendrons blooming, let alone azaleas.'

But they did – I know they did.

'You misremember, fantasise.'

Poor Millie's mind is wandering. I know when certain flowers bloom, as they did in that hot July.

I squat on the ash-stained carpet, girdled round with photo albums. Curled press cuttings; dull, buff, scrapbooks, biscuit brown with age. Glue marks crackle through the surface; random photographs tied down with shoddy fixative. There, you see the cloche hats and the garden parties of our youth, stiffened family set pieces, framed by the wisteria. Gruffly unconvincing uncles peer into the next decade; summer frocks and parasols and tea beneath the cypress trees.

And there she is – as plain as day. Faded from exposure to the sun. Pale, enquiring cornflower eyes, the lips half parted, questioning. Isobel – young Rosalind. One single tattered photograph salvaged from the years. For there she is – that four in the morning dream in a sunburnt photograph, where seas run dry and rocks melt in the sun.

Chapter Two

It was Christopher who opened up the world of Connaught Hall, Christopher who drew the curtain, ushered in a world where hope and disappointment played a deadly game.

Christopher, her brother and the rakish son of a Brigadier; Christopher, who did not care a jot for the conventions of a buttoned public school. His scarf was an Edwardian knot, with the flash of a quiff that seemed to say 'I'll sail as close to the wind as I can'; he stood out like a beacon from stiff collared post-War men. Christopher captained the Second XV, though he could have made the First with ease, but for the effort of keeping himself in trim. Happy to lead his band of men across the Lower Common, instead of enjoying the roars of the crowd as Bloods trotted out from Top Pavilion in peacock blue and gold.

Early days at the Abbey School; a skittish new boy, struggling with rituals and unspoken rules, I wandered down the narrow High Street, after a stamp for a letter home; brief, staccato lines, whose blandness must have made the raw homesickness sharper than a gush of grief. There, before me, in the High Street, lay a curious erection, built of yellow sandstone, glowing in the light of afternoon. Hexagonal and buttressed, with an arch on either side, it seemed as if the monks, who were expelled by Thomas Cromwell, had left an exotic summer house standing alone in the market square.

Anxious not to miss roll call, I turned to hurry through.

'Hey! Watch your step! Don't break the spell!'

Two lofty men in boaters towered above me.

'Oh.'

'You're new.'

'Yes, Sir.'

'You don't 'Sir' me. I'm Mountjoy. This is Parsons. You're in Abbey House. I've seen you.'

'Well –'

'It's tough, your first few weeks. But you'll get over it.'

'Oh yes. I'm sure,' I muttered, flushed, embarrassed.

'What's your name?'

'It's Wallace.'

'Well, this is the Conduit, Wallace.' Mountjoy tapped the ribbed stone wall. 'Know what a conduit is?'

'I –'

'No, of course you don't. How could you? It's an ancient washing place, where monks came for ablutions. After the Dissolution, the townsfolk took her away and plonked her in the midst of all the mire. We've never forgiven them, you see. People say that in revenge the monks put a curse on the Conduit. No boy from the School must ever walk through it from arch to arch. Walking through brings misery to anyone who breaks the spell.'

I gazed up at these tall and worldly fellows. 'Thanks. I'll take more care.'

'OK, Wallace. Better cut along to House. It's nearly tea.'

Scurrying up Market Street, I glanced back at the pair who ducked into the Luckpenny, where sporting men were gathering for post-match toast and teacakes.

Back at the grey forbidding House, which was to be my home, I pushed the groaning side door, signed my name upon a ruled off sheet and hung a pristine boater on a hook along the corridor.

What shook me was not talk of monks or of the cursed Conduit. It was the fact that these two men spoke to me at all. For it was forcefully explained on our arrival at the school that boys from different year groups simply *never spoke* to one another.

1947. And Austerity had come to stay. Dispatched by train, with a trunk in tow and a small allowance of ration cards, I'd waved a wild white handkerchief as the train pulled out of Waterloo. Huddled in an overheated corner of the carriage, I counted stations, as the shuffling engine crawled to the West. It was unreal, like a dream. My father sent a telegram from somewhere east of Suez, full of the kind of chin-up talk he must have used to jolly crews in battle worn destroyers on those endless Russian convoys. Glimpses of this absent hero interspersed the War Years. There he was among us, in a sudden blaze of light, glittering with golden braid, briefly resting from the battle. Then, before you knew it, he was gone, leaving a whiff of Brylcreem and an empty box of RN issue cigarettes.

Few boys at the day school where I spent my early years had fathers living near to home. Anyone who did was suspect – or considered weak and frail, like Charlie Allan's old man who survived the mud of Passchendaele. Fathers were like household gods, remote and otherworldly; something to boast about at school, their deeds the stuff of lofty and dramatic tales of fiction.

Still, as the train tracked westwards, I could have done with a stout companion, one of those brave stalwarts featured in *The Hotspur* or *The Boy Scout's Magazine.* I nodded off amid the button cloth and smell of steam, waking in the desperate hope that I had missed my destination and was rolling on towards Land's End.

New Bugs were summoned back a day before the term began, to settle in before the rest arrived. We spent our first night in the echoing vault of an empty Boarding House. Shunted into 'Matron's room', confronted by a group of boys, decked out, like me, in stiff white collars bulging gently sideways, the odour of cooked dog meat was enough to daunt the strongest from the curling sandwiches that lay uneaten in the corner.

On the second floor, stood rows of iron beds, with scarlet blankets. Down below we found the Day Room. This was where we were to live.

Strange how ancient photographs present a world of grey – not black and white as in Art Deco, but in grainy tedium, as if the sky were always full of rain. Memories of happiness are bathed in light and dappled sunshine. From the start, this Day Room was a world of monochrome.

Two oak tables ran along the centre to the pale green lockers; at the other end, a rack for laying out the newspapers. Four more rows of wooden lockers also served as benches. Not a single picture hid the peeling paint of the barrack room, whilst in a corner by the window stood an odd contraption, a wooden stall, a metre high, designed for waste and rubbish. Below the stall was a small, hinged flap from which the daily waste was drawn.

I was not horrified. I had few expectations of the joys awaiting at the Abbey School. I *was* a little startled by my first acquaintance with the toilets. These contained no doors. ('To foil self-abuse and sodomy.') For a child brought up in the modesty of flapping towels on a windy beach, to shit in public view would make for several years of constipation.

Just before bed, we were ushered to meet Bill, our new Housemaster, a greying, kindly bachelor, whom I remembered visiting with Mother just a year before. He gazed at us through cloudy, bluish eyes.

Housemasters, as a rule, were chosen from the Oxbridge men, sporting types with a couple of blues, who could rattle through Homer and Cicero whilst running the Colts or the Second XI. But Wartime meant that all the dashing heroes had been whisked away. Bill, who taught P.T. had been considered past his best, but there were few alternatives and he had been in place since Alamein.

'I trust my boys to run the House effectively and efficiently,' he once assured a nervous parent. 'Rarely do I intervene.'

'Well, well, well – I'm pleased to see you all. I hope –.' He paused, distracted. 'Are you sure that all of you are here? Goodness me, is someone missing? I thought there were eight of you – and I see only seven.' He seized a list from the wooden desk. 'You'd better answer who you are.'

Bill was right. One of our number had absconded early – a small and freckled boy called Mumford, whom I'd noticed squeezed behind the door in Matron's room. Mumford had looked at his lodgings and decided that they lacked the charm. He was apprehended buying a second-class ticket to Frome. Later, I spotted him in bed, a pillow curled around his shoulder, shocked and silent and ashamed.

'Yes,' said Bill, when we had reassembled one hour later, 'Yes – well, you must do your best. Each one of you must do your best. That is all that any school requires. Do your best at work and – Once again, he paused and gazed towards the blackout curtains, where the photo of a younger, happier Bill had gathered dust. A youthful, smiling Bill was holding up a trophy.

'But I won't stand for beastliness.' His voice had reached a higher pitch. 'Let me be clear about one thing. I will not stand for beastliness.'

Mystified, we gazed at one another. After a moment's pause, Bill continued. 'Well then, do your best and let us see how things evolve.'

Pondering these pearls of wisdom, we were dispatched to the echoing dorm, to be overseen by a towering chap with a manly stubble, who told us to prepare for bed.

I lay in the cavernous dormitory, listening to the quiet chat of other nervous boys, crew mates on a journey to an undiscovered land. An owl flew by. From time to time, the Abbey clock rang out the hour, ten…eleven… Not long before midnight, silence fell.

At eight o'clock, we took a silent breakfast in the panelled Hall, stacked with gleaming cups and Honours Boards. Steaming tea and stodgy porridge were the order of the day. Then the Head of House appeared.

Tall and slightly balding, he addressed us from a wooden throne, decked out in a stylish suit, whose front revealed a crimson waistcoat and the blue and golden tie worn by all the Prefects.

"Last night was your first and very last night without discipline. This is the Abbey House. We have a proud tradition here. Some of you may think our ways old fashioned or Victorian. Some may not like what they find. But let me warn you: anyone who takes a stand, steps out of line or thinks himself above his station will not last here very long. Do your duty. Show respect and keep your head down. Then you will survive.'

Sharp, surreal images of early days at school float across my dreams from time to time. The sudden shrill alarm, as you sit upright in the dark. The fire alarm? A crack of light and stumbling lines of bodies trample through the draughty dormitory. Down the iron bannisters and cold stone stairs towards the shower rooms we march, somnambulant as cattle. Smack and shock of icy water, as you plunge into the trough; gasping, scrambling out to miss the next pink wave of flesh that comes a-crashing through the spray.

Dressing in the icy dark, you fumble for a collar stud that spins across the wooden floor; fiddling the stiff, unbending starch that will not stay; pinching it against the chin; flapping ties through curious odd knots like ugly boluses.

There was ritual 'Calling', whereby miscreants woke sleeping prefects, having dressed; then in pyjamas and a third time fully clothed. Some offenders did the business dressed in uniform, complete with shining brass and polished boots.

New Bugs were the lowest of the low. Two weeks 'grace' was given for the fresh intake to settle down, during which the last term's fags were working through their final days. Like prisoners on the verge of their parole, the old hands eyed the anxious newcomers with scorn and muttered 'Your turn next, old chap – it won't be long.'

I knew about fagging – it was slavery of sorts, the '*doulos*', called to serve the Bloods and Prefects of the House. Not that it was all unpleasant. Who would not be willing, after all, to serve those lofty souls who lounged at the Top Table, swilling tea and swapping tales of sporting glory?

A bell would ring – a cloud of fags would hurtle to the study, where Abrahams, the Head of House and Hopkinson, the Deputy sprawled on mothy sofas. Last to arrive was given the task. 'Cut along to School House. Find Le Mesurier and tell him that he's playing wing for the Seconds tomorrow.'

'Right-oh, Hopkinson. Is any answer needed?'

'Just say 'Don't forget.''

The emissary sped off, laden with the message from Olympus.

Far more chilling, after those two weeks, was Day Room duty. This entailed a day of sweeping, cleaning tables, dusting every nook and cranny of that barren hall. More than a question of simply removing yesterday's grimy residue, the whole room had to sparkle, if a soulless underworld could ever sparkle in the sun.

Known as The Boxing Party, Day Room monitors would carry out inspections, running fingers round the cracks of cupboard doors, stooping low at long oak tables to discover any patch of dust. Failure to complete the work could lead to further impositions on the next day – and the next.

Not that there was time to spare before the two weeks' grace was done. There was a dreaded 'Colours Test'. Every boy must know the Colours worn by every House, names of every beak, the whereabouts of playing fields, the casual slang of the Abbey School ('What is the Upper? Where is the To-ey?' 'Who is Abe?' 'Who is the John?') Above all, there were rules of dress – who might sport a brolly, wear a cap adorned with golden tassels, walk with coat buttons undone or put his hands in his trouser pocket? Each step was a privilege permitted to the few.

Then there were the Locker Pegs – a special saga of their own. Every locker in the Day Room had been fitted with a peg. Shaped in a 'Y', this neatly carved and sanded twig slipped through the latch and held the locker shut. Locker pegs were a work of art. The wood must be a perfect Y, straight without a knot or scar, sloping and symmetrical as a medieval crucifix.

Days and hours of afternoons, we scanned the Slopes above the Abbey for a branch or twig to render up that perfect peg. How many broken Boy Scout knives were blunted in our desperation! Then, after the hours of labour, thoughtless fingers seized the product, bruised with sandpaper and slicing, held it to the light – 'No – that is not symmetrical. That will not do at all' – and crushed the fragile offering with a sharp, quick snap, like a broken bone.

The Colours Test had come and gone and most of us scraped through – even though we had no clue how many pubs there were in Town, still less the name of the Labrador owned by the Headmaster. But we were fledged and recognised as members of the School, no longer allowed the 'New Boy's Privilege' of a tie below the stud. We had been admitted to the cult, with all its rituals. We stood at the foot of a ladder that might lead us to the stars.

There were many hidden dangers lurking on our path. The Boxing Party ruled the world and as with every petty ruler, statutes, rulings and decrees were handed down with no appeal. Even to address these fellows, twelve months older than ourselves, boys stood rigid to attention, prefacing each sentence with a prayer.

'Please, Wilson, please may I fetch my books?'

'Please Harvey, please – will you inspect the Day Room?'

The rituals of old Versailles could teach these Sons of Empire nothing new. Sunday mornings witnessed state occasions when the threat of execution gave a frisson to the whole affair.

A fellow called Trelawney had arrived two terms before. He wore a friendly smile that spread as wide as any Harvest Moon, together with a streak of sandy hair. Trelawney often grinned, as if enjoying some obscure joke; he whistled in the changing rooms or when he cleaned his rugby boots. But then one fatal Friday, there was rather less to laugh about.

A member of the Boxing team, a fair-haired, acned boy called Deal, was busy inspecting the work of the Day Room fag. Trelawney whittled wood. Shavings lay around the floor.

'Clear that up,' said Deal.

Trelawney whistled on, quite unaware.

Deal, who was known as 'Squeal', turned deep red. 'Right, clear that up.'

Trelawney grinned. 'Of course, old man. Everything in good time.'

Blushing to the roots, Deal froze and in a voice that shot through several octaves screamed '*At once*! Do you hear?'

Silence fell. In frozen time, boys who reached for books in lockers, boys who read the paper paused to watch the drama run its course. Trelawney grinned, then slowly, slowly stretched a paw and like a poker player pulling in his winnings, gathered up the wooden fragments, gazing at the overseer with a beatific smile.

Prep began. And life passed on. The clock ticked on to Sunday.

Sunday always raised the soul – an extra hour in bed before fresh hot rolls were served for breakfast. But by Sunday 'Hall' – a silent hour of letter writing – anti-climax followed, like the rain after a golden dawn. The Boxing Party held their weekly meeting in The Reading Room. This was followed by a stern address. A senior fourth former had been left in charge to keep good order. Pens scratched listlessly; on frosted panes, a bluebottle was buzzing.

Then with a rush of feet, the Boxing Party made their rounds. We stood to lift the lid of lockers. while behind us tramped the Boxing troupe, eyeing each for tidiness or, in some cases, contraband. Next came all the book lockers, where pegs had been removed. Doors slammed to, like nutcrackers; defaulters were instructed to report directly after Hall. And then, as they reached the end of the line, the trio turned in unison, strode towards Trelawney, where they seized him by the shoulders and frog marched him towards the wooden box.

Shaken and surprised, the boy attempted to resist. In vain. He was upended, pitched headfirst into a mass of paper, string and bits of cardboard, empty bottles, broken laces. Muffled, gagging sounds emerged, as two boys jumped up on the bench and placed their feet on top of him, forcing him right down. There came a scrabbling sound; the flap below the box was quivering.

'Get down – you filthy tick!' yelled Harvey, Head of Day Room. 'Grovel out, you scum. Come on, let's see you grovel.'

No-one moved. We gazed in shock. The trio howled like wolves.

'Sort the bastard – let him crawl.'

'He's coming out – he's coming now.'

A hand appeared, an arm poked through the wooden flap below; another hand and then a head, or what seemed like Trelawney's scalp, all painted red, with one great smear that bruised the left-hand cheek. His hair was matted and, as it emerged, we saw his coat was torn; the rents upon his trousers showed a whitened knee. A shoe was missing.

Suddenly, the shouting stopped. Up on the box, the Party towered. Trelawney lay quite still. The blood was coursing from his temple.

'Get up, now,' yelled Harvey. 'Go and clean up. And remember – that's what comes of bolshy ticks. Anybody else require a lesson while we're here?

'Good. Well, just bear that in mind. Right, Trelawney. On your feet.'

The shambling figure struggled to the door, a scarlet handkerchief clasped tightly to his cheek. We heard a choking sound, a whimper and a groan.

Stunned and silent, we were herded off towards the Chapel, a barrel vaulted, stain glass barn above the Undercroft, where monks had stored their wine in former times. Chapel was a sanctuary. No prefect there could hand a pair of muddy boots for polishing; no leering Boxing Party could disturb your peace of mind. Like all prescribed activity, Chapel was compulsory. It brought a sense of unity, from smallest conscript to the top. And whether or not you believed in God, well-worn hymns were bellowed to the rafters in a battle cry.

My voice had yet to break and I had lately joined the Choir, though music and musicianship were not a thing to boast about. My quiver would need sharper arrows, if I were to count for more than just another odd, eccentric scum. There was a military air to almost every hymn we sang. For lads brought up in the heat of war, '*Fight the Good Fight*' and '*Onward Christian Soldiers*' were staple fare. '*The strife is o'er, the Battle won*,' we thundered, baying lustily of '*toil and tribulation/ And tumult of the war…*'

We reached the final verse which ran '*yet saints their watch are keeping*', when my eye was caught by a painted angel, perched on a beam from the barrel vault.

Where was Trelawney's guardian angel when he was upended? I mouthed the last two cheerful lines. No-one wept at public school. When they boxed you, then you bled and when they kicked, then you whimpered.

As I turned away, I noticed someone watching from the serried ranks of congregation.

Mountjoy. It was Mountjoy – the enormous chap I'd met in Town.

Blushing at such close attention from a senior boy, I looked back at the painted angel in the barrel roof. Clad in blue with golden wings, it leant across the nave and in its mouth, a tiny trumpet.

Something in the jaunty angel's poise held my gaze. Then I saw it, sharp and clear. That was no trumpet. In his lips, the angel held a cigarette. The glittering blue angel smoked.

Mountjoy nodded, raised his chin and slowly winked at me.

Chapter Three

About suffering, the Old Masters were never wrong – so Auden tells us, as we turn away. Life continues, even as a boy falls from the sky. The sun shines, children play and horses scratch their bottoms on a tree.

Our young lives, Millie, did not feature flowers flung by wailing crowds across the cortege of a dead princess. Outpourings of grief were not in keeping in a world of refugees who trailed the dusty roads of Europe; a shattered world of bombsites, ragged children playing in the ruins. Nobody had any time for tears.

Tears are all the fashion now. They are in demand today. 'How do you feel?' importunate reporters ask a victim. There was no time to sit and wail. Life must carry on.

Back in 1941, we huddled in our garden shelter. Bombs were raining down on Portsmouth Harbour. Peeping out from time to time, we'd catch a hail of fireworks, the orange glow of the brewery, a minesweeper ablaze. Others down in Southsea lost their homes, a whole street carved in two; massive craters near the old Cathedral and the Hilsea Gas Works blown to smithereens.

The city furnace lit the Isle of Wight; the Solent glowed till dawn. Firemen on the roofs of shops along Commercial Road watched a licking tidal wave of flame. Listening in the dark womb of the shelter to the crash of thunder, I was more afraid than I can say. But as grey dawn leaked across the January skyline, we emerged from hibernation, crossed the patch of lawn and back into the lightless kitchen. Plates from last night's supper lay unwashed upon the tablecloth. Mother drew the blackout curtains, riddled ash from an ancient stove and blew fragments of the coke into a shallow flame. We dusted down and waited for the world to start again.

It wasn't just the Pathe News or patriotic films. Coward's part '*In Which We Serve*' caught the clipped and buttoned tones of people trained to keep the panic down. Life in all its tragedy meant there was little time to mourn. And if they danced in palace fountains at the news of Victory, there was suffering to follow; hunger and, for some, starvation and the bitter cold.

A bullied boy in a boarding school was scarcely worth a thought, besides the few who watched and wondered who was next in line.

Life was a race of obstacles, often high as Beechers Brook. Naturally, there would be fallers. Let us hope it won't be you. Happiness? No-one expected happiness, not yet. As for those who missed their footing, well, there would be broken ribs.

After the Boxing Party show, the daily round began again. Hours passed, with lessons, rugby, routine bouts of fagging. Summoned during tea to 'Fetch my jam from the kitchen cupboard,' I was not unwilling, though at times a mite forgetful.

One or two good friends appeared; quiet, thoughtful characters, who watched the daily ritual through careful, hooded eyes. It seemed for a while that a truce was signed. The Boxing Party kept their peace after that awful Sunday.

Lessons passed amid a haze of dusty pre-War books. Latin, Greek and Maths were taught by aged masters, armed with sticks, limping through the Courtyards, clad in battered gowns and tweedy suits.

Our form master, a Mr Vaughan, lived in a kind of mausoleum crammed with pottery and photographs of ancient ruins. Rough benches in the classroom bore the names of former residents, carved into the antique wood, as convicts carve memorials of their captivity.

The days were not all grim and grey. One grows accustomed to a life, however bleak it may appear – and boys are natural optimists. Sometimes, we sat at ink-stained desks inscribed with all those chiselled names of pupils fallen at the Somme or Balaclava, whilst a young, enthusiastic beak, relieved from active service, read to us. He gave us Fagin's last dark panic-stricken night from Dickens or some rural chunks of Hardy.

Mr Melvin was the only youngish teacher visible. His pale straw hair was thinning out; he would be bald in ten years' time. His blue eyes flickered as he read about Bathsheba Everdene. We sat transfixed to hear the tales of wooing, separating, parting and uniting once again.

'Mel' was a defiant actor, giving each dramatic page his all. It was, in retrospect, a little overdone. In Warren's Malthouse, Mel slipped into broadest Dorset dialect, where rough farm hands, like Jacob Smallberry and Coggan came alive. Mel was like no other teacher I had met, a real thesp.

But there was something melancholy in him, all the same. Locked away in a country town, far from female company, we watched him tidy books away, hunched across the dais and noticed that his life was passing by. Soon he would be tweedy, middle aged, like all the rest of them.

Only on the rugby field was there space and freedom, space to run and breathe the clear, uncluttered country air. I was a scrawny wing three quarter and a fearsome tackler. Most of my contemporaries were tougher and more skillful. A clever lad called Hayes, who'd won an Open Scholarship, boasted of his prowess on the field. Alas, poor Hayes was tackled in the opening minutes of a game. I, by chance, was marking him and as the ball flew from the scrum, I pitched into him, caught his leg and heard it crack like a walnut shell. He spent the rest of term head bowed and hobbling between class and House.

'Rotten luck,' we muttered, as we took our turn to bring his books. Hayes was left to face his lot alone. A boy falls from the sky, the ship of state sails calmly on.

All the same, a shadow hovered. After the Sunday massacre, we waited for another thrashing from the Boxing Party. Misdemeanors, mud upon your shoe or careless cleaning meant an extra chore, together with a point against your name. Eight whole points and you were summoned after bedtime to the shower room, where the Head of House awaited with a supple cane.

No-one looked for trouble. Trouble seemed to follow me. Like a careless driver who has failed to see the baker's van, I was foolish and imprudent, ever prone to rushing in.

Bill had introduced a female presence to the House in the shape of Charity, his sister. Housekeeping was never meant to be a bed of roses. Charity may well have wondered. how it was that fate had thrown her to a life of cleaners, cooks and crowded laundry lists.

School food in Austerity was sometimes barely edible. Lumpy porridge, semolina, burnt rice pudding, boiled cabbage – expectations were not high and they were rarely met. Red letter days might feature tinned sardines or even spam. But there was a nasty interlude when a curious fish called snoek was served. Oily as an eel, it could be only downed with mugs of tea.

Sister Charity was named after St Paul's sermon that *the greatest gift is Charity'* – words that met with furtive sniggers when declaimed in Chapel. Still, apart from Matron, Charity remained the only woman in the House. Clad in brownish tweed, she rarely ventured past the door that linked our world to hers. Except at lunch.

Conversation was a challenge. What had we to offer to this pale lady, serving stew? Every day, we moved a place or two around the table and so, one Friday lunchtime, I was placed next door to Charity, charged with desperate commands for 'just a tiny helping please'.

All around, the roar of lunch time gossip ebbed and flowed. Lost for words, I turned towards my neighbour.

'What do I talk about?'

A friendly, bovine chap, he whispered 'Ask her if she knows why women don't go bald.'

I spouted automatically, 'Miss Tucker, why aren't women bald?'

And suddenly, it seemed as if a hush descended on the hall. Faces turned in my direction. Charity flushed, one hand suspended on a cooling dish of stew. The ladle sank into the gravy. Heads craned from a nearby table. Flanked by senior prefects, Bill had raised his head, a patch of sunlight silvering his dome. Time hung in a heartbeat. Like a photograph, the scene was seared deep into the memory.

And then the whole kaleidoscope of lunchtime bustle filled the void. Small boys cleared the plates, another stretched towards a water jug. China clattered to the hum of fifty different dinners.

Charity replaced the ladle. One small knot of meat and gravy stained the whiteness of her plate.

'Well – ' she smiled ironically. Our eyes met for a second. Then she paused and turned away.

'Hm – you've done it now,' my neighbour muttered through the mashed potato. 'Don't you know that Charity wears a wig?'

Crimson faced, I bowed my head, a new boy in this world of men, knowing that I was a cad; no gentleman, a thoughtless cad, who made fun of the sister of our boss.

Now, we were reciting Latin Grace. I bowed in shock and shame. The rumble of dull bodies bore me out. I headed for the yard.

'Wallace!'

'Yes?'

I turned around. Wilson stood behind me.

Wilson was Deputy Head of the Dayroom, senior to Squeal. A large boy with a button face, high cheeks and narrowed eyebrows.

'Come here, Wallace.'

Wilson loomed a good three inches over me. He pressed his nose into my face and growled 'What's the idea?'

'What do you mean?'

'I think you know. What's your game, eh Wallace?'

'I don't know what you mean, please Wilson.'

'Don't be a fool, you little tic. We heard you. What's the game?

'There isn't a game.'

It's after lunch. It's time to change – it's Junior Leagues. Boys are throwing tennis balls around the yard. In the road outside, a motor bike roars by and I am locked in time and space before a towering teenager, a single year my senior, who holds me in an iron grip.

'You're just a tic, a bolshy tic. What do you think you're playing at?' Grey eyes bore through my skull. 'You're going to pay for this, you know. You're going to wish you never joined.'

Then from nowhere, comes an arm that sweeps and knocks my ear. I shy away. I'm scared of course. But somehow, I can't run.

'Don't do that.'

'Do what?'

'You hit me.'

'No, I haven't hit you – yet.'

Another movement – it's a feint. The arm moves up, another flicker. Every time I shrink from an impending blow, I quiver – flick. The bare hand swishes at my ear. I feel the wind.

'Don't do that, please.'

'Why not, you tic? It could be worse. There's worse to come for tics like you. You wait till Sunday. Wait until the Boxing Party meets.' Flick. 'There isn't room for tics. We'll sort you out and then we'll send you down to Abrahams. Want to know what it feels like to be boxed on a Sunday morning?'

'Wilson, what are you playing at?'

A voice I recognise. 'Pick on someone your own size.'

A streak of red has flushed across the sallow cheeks of my assailant.

'I'm teaching this young tic a lesson, Mountjoy.'

'Scare the shit out of him?'

'Mountjoy – '

'Leave the lad alone.'

Slowly, very slowly, Wilson turns and faces Mountjoy.

Mountjoy is a good six inches taller, like a battleship above the little frigates. 'Just be careful, Wilson. You won't be in Dayroom that much longer. Nobody would want to hurt you once you're up amongst the studies.'

This time it was Mountjoy's turn to lean close up. He paused. 'A reputation as a bully? Something might go wrong for you. Leave the boy alone or you will wish we hadn't met.'

Mountjoy turned and sauntered back across the tarmac of the yard. Wilson watched him go, he glared and muttered something horrible; then disappeared into the junior lats.

Stunned and grateful, wary of another brusque encounter, I wandered back towards the changing rooms. Lacing boots with shaky fingers in a corner of the Boot Room, I was startled by another shadow.

'Wallace. You OK?'

I nodded, trying not to shudder. 'Take it easy. They'll back off.'

Mountjoy grinned. 'They know the limits, Harvey and his crew; know we'll keep an eye on them. Things have not been good of late. They're beginning to think they rule the roost. But I'm willing to bet you don't have too much trouble from them now. Besides – ' he grinned. 'She doesn't.'

'What?'

'She doesn't wear a wig. And anyway, she didn't hear you.'

With a thump of polished boots, Mountjoy disappeared.

Chapter Four

Trelawney came from Hospital with ugly stitches on his cheek. The Boxing Party left me on my own.

But news had spread of Mountjoy's intervention in the Yard. Was I Mountjoy's lush? – a phrase that ended with a sneer.

Mountjoy showed no interest in a world of petty rules. He sauntered into breakfast, prayers or lessons in a carefree way, as if he might be dropping in for tea with friends from home. Walking back from games, I dawdled past the Seconds' training ground, hoping for a glimpse of magic, as the fly-half looped the loop or dummied 'Scissors' like a conjuror.

In the squash courts or the Chapel, underneath the watching angel, I was constantly aware of my own Raphael. Weeks went by. We rarely spoke. I never thanked him for his help. All the same, there was a bond between us, mutual respect, as brother looks to brother.

I practised how to wear my tie in an enormous Windsor knot, how to wrap a scarf around the neck and leave it trailing; how to flick a casual forelock, as you track across the Courtyard, never seeming ill at ease or hurrying for Chapel. Merriman, a Dayroom chum, called me 'Mini-Mountjoy'.

In the world at large, an Iron Curtain had descended. War had ended, but another war was on the cards. To counter which, on Monday afternoons, we must parade in combat kit to drill and march, to be inspected, square bashed, bellowed at. In gleaming belts and blanco-ed spats and spit and polished boots, we trudged around the gravel to the shrieks of NCOs.

The banshee scream of adolescents ricocheted around the walls. Teenagers who missed the war were given scope to browbeat. Old Lee Enfields from the First World War had been re-issued, ready to be cleaned and oiled in case the Russians started to invade. On Field Days, we marched up on the Slopes above the town, attacked the ridge and took a verbal lashing from the RSM, who criticised our sloppy camouflage and feeble planning.

A bigwig from the Fighting Fleet had been engaged to spend a day inspecting our platoons. The beaks, transformed from gown to uniform and now our proud commanders, ordered ever more parades, more brasses scrubbed and buttons sewed. Barber's shops throughout the town were crowded out by eager youth instructed to demand 'the shortest back and sides' the world had ever seen.

The officer in charge, a pale, dyspeptic chap, whose weeping eye and bristled cheekbones were a constant source of mockery, took the names of anyone with parents serving in the Royal Navy. After the inspection, we would stand in rigid lines, to greet this giant of the seas.

Time and again, we turned and turned across the windy Courtyard, numbered off ('Eyes left – two, three four – eye-es front'), stood grimly to attention as lance corporals flicked the angles of our caps and sniffed the Brasso on our belts or told us to stand tall.

Come the day of the Admiral's visit, we were summoned early on parade.

Never the best at storing clothes or papers tidily, I made sure my kit was neat and ready. After meagre lunch, we poured into the changing rooms. The prospect of parading before one of Britain's fighting beasts lent a whiff of genuine excitement to the day. This was our First Night, a chance to show what we were made of. We strapped our spats and buckled belts, inspected one another's battle dress for hairs and specs of dirt.

'Right, lads,' our sergeant bellowed 'Time to move. Caps on.'

I looked around. My cap had disappeared.

I'd seen it on the wooden locker, just above the pegs. I glanced at my fellow cadets. Each wore a khaki beret, right side down.

'Anyone seen my cap?'

'Try under the locker.'

'Look on the floor.'

'Come on men, let's go.'

A rumble of boots on the tiled floor. And the changing room was bare – except for a single young cadet scrabbling under the lockers.

Somebody had pinched my cap. It wasn't hard to do. You just reach up when no-one's looking, help yourself and slip it back when the parade is over.

To show up on parade without a cap was a hanging offence. To miss the parade was unthinkable. I clambered along the benches wiping hands from shelf to shelf. Nothing but an unwashed sock, a broken lace and a grubby jock strap. Seconds ticked away and I was seized with real panic. Once, I had seen a blackbird caught in a ragged raspberry net. It threw itself in desperation onto prison walls. I was now that blackbird, throwing myself at the dusty floor, at empty pegs, as if by magic I might conjure up that stolen cap. Fate had played a joker. I was lost beyond recall.

I punched the wooden panel, sobbed in anger. Bloody cuts appeared along my knuckles and my fingers were aflame, when, looking down, I saw a pair of polished leather shoes.

'What's up, Wallace? Lost something?'

'I've lost my cap.'

'You mean that someone borrowed it, more like. Better shift or you'll be late.'

'I can't – I can't go out without – '

'Your cap. Of course. I'll sort you out. Use mine.'

I gasped – 'But – '

'Worry not. I'm not parading. Sprained an ankle. Look.' he waved a crumpled scrap of paper. 'Note from Matron.'

'You're missing the parade?'

'Indeed. Now quick or you'll be late.' Racing round the other side to where the Seniors changed, Mountjoy grabbed his army beret, hurtled back and placed it on my head.

'It fits you well enough. Now cut along or there'll be hell to pay.'

The next two hours, the whole triumphant bally-hoo, passed in a dream. We hit the well-known drill manoeuvres like a *corps de ballet*, stamping, lining, shouldering arms, all in perfect synchrony, marching to the hybrid strains of *'Hearts of Oak'* and *'Colonel Bogey'*, as the squat moustachioed band master waved his silver stick.

On the steps of Big School, stood the braided Admiral ('Eyes left!), bushy eyebrows glowering. A wave of pure elation made it feel as if we trod the air, lifted from the jaws of death to partake in this cavalcade.

We stood at ease to hear his gruff words echo round the Courtyard. A gentle spray of falling rain sparkled on the braid.

'Soldiers and cadets, Headmaster – Greetings from the Front. We live in exciting times. Dangerous times and hopeful times. Right across the British

Empire, members of His Majesty's armed forces are deployed to keep the peace, after a war of which the world has never seen the like.

'Today in India, there is still fighting in Kashmir. Many lives have now been lost. As for Europe, communist expansion from the Soviet Republics threatens the very peace for which we have all fought. And so, the price of liberty remains eternal vigilance. Let that be your watchword, a symbol of your resolution to defend our freedom. Other Empires rise and fall, but with your help Great Britain will be free.

'This afternoon's parade was quite the finest I have seen in any Public School. My thanks to everyone involved and good luck for the future.'

I watched the craggy legend make his way along the line, springing to attention 'Sir, my father is Commander Wallace – HMS Scorpion, '43.'

'Sinking of the Scharnhorst, eh? Do convey my compliments when you next write to him.'

And he was gone. The moment passed. The limousine rolled slowly off and through the golden archway, leaving a whiff of magic dust before we settled back to *terra firma*.

Looking back upon the thrills and spills of any childhood, how these small events still loom as large as bogeymen. Empires rose and fell and the survival of the very planet seemed to be at stake and yet my insignificance could not affect the strong impression that I'd had a magical escape. The saga of the lost cap had significance for me alone. The earth continued on her path. No seismic monitor would trace the path from grief to soaring joy. But young life must be lived right in the raw through every incident and, like a dress rehearsal, look to joys and tragedies to come.

I had grown up with heroes. Hector of the gleaming helm, brave Achilles and his Myrmidons. Drake and Raleigh, Wellington and Woolf. What remains to take their place, but hollow men with feet of clay? But, Millie, we believed in them, our ghostly forebears of the past. Life was hazardous enough and vigilance remained the watchword. Notices were fixed to battered boards throughout the school, echoing the Admiral's rousing words that in a small West Country town, the realm remained secure.

Showering after games, one afternoon in late November, adult voices filtered through the stalls of a steamy changing room.

'What about that waitress in the Luckpenny on Saturday? You could have had her for the afternoon.'

'I was late. Bill called me in. Wanted another little chat.'

'What did he say?'

'He asked me if I wank.'

'And you said –'

'Yes, of course. And then he said, 'How often?''

'And you told him?'

Loud guffaws.

'I said, I wasn't sure. But maybe ten or more a week.'

'Good lord!'

'That's what *he* said! 'Good Lord! That's nearly twice a day!'

'You horny bastard, Mountjoy.'

Howls of laughter shook the wooden panels.

I had some idea what 'wanking' meant. But I was still a novice, ignorant of sex, despite a chat from the Headmaster on my final night at prep school. He said if I touched my private parts I would 'produce the seed'.

But with an absent father out at sea, I asked the boy next door if he knew any more than I did about matters of the flesh. A well brought up, clean living scout, I watched him blush and turn away and change the subject back to cricket scores.

Whispers after lights out in the dormitory at prep school had told me something of the plumbing parts of procreation. Much of it seemed laughable and frankly most unlikely.

But something dark and lingering still hung about those words, the careless talk of grown-up men towelling in the shower room. I dried myself and left the room, musing on the fellows who knew all about the world.

The final weeks of term sprang in a welter of exams. Trunks appeared from nowhere and a distant light began to glow at the end of a seemingly endless tunnel. Choirs sang *Ding, Dong Merrily* and descants soared with *Hark, The Herald*. Sprigs of mistletoe and holly decked the narrow High Street. Misty dawns and early evenings spoke of 'coming to an end. Only the drab Day Room was unchanged. No hint of paper chains, no silvered ivy daubed the barrack walls. Life continued on its way from shrieking bell to lights out.

Amid this activity, I lost the scope for vigilance. The rash belief that Fate was on my side meant that I dropped my guard. So, as the days went by, I racked up several Day Room points. A book left on the table or a locker filled with sweet papers; each point meant another chore. One fateful afternoon, I was approached by Harvey in the Dayroom.

'Wallace, you were substitute for Day Room duty. On the list. The fag on duty's in the San and look, the place is filthy.'

'Sorry. Didn't see my name.'

'The list was up by breakfast.'

'Oh – '

'You didn't look. You'd better clean the place out now.'

'But Harvey – '

'Don't you 'Harvey' me.'

'Please, Harvey. I must go to choir.'

'Well, suit yourself – two Day Room points. And do the dusting after prayers.

At Choir, *The Holly and the Ivy* seemed a mournful elegy. Those two points would take the tally up to seven; one point more and there'd be an appointment in the Shower Room in thin pyjamas. Silently, I begged the pale blue angel for assistance. With five days to go, it should easy keeping out of trouble.

Next day, on the noticeboard, my name was on the dreaded list.

'Please, Harvey, I've been told to see you.'

Harvey was revising Latin verbs; a dog-eared primer opened at the fourth declension.

Silence. Then he closed the book and handed it to me.

'Yours, I think.'

'Oh, is it? Thank-you.'

'Left out on the windowsill.' A pause. My heart had stopped. 'You know what that means.'

Dry throated, I nodded 'Yes.'

So, to the execution, which took place with all due ceremony. Hushed words in the dormitory, though it was the end of term, the atmosphere expectant and subdued. One or two friends whispered 'Bad luck', but like Icarus, I fell alone. A minute before lights out, Hopkinson appeared and beckoned to me. Clad in camel hair and slippers, trekking like a traitor to the Tower, I reached the white tiled shower room, where four giant Bloods in scarlet waistcoats waited like so many Yeomen.

The ritual solemnity is what I most recall, bending low, before the switch. It hurt of course. That was the point, in retribution for what had been done and left undone. Each stroke was like a cut, a savage slice, a cutting down to size – as if some magic powder had been ministered for shrinking me. The prisoner must be violated in accordance with the law.

Mumbling a hurried 'Thanks' to Abrahams, I climbed back along the staircase, hoping nobody would spot the tears in my eyes. But as I reached the first floor, a familiar voice was whispering.

'Chin up, Wallace. Welcome to the Club.'

Chapter Five

Summer 1949.

Mountjoy put his head around the flaking Day Room door.

'Got much on, this afternoon? Want to help us out?'

'What for?'

'Commemoration Play, you know. Should be very jolly. There's a part for me. They're looking for a footman. Will you do it?'

'Footman?'

'Yes – you don't say much. In fact, you don't say anything. Still, you get a ripping costume. Gorgeous says it's quite the best.'

Mountjoy had been cast as Algernon in Oscar Wilde's play *The Importance of Being Earnest*. He would be the laddish rake, a part which one suspected Wilde had based upon himself.

Thursday afternoon and we are on the Big School stage, sunshine beating on the Courtyard. From a distance comes the sound of willow bat on leather.

One hand on a doorknob, Lady Bracknell speaks to Mr Worthing.

'What is it to do with me? You can hardly imagine that I and Lord Bracknell would dream of allowing our daughter to marry into a cloakroom and form an alliance with a parcel?'

After which, she sweeps into the wings.

'One moment – please. False exit, Tait. You reach the door; try turning – wait a beat before the final word. And that should get a round.'

Perched on hard metallic seats, we gaze in awe at elegance and wit from another world. A world where people live for pleasure of a superficial hue, a world where social norms are turned completely upside down – where nothing can be everything, where truth is rarely pure and never simple.

Scene by scene, I gather up the threads of Wilde's play; a tale about a man who changes names from town to countryside. At home, his name is Jack but when in London, he is Earnest. And nobody suspects a double life. He *thinks* his real name is Jack and Earnest is a lie. But then a twist of fate reveals that he is truly Earnest. He thinks that he's been lying, but discovers he's been telling truths – and what he thought was true was just a lie.

Play performances had been suspended in the War. Now, at the end of my second year, this bold revival promises a glimpse of things to come.

'Gorgeous George' – his real name was 'Mr Gallier' – was a fleshy Scot from Morningside; passionate, grey haired and to our eyes the last word in flamboyance. George wore green carnations in his buttonhole throughout the summer, sent from London on the morning train.

Two fourth formers of my age had been cast as *ingenues*, the catty, knowing Gwendoline and then the artless Celia. Another boy, whose voice had not yet broken played the Governess, Miss Prism, whilst a sixth former, whom I had never met before, took the role of Lady Bracknell.

Boys acting girls was nothing new. There were no girls to play them. Jonny Tait, who played the Lady, did not count among the Bloods. He spoke with a curious dreamy lisp that later would be known as 'camp'. As Lady Bracknell, he delivered lines in a languid drawl. Despite the regulation collar, tie and highly polished shoes, Tait possessed the posture and the diction of my grandmother, a relic from an age of bustles, jewelled necklaces and corsets.

During one of the endless gaps between liver and semolina, I let slip to Bill that I was part of George's acting troupe. His face grew dark and after lunch, he called me in for a dressing down.

'I don't approve of this at all. Acting, Wallace? Showing off. You've better ways to spend your time.'

'But I'm not doing much, sir. I just stand there with a silver tray.'

'That's bad enough. You're dressing up. Besides, if I know anything, this means fellows dressed as girls. I call that very dangerous.'

'But sir, it's just a play for parents.'

'Don't you understand? A boy dressed up in flummery could look, I don't know – dangerous.'

I did not fully understand. But I knew from the way he filled his pipe with strands of Old Gold and the papers round his desk that Bill was more upset than me.

'Sir, I've told my parents. And my mother said it's fine. Besides, it's not just me, Sir. Mountjoy's also in the play.'

Bill blinked and sat back on the captain's chair.

'Mountjoy?' He scratched at the box of matches. 'Mountjoy. That makes matters worse. I rarely speak with boys about their friends.'

In fact, Bill rarely spoke to me at all. This was a first. No praise or blame had passed his lips about my progress through the school. Progress there had been of course, just as a neglected tree continues to put forth its leaves, so I had grown and learnt a little of the ways of men. But the Olympian masters, who instructed us, had kept their distance. Clad in gowns and mortar boards, perched on lofty daises, why should they be concerned with how the lesser beings lived, provided they were kept in decent order?

Now the conversation took a rare and unexpected turn.

'Mountjoy,' Bill repeated. 'Yes. I heard that there were rumours.'

'Rumours, sir?'

'Of you and Mountjoy spending time together.'

Through the clouds of pipe smoke, Bill was gazing balefully. Doubt, bewilderment and plain anxiety were evident from the way his eyebrows twitched.

'Wallace, I made you Head of Day Room at the start of term. Prefects told me your appointment was a risky one. I did not ask them why. But all I say now, Wallace, is Take care. Be very, *very* careful.'

Dismissed in a darkened corridor, I felt bewildered at the muddle that was clouding poor Bill's mind. After two years, I was not the artless scum that I had been. But to be told point blank I must avoid the only character who made my life endurable – and, frankly, much more fun – was more than I had bargained for.

The thought that Mountjoy, like his *alter ego* Algernon, might lead a double life was no surprise. I too had heard the rumours of strange incidents, long after dark, of windows opened after careful checking by the monitors, of how the backdoor to the yard was left ajar one Friday night; trivia, ascribed, like so much else at school, to the resident ghost. Mountjoy's role in any of this talk would not surprise me, although he never gave a hint of what he might be up to.

Mountjoy was our talisman, a go-between, on easy terms with the Head of School, the Captain of the 1st XV, as well as several fags. He was the oil that helped the House move effortlessly on its way. Now, in the Middle Sixth, the opportunities were beckoning. Next year, if he cared, he could be Captain of the Team.

So, despite the iron law of separation of the years, I would often flee the drabness of the Day Room, choosing now to spend the afternoons on Mountjoy's battered horsehair sofa, whilst he read an extract from a novel just received from home.

Censorship was rife at School, where every piece of literature was vetted by a careful tutor. Saucy tales and dodgy titles, like notorious *'Fanny Hill',* would lead to trouble and the cane.

But Mountjoy's private library, ranged on bookshelves made of bricks, offered much more interesting fare. After the dust of Xenophon, Thucydides and Cicero, the racy tales of Evelyn Waugh and Huxley were a breath of air. One felt as if a window had been opened on a secret world. Silhouetted by the panes that overlooked the Armoury, he spoke of poets I had never known; how April was the cruellest month, breeding lilacs out of the dead land.

One dank afternoon in May, when cricket was abandoned and the smell of damp Viyella shirts, wet wool and grass crept up the stairway, Mountjoy read the opening lines of *Ode to a Nightingale.*

'My heart aches and a drowsy numbness pains
My sense, as though on hemlock I had drunk.'

Curious, the fairy tale spell that words can cast. Throwing open casements onto faery lands forlorn seemed the very opposite of everything I'd known at School. Suddenly, the tight and narrow room in which I lived was bathed in golden summer sun. Hitherto, all poetry was little more than thumping tones of *'Flores in the Azores'* and *'How Horatius Held the Bridge'.* Now, I was exposed to knights *'alone and palely loitering',* to scenes of mellow fruitfulness, unravish'd brides and weeping clouds.

'Never read any Keats before,' he smirked. 'Where have you been?'

'Borrow the book,' he added, carelessly lobbing it onto the sofa. 'After all, one should have something sensational to read.'

The book was bound in ancient leather, with a crest embossed along the spine. On the flyleaf were the words *'Ex libris Christopher Mountjoy'* and above, in neat round childish writing, *'Christopher, with love from Isobel.'*

Pages crackled and the leather bore a whiff of apricots.

Christopher. No Christian name was uttered while at School. Talk of family and home was generally taboo. There were letters written on a Sunday, carved in strictest silence, full of predictable information, such as the score of the 1st XV and endless calls for cash. Letters from home were delivered at breakfast by the duty fag – but they were never read in public. Home thoughts from a boarding school might well encourage homesickness. Such a loss of manly virtue was unthinkable.

So, Mountjoy's name was Christopher. A curtain had been parted, the rabbit and the conjuror's top hat revealed behind the scene. Christopher. It conjured up a softer, simpler character, quite different to the buccaneering rascal that I knew. And Isobel must be an aunt, anxious to improve her nephew's mind.

I turned the fragile tissue pages, captured by this sensuous bright world of words and feelings. This was what Bill thought so dangerous.

'No, no, got to Lethe, neither twist
Wolf's bane tight rooted for its poisonous wine:
Nor suffer thy pale forehead to be kissed
By nightshade, ruby grape of Proserpine.'

'Do they speak to you?' said Mountjoy. 'Black words on a cold white page? Listen – look! They're so intense. They live and breathe. It's like he's speaking now and in this room. That's why poetry's a drug. Because it's still alive.'

Of course, I was naive and did not see the road ahead. But nothing short of rustication could persuade me now to close the window, draw the blinds and turn my face back to the wall.

Rehearsals rumbled on, though mine were few and far between. George was in his element. 'A little louder if you please. Crispy epigrams – enjoy! Gwendolen – '*This is no time for wearing the shallow mask of manners.*' Scratch each other's eyes out with a hatpin.'

Little was asked of me except to swell a scene, to start a progress, bear a silver salver, lay the tea and muffins, bread and butter; then in the final act to enter, bearing all the weighty tomes of ancient Army lists.

Big School was a dusty barn and not ideal for drama. Portraits of Headmasters glowered down from every side. Sound bounced off the walls; the place was echoing and cavernous. Big School was a concert hall, assembly room and theatre – whilst in former times, it also acted as a gym, complete with wall bars, vaulting horse and a full-sized boxing ring.

Transforming the stage to a late Victorian garden, packed with roses, elegance and whimsy was a challenge. A posse of scene painters had been press ganged into service and ten-foot flats were shuffled to and fro. Under the direction of the ageing Drawing Master, Mr Antsy ('Pantsy-Bean'), they painted red and yellow roses, hollyhocks and cyclamen, with leafy hedgerows in the distance, fleecy clouds and azure skies. The 'Garden of the Manor House', the setting for the Second Act, had surely never looked so fine, complete with real trellising and sundial from the woodwork team.

A trunk of costumes was delivered from the London train, full of chokers, creams and crinolines. Our cup was full. My lowly footman's costume was replete with white silk stockings, patent leather shoes and scarlet livery. It glowed. Few of the other male actors could outshine my plumage, which, despite the smallness of the part, filled me with heady self-regard.

Such vanity as I had gained was also stoked by being cast as current Head of Day Room. Boys stood stiffly to attention when addressing me. 'Please Wallace, may I get a book?' 'Please Wallace, I have finished Prep.'

How easily, we glide from one allotted role into another. Eighteen months before, I was the meek, submissive new bug. Now, the Monarch of the Glen, with antlers broad and blossoming, I held the fate of fifteen other youngsters in my hand.

I played the wise and generous ruler, balancing the common good with temperance and justice, handing retribution out with mercy. Those on lower levels may have thought about it differently. Fortune dealt the cards; the ancient system never missed a beat. I played the role which she had granted me and my two comrades, marching round on Sundays as the Day Room stood at full attention. Had I then forgotten what life was for those less fortunate? God had given us the Day Room and we would enjoy it.

Every evening before Prep, I wandered round, the fag in tow, wetting a forefinger before running it along the lockers.

'Look at this – you said you cleaned it.' Mimicking disgust; crouching low before the long oak tables, spying out the streaks.

'Boxing' as I'd witnessed it that memorable Sunday, had continued off and on, though not upon my watch, and never quite so brutally as that day with Trelawney. The wretch had vanished to a dismal room up on the second floor and these days rarely braved the light. By half term, there had been scant talk of Boxing. But the Box remained, squatting sternly in the corner, just as the sight of the torturer's instruments can be a useful ploy to force a prisoner to blab before they are ever needed. 'Remember me,' it whispered. 'I am still the last resort.'

A small boy with a gleaming 'New Boy's Privilege', stood right beside me.

'Please, Wallace.' Scuff marks stained his suit, the sign of servitude; grey herring too – when most of us wore uniform of sober black. He stood out like a new-born lamb. 'Please, Wallace,' the boy bleated.

I raised a lazy eye. 'What is it?' noticing a tell-tale tear across the cheek.

'Please Wallace, I've lost my – ' stammering through lips that quivered, ashen faced, with greased and pale hair.

'You've lost your...?'

'Latin book. I had it after Prep. And now it's – '

'Gone,' I added, rising to my feet and reaching in the locker. 'Here, I think this must be yours.' The faded, green-clad tome, engraved with inked-in alterations, had 'Latin Primer', now transformed in blue Quink into 'Eating Primer'. Scratched inside, the cartoon of a boy force fed on Latin verbs.

'Your graffiti?'

'No, of course. I bought it from the Book Pound.'

'Nobody would sell a Latin Primer in that sort of state. Which means you've inked it in yourself.'

'I didn't, I swear I didn't, Wallace.'

'Don't lie to me, Stevenson.'

'I promise you, I didn't.'

'You left this book out after Prep – *after* you'd written all over it. Listen, this is serious.'

I rub my chin and feel the few rough hairs across the upper lip. I need a shave, I realise.

Whatever my decision, it will meet with no appeal. My fellow Boxing Party chums will always back me to the hilt.

Outside in the corridor, familiar voices echo. 'Fancy a spot of Bunburying tonight?'

Seconds pass. The voice outside is like a tolling bell, to roll me back towards another boy, another Latin Primer.

'Look, Stevenson, you're getting close to eight full Day Room points. I think you know what happens then.' I pause theatrically. 'So, let this be the last time you and I have any conversation. Otherwise – '

Another pause. I hand over the dogeared book.

'Just be very, *very* careful.'

Wise as Solomon, I sit and wave the thanks away. Onward, ever upwards – seldom looking down below, moving slowly through the pecking order. No longer a nightingale, soaring high above the clef, my voice had started on a slow descent. I'd joined the altos.

No-one spoke of puberty. But it was unignorable. Every day we plunged in naked file into the trough. Who could fail to see the changes taking place in all of us? Steady growth of pubic hair, swelling of the testicles, the unexpected surge of an erection at an awkward moment. Furtively aware of one another's progress into manhood, anxious to keep up with it and fearful to be left behind, amid the acne and the odours, we lurched into adolescence.

Horny, yes, I did feel horny. Now I knew what wanking was, midnight throbbing underneath the cover of the dark. I wanked as well as anyone. Semen stains could be disguised, as well as dank pyjamas, witnesses to strange, erotic early morning dreams. Sex was an embarrassment, a secret unattainable, hidden in the shadows, undiscussed and often undisclosed.

I admired the lofty Bloods, who strode about when I arrived, and who seemed effortlessly passing into adulthood. Who could ever think that they once had unbroken voices – or struggled with a collar stud or ever been a fag? Now, at the end of my second year, like a man who aims for a distant peak and climbs the lower foothills, lofty summits looked far less imposing. Men higher up seemed neither superhuman nor heroic. They were merely grander versions of my adolescent self; certainly, more knowing and experienced, but mortal too, endued with mortal faults, some lazy, some conniving, some enthusiastic, generous at times. Some were pinched and anxious; one or two upstanding, principled. Each was locked within a system where one rose and fell, according to the way one played the part for which we had been cast.

The gods of my first year had gone, to be replaced by lesser heroes. Now their days were numbered too and like the veterans of old, we shook our heads and swore that we would never see their like again. In their wake, a group of ordinary legionnaires, tolerably decent types, who carried on without distinction, lacked the glitter and the dash of what had come before. Many would be civil servants in their future years, tracking rules and regulations, never stepping out of line.

Only Mountjoy stood out, as the maverick, the nonconformist. Not that he rebelled. But his careless *joie de vivre* was enough to ruffle others' plumage. Charm and sporting prowess did not make for comradeship with some of those whom he outclassed. Add to that his flouting of the rigid social system and Mountjoy's list of critics might have outweighed his admirers.

Conversation had already turned to the succession. Barratt, the talented Head of House was due to leave at the end of term. A chip off the old block, he played at full back for the 1st XV, lounging happily in crested cap and waistcoat at Top Table. Genial, but with a firm hold on authority; lazy when it came to work (Oxford colleges, less keen to hear of sporting skills, now demanded academic rigour). Barratt would be on his way. The generation waiting in the wings looked mediocre.

No-one thought of Mountjoy as a future Head of House. Even Bloods could recognise an oddball. It was widely touted that a character called Ainslie, a studious, umbrella wielding, buttoned Exhibitioner was tipped to win the prize. Ainslie was ambitious in a calculating way and formed a group of similar companions. The House would go to the dogs, we thought, if ruled by a cold bureaucracy that lacked the golden glamour of the past.

Ainslie disliked Mountjoy too. 'That fellow's riding for a fall,' he whispered to his stooges, as they gathered by the noticeboard.

'He's good for House morale,' another chap replied. 'And he's our best hope in the Three Cock. We'd be lost without him.'

'Just supposing that he lasts that long,' said Ainslie. 'Mountjoy sails close to the wind. I wouldn't bet on him surviving through the coming term.'

I wondered about Mountjoy. I had heard him mention 'Bunbury', who, as I knew from Wilde's play, was a fictional friend of Algernon – a priceless invalid, whose needs enabled him to cancel disagreeable engagements and to choose instead a life of pleasure. Algy lived a double life of unlocked doors and open windows. It was no surprise that Mountjoy relished such a role.

I, too, led a double life, although unwilling to admit it. Clothed in brief authority to suit my Day Room character, I doubled as an acolyte in Mountjoy's company, happy as an also-ran behind the cavalcade.

Now the cavalcade had moved beneath the Big School stage. Here were two neat alcoves, which were used as Green Rooms for the play. Since I was rarely up on stage, much of my time was spent amid the shifting company. Actors would appear, then disappear as they were called, but an endless bubble of gossip drifted round the little rooms, like laughing gas in a cosy underworld. Actors would make forays to the floodlit stage above, to draw applause and laughter, before climbing back into the burrow.

Central to this world was Jonny Tait, who loved an audience. Couched in the only armchair, like a queen weighed down by crinolines, he told us of his escapades in Paris in the Spring.

'Well – I somehow found myself inside a steamy nightclub, somewhere on the Left Bank in a basement. There were black men playing jazz. Well, I thought, this *is* exciting…' Then a stagehand whispered 'Call for Lady Bracknell. Call for Gwendolen.'

Jonny rose and grabbed a wide brimmed hat and turned before the exit. 'Cliff hanger – just wait until Act Two!'

It was the night of the Dress Rehearsal. After it was over, Gorgeous stepped into the Green Room, where the stench of male sweat and make-up powder made it hard to breathe.

'Well done, men. A hearty run. It needs to crack on still. Watch those consonants. Remember the ninepenny seats in the gallery, craning their necks for every syllable. Don't just play the second row – there's honest punters in the gods.'

He mopped a lime green handkerchief across his brow and added 'Notes will be on the noticeboard by Chapel. Read with care. And make sure you are ready for tomorrow.'

Thursday was the opening night, when the school invited townsfolk. On Friday, the rest of the school would watch; but Saturday would see Commemoration Weekend in full flow and the place awash with proud, adoring parents.

'Three shows and a sell-out,' murmured Jonny. 'This'll need some form of celebration when it's over. Mountjoy, you will see to it, I'm sure?'

Chapter Six

That May weekend saw Mountjoy triumph. Star of stage and sporting titan, suddenly the world lay at his feet.

Commemoration Weekend was a promise of the Spring. Hostelries around the town had groaned with bookings months before. Late comers were forced to come from many miles around. On this one weekend, the school threw down the drawbridge and monastic isolation was replaced with dinners and displays.

Bentleys and Rolls Royces lined the streets before the War, bringing wealth to coaching inns throughout the little town. 1949 would see another lifting of restraint. By Easter, all the best hotels were stocked with every fancy ration that the market could supply. After several fruitless letters, Mother had secured a room in a public house on the edge of town. Father sent regrets from Singapore.

I met her at the station. She was dressed in navy blue, with tilted hat and netting and a pair of brand new shoes. She looked the height of fashion with those neatly padded shoulders, knee length skirt and nylon gloves I'd never seen before. Oddly vulnerable too, a lady travelling alone. I noticed, as I kissed her cheek, that I was now the taller.

We took tea at the Luckpenny in one of those strange public meals and swapped polite and formal words, whilst starched and aproned waitresses delivered cakes and scones.

'Father's sad to miss you and he hopes you're doing well. He should be back for Christmas.'

'Jolly good.'

'He writes such interesting letters – rather better ones than you. But Charles, if there is time, I'd like to meet some of your friends.'

'Yes,' I murmured, reaching for a second buttered teacake. 'I'm not sure what they're up to now. I guess we may bump into them.'

Home and School must not collide. Of that much I was certain. My own friends were planning festive dinners with their families. I doubted whether Mother would bump into Mountjoy's clan.

I left her, with a twinge of guilt at going off so soon and sped along the cobbled street to change for the performance. The prospect of the next two hours on stage and in the Green Room were like forbidden pleasures, dangerous and captivating.

Saturday dawned bright and blue. A veil of mist hung on the Slopes. 'It's bound to be a scorcher,' we agreed.

Last year had been wretched. I had hated every moment, moping in an empty House and cursing both the Royal Navy and the weather gods. Now, today, I felt a thrill which I could only half explain. Even the thought of an hour or two, commemorating benefactors could not crush that rising sense of hope and expectation, like waking early on that first day of the summer holidays, luxuriating in the thought of eight long weeks of freedom.

Last night was a triumph with an audience that clapped and cheered. Jonny Tait had been a revelation. Milking lines and pauses and refining every epigram, his timing was unbeatable. With one twitch of a parasol, a half-raised eyebrow to the gods, the whole Big School had rocked and roared at Lady Bracknell to a 't'. Edith Evans scarcely could have mastered that immortal line 'A handbag?' and the rest of us were swept up in the acclamation. There remained one final chance to feed upon that wild applause.

Even Bill appeared to feel a little of the glow that radiated off the sandstone walls that early morning. One by one, he summoned us from Head of House to lowest fag into the high walled garden, where he tended climbing roses – Zephyrines and Golden Showers, Don Juans and Blazes. For each, he chose a buttonhole to wear throughout the Abbey Service, handling them like sacramental bread.

Thus garlanded, we took our places in the ancient choir stalls. Although we wore no vestments, unlike most cathedral choristers, there was a sense that once again we stood upon the stage, leading Parry's setting of the psalmist's paean '*I was glad.*'

High above us, hung the vaulted ceiling, made of golden lace; each interlocking rib part of one glorious cat's cradle, echoing each curve and angle in a perfect symmetry. Did this patterning reflect the mystery of life? All its elements were not divided or a double life, but interwoven, part of some unfathomable unity.

It continued through the service, through the grand delivery of Parry's lusty chords. I was part of Jonny's tribe, with Mountjoy and the other boys. My feet stood on Big School stage, engulfed with wild applause. The organ boomed; we trooped into the sunlight, where our parents waited.

Speeches followed in Big School, with mothers decked in wide brimmed hats and fathers in their Sunday best. Throughout the tedium, I gazed towards the scarlet curtain, as if I alone knew of the magic world that lay beyond.

Lunch was at The Luckpenny; then cricket on the Upper Meadow, where the 1st XI faced the Old Boys. Mother bore the whole charade with all her usual fortitude. Even if I had not been distracted and preoccupied, it must have been a strange ordeal to spend a long day with a son she had not seen for many months, making stilted conversation in a restaurant.

Wandering the narrow streets towards the Upper Meadow, we passed a group of parents talking animatedly.

'Wallace!'

It was Jonny Tait, a red rose in his buttonhole.

'Mother – this is Wallace, whom I told you all about at lunch. For a chap who doesn't say a word, he gives a great performance. He has nothing, but he looks the part. He simply steals the show.'

Decked out as a dowager in shawls and layers of silk, Jonny's mother pressed a powdered hand in mine, whilst Father Tait conferred a chalky smile. Clearly, it was proving quite a long day for them both.

'But I must not detain you,' Jonny went on, unabashed. 'Your friend Mountjoy's making hay – not that I understand the game.'

As he spoke, a cheer came from the cricket field, a street away, followed by polite applause, that drifted up like scattered leaves. 'Good to meet you. Come on, Mother. Time for tea and crumpets.'

By the grassy boundary, smooth as any billiard table, groups of parents lay in deckchairs, like exhausted seals. Mother sank with some relief into a proffered wicker chair, gazing shyly up and down for someone she might recognise. On a tartan rug beside us, sat a boy I partly knew. I think his name was Hardcastle and we did French together. We nodded formally to one another. In a canvas chair, his father gently snored, a panama across his nose and frayed cuffs of an Old Boys' blazer halfway up his arm.

'Mountjoy's giving it a biff,' the boy said, as a sudden thwack saw the ball coast skyward, to land beyond the boundary rope.

'Smashing shot!' he added. 'That's his second six this afternoon. One more and the fifty's up.'

Flannelled figures spread a little wider round the field, as Mountjoy took his guard again, looking utterly at ease, whilst a former Captain of the School, a chap called Millard, scowled and paced back to his mark in readiness to bowl.

'Millard's up at Christchurch,' said my new companion 'He plays for the Varsity. And Middlesex is after him, they say.'

Millard did not look too friendly, as he steamed in twenty yards and flung a thunderbolt which reared and might have taken Mountjoy's head off. Mountjoy ducked beneath it just in time.

'Do they let them do that?' Mother sat up, suddenly alert.

'It's frightfully unsporting,' said my comrade. 'Might have killed the fellow.'

Mountjoy leant back on his bat, as once again the bowler set himself to hurl a cannonade. The next ball pitched a shorter length and rocketed head high. Mountjoy steadied, stepped to leg and helped to guide it on its way towards the long leg boundary. A ripple of applause greeted an unbeaten half century.

'Topping player,' said my friend. 'You lucky chap. He's in your House He's bound to get his colours after this.'

The afternoon wore on, as the thermometer began to rise and bowlers tired and Mountjoy stood his ground. Batsmen came and went; it seemed my friend could do no harm. A stylish cut right through covers, then a graceful pull to leg; a glance between the slips for four; the tin plates on the scoreboard clattered, as the fellows on the Tally tried to keep up with the score.

I sat entranced by the unfolding drama. Mountjoy, hero of the hour appeared the sole protagonist, whilst other neat white figures crouched around were little more than extras, walk-ons, scraps of scenery.

During a lull between the overs, Hardcastle turned and gazed at me. 'I saw you in the play,' he said. 'By golly, it was good.'

I blushed a little, hoping Mother overheard the compliment. 'Thanks,' I said. 'It is a ripping show.'

'That Jonny Tait, he takes the biscuit, mincing round about like that. Haven't laughed so much in ages. But he is a queer cove.'

'He's clever though,' I said.

'I guess. I bet he takes a lot of stick. I'd rather have the part that Mountjoy plays. But as for you – you didn't have an awful lot to say. What was the point of coming on?'

I swallowed. 'Well, I'm like a footman.'

'Yes?'

'I lay the table in this country house. I do the chores.'

'You don't do all that much onstage. You don't have any lines.' I bit my lower lip. 'I really couldn't see the point of you.'

Out of the corner of my eye, I spotted Mother studiously reading from a magazine.

'Must be rather dull for you to wait around all evening. No-one notices when you appear.'

Mother closed her eyes again; the carnage of the field began again. Meanwhile, the audience had grown – drawn more by the thought of tea than by the prospect of the School trouncing a team of Old Boys. Summer hats and boaters, cotton dresses and bright blazers decked the narrow boundary. The scoreboard read: 'Runs: 158. Wickets: 8.' Batsman number 5 was nearing 90. Then, with a buccaneering heave, Mountjoy struck an easy four through mid-wicket's legs. The applause was louder now. A century on Commemoration Day was a thing to be talked about.

Mountjoy's cavalier approach was well tuned to the festive mood, the sunshine and the sense that all Austerity was brushed aside like cobwebs in the Spring.

Millard, looking puffed and angry, had been exiled to long-on and the ball was thrown to a chap with tousled hair and military moustache. He trotted to the popping crease and lobbed a slow full toss. Mountjoy struck the ball full on towards a stocky fielder.

'This'll be fun,' said Hardcastle. 'They've brought the carthorse on. Now we'll see some fireworks. Stand back everyone.'

The carthorse rolled his arm with yet another gentle lob. This was too much for Mountjoy, who, like Trumper in his pomp, charged up the pitch to catch the ball half volley. A rattle of bails, a cry 'Owzat!'; the square leg umpire's finger pointed upwards to the sky. My hero had been trapped by spin and guile. He stood mid-pitch, marooned, his shoulders slumped; the opposition cheered.

Five runs short of a century. 'Still, he did play jolly well. Our men would have struggled without Mountjoy,' my companion said. 'Stumping seems a sneaky way to get a fellow out.'

I joined the applause, as Mountjoy dragged himself to the pavilion, like a man in chains.

The last chap in could offer only nominal resistance. Very soon the players were all trooping off for tea. We made our way to the marquee, where steaming urns and plates of scones and jam tarts filled the trestle tables.

Finding Mother an empty chair, I waded back into the throng.

'Steady on!' a voice called out. 'Why, it's the Footman serving tea.'

In the half light of the tent, Mountjoy seemed to glow, his brief despair completely gone, along with gloves and batting pads. 'Hey, Wallace, meet my family.'

The Mountjoy clan was gathered round a table crammed with cups and saucers, plates and jugs and sugar bowls and cake. 'Mother – this is Wallace. You will see him on the stage tonight. Father – this is Wallace. He's an excellent recruit.'

Mountjoy Senior, the Brigadier, had thick black bushy eyebrows and a white moustache. His head was like a walnut; on his cheek there lay a heavy scar. He cleared his throat by way of greeting. Seated at the trestle table, Lady Mountjoy beamed, 'A pleasure, Wallace. So, you tread the boards?'

'Well, just a bit,' I said recalling Hardcastle's rough words. 'But if you blink, I think you'll miss me.'

'Not at all. I'm sure you're *perfect*.'

Even I had heard the talk of Madeleine Mountjoy, an heiress around whom the scent of scandal wafted in the '20s, just before the Wall Street Crash. A debutante, 'Miss Bailey' had attracted her admirers, winning hearts wherever she bestowed a captivating smile. She was one of the girls who in former times had danced with the Prince of Wales, whilst titled youths and one Viscount were rumoured to be hovering. Then, at the height of the Seasonal Round, she had slipped away from the demi-monde to spend her nights with a rather fast set, hell bent on the stage.

There followed a series of strange affairs, which her desperate parents tried to prevent, before she eloped with a juvenile lead from the Northern Touring Company.

I need not explain how a firm of detectives finally tracked her down, nor detail the unfinished suits for slander, seduction and larceny. Madeleine was underage and her family sued to Chancery and brought the penniless prodigal home, thrilled but unrepentant.

Home. But with none of her love of the greasepaint lost; indeed, to the contrary. Ruined of course, but her family begged and bullied her into a decent match. And since she was good enough for some, and highly priced as well, she set her cap for a genial Captain of Guards and later Brigadier, Arthur Mountjoy MC. They settled down in Surrey. The Estate was known as Connaught Hall.

Madeleine gave a radiant smile and proffered one gloved hand.

'A real pleasure to meet you, Wallace.'

Balancing cups of milky tea, I made a little bow, swilling half the contents on the grass.

'Jolly nice to meet you too.' I turned away to the lonely table where my mother sat.

'Sorry to be quite so long. I just met Mountjoy's family.'

'Mountjoy?'

'He's the man who batted so tremendously.'

She frowned. 'I've heard the name. So, that boy is a friend of yours? I thought he looked much older.'

'Yes, he's in the Middle Sixth, but we're in the play together.'

Mother stirred her tea. 'So, he's not a close friend?'

'Well – '

But we were interrupted.

'Wallace – this is Isobel. And this must be your mother. Mrs Wallace, what a pleasure. Please forgive the interruption.'

Mother raised her eyes to meet the full force of the Mountjoy smile. 'Please do not get up. It's just that Wallace here was passing by and met my parents, but there wasn't time for Isobel.'

Isobel, at seventeen, must have looked as her mother did when causing a sensation all those many years ago. She wore a pleated tennis skirt, her blond hair in a simple band. Slim, light boned, her lips parted and her neck pure porcelain.

Isobel. No maiden aunt, anxious to inspire her nephew with a love of poetry. Mountjoy placed an arm around her shoulder.

'Very pleased to meet you,' Mother said, her stiffness melting in the glow.

Years afterwards, that moment in the tent remains as clear as day. A switch was thrown – that pale Madonna face that made the world stand still; the clatter of cups and murmured buzz of conversation faded. I was transfixed. Girls, as I said, were not a feature of our lives. The only women in my life were motherly or matrons. What they called the Fairer Sex was still a universe apart. I blushed and muttered something dull.

Yet there was something else. A glimmer, something much less biddable than any cold Madonna frescoed on a Tuscan wall; something almost devilish about the sparkle of her eyes, something so alluring in the corners of her smile. They seemed to promise risk and danger. Rapidly, I turned away. I had a sudden hard-on. I was mortified with shame.

'Gosh, is that the time? I'd better get my pads on smartish now.' Mountjoy was the wicket keeper. 'I'll see you tonight – and don't be late.' He hurried off with Isobel and vanished in the crowd.

Never before had I been drunk, as I was on that night. Drunk with alcohol, of course, but also drunk with something else – with lust or love and wonder at the sight of Isobel. Beyond the stage, beyond the crude electric footlights, was a shape, a figure seated at the front, a presence that observed our brave performance like a charm.

'My family are all out there,' said Mountjoy before Curtain Up. 'Make sure it's a ripping show. Break a leg, my hearties.'

If ever footman gave his best, I was to be that footman, glad to bathe for one brief moment in the dancing limelight. Surely, she had noticed all my gorgeous finery, insignificant to all but that one lovely countenance. We gave our all, that final night, and though I knew the roars of laughter and applause were not for me, like one who has been blinded by the sunlight, I was acting just for her.

After it was over, after we had wiped the make-up from our faces, Leichner Numbers Five and Nine streaked with Lake and sticks of white, I asked 'What did she make of it?'

'Who? Isobel? I bet she loved it. Did you notice her out there, you Footman? Weren't you concentrating?'

'Bet you half a crown I did.'

He grinned. 'They loved it, every minute.'

'What do we do now?'

'Well, first, we sign in back at House.'

'And then?'

He tapped his nose. 'You follow me.'

We sauntered back beneath a sky of darkest summer blue. A few bright stars were shining. It was three weeks to the solstice. Footsteps crunched the gravel Court.

'You enjoy this sort of thing?' said Mountjoy.

'Theatre? Yes – well, it was good, although I hadn't much to do.'

'You want to do more acting, proper acting, in the summer?'

'What do you mean?

We reached the big arched door that led beyond the Courtyard. Mountjoy stopped and leant against the ancient sandstone, where the motto 'Omnibus fidelis' – 'True in everything' – was flecked in gold above his head.

'So, you've met my sister now. Bet you think she's wonderful?'

'Hm – ' I hesitated. 'She is – well, I don't know what to say.'

'Stunning, isn't she?' He nodded. 'Well, you'll see her on the stage.'

'Isobel?'

'Yes, in July. Mother's planning something special. It's a Festival – It's called The Connaught Shakespeare Festival. Outdoor Shakespeare's all the rage. Jonny's coming too.'

'I'd have to ask my parents.'

'Tell your mother in the morning. Come on – we must sign back in before the entertainment.'

What followed that evening, I can only hazily recall. The icy cold of concrete flooring, as the Abbey clock chimed midnight; then a creak of hinges, as the bolts slid on the outer door and silence in the street outside, where one small lamp was burning. Through the kitchen garden on the slope behind the Gym, lettuces and green tomatoes gleaming in the starlight; up towards the squash courts and the wooden huts of the Armoury, crouching bleakly underneath the stars.

The squash court door lay open. Someone had purloined a key. Inside, barely silhouetted by the pale skylight, huddled figures lay as if for ambush.

A whispered summons: ''What brings you to town?

'Why, pleasure, pleasure! What else would bring one anywhere?'

Two dark shadows greeted us. Jonny Tait, who lugged a rucksack and a chap called Nightingale who'd been playing Gwendolen. A rug was spread across the floor; there was a hiss, a splash – a bottle of what sounded like champagne appeared. Another followed.

'Drink and be merry,' whispered Jonny, raising a glass towards us all. A lighter flashed an orange glow and there was a wave of rich tobacco. Someone passed a silver cigarette box round the circle. I had never smoked before. I lay back on a rucksack as the bubbles danced along my throat.

'Try one,' Nightingale suggested, placing it between my lips. 'Just be careful. Don't inhale.'

Too late – I was asphyxiated, choking up champagne and smoke to the delight of everyone. The burst of laughter should have brought the watchman running to our hide. We lay silent, listening to an owl swooping by.

Mountjoy murmured 'Lane, I see that on Saturday night, nine bottles of champagne are entered as having been consumed. Why is it that the servants invariably drink champagne?'

Nine bottles were a lot more than we brought along that night. But quite enough had been consumed before the darkness deepened and the stars began to spin. Nor was I the only one unused to alcohol. Two other boys were soon the worse for wear. One of them was Nightingale, who started up a rustic song, which Jonny hushed, but Nightingale resisted. Mountjoy fared no better and the music wafted gently up towards the iron girders and out across the shadowed beds of cauliflowers and cabbages.

'Now I am a bachelor, I live with my son
And I work on the weaver's trade – '

'Keep it down, you idiot!' They threw a rug over his head. But Nightingale fought on, undaunted, with his melancholy tale.

'And the only, only thing that I ever did wrong
Was to woo a fair young maid.'

'Shut it, cretin. Hold your noise.'

The bubbles of champagne had done their business. Nightingale escaped, stood up, continued amid giggles, hiccoughs and increasingly hysterical attempts to silence him.

'She sighed, she cried, she damn near died.
Alas what I could I do?

So, I took her into bed and covered up her head
Just to keep her from the foggy, foggy dew.'

The ballad ended and the boy gazed up into the shadows. Echoes of the plaintive notes had drifted through the courts, whose painted lines were more used to the heavy thud of squash balls. Silence followed – until Jonny murmured 'Hell, you've done it now.'

As if on cue, a flashlight threw a beam across the room, caught the singer's profile like the spotlight in a cabaret. Giant shadows danced across wall.

'Scuppered,' Jonny murmured; then, because no movement followed, he called out 'Who goes there?'

There was no reply.

'Friend or foe? Stand and unfold yourself.'

We huddled in the headlights like a colony of rabbits. The torchlight wavered. Peering through the gloom, we saw the roughened features of a boy. No cunning Beak sent out to spy on revellers; no, it was one of us, or so we hoped.

But all the same, we had been trapped, carousing like a bunch of sailors. Now I recognised the figure with the gleaming flashlight. Ainslie of the Middle Sixth, scarfed and muffled in the dark.

'Ainslie!' whispered Mountjoy 'Come and join us, have a glass.'

Ainslie did not flinch; the torch was shining on the wooden floor.

'Come on, lad. You're safe with us. A quick one, then we'll pack up and go quietly to bed.'

Ainslie glared. 'You must be mad. Look at you – with a bunch of junior boys. You could get canned for this.'

'Unless we're not discovered. And if no-one breathes a word about it.'

Ainslie looked a little sheepish, even in the dark. 'Would you?' Mountjoy added. 'Even though you're after some promotion. No, you wouldn't sneak on us to Bill to help your chances?'

'Look,' said Ainslie 'you chaps think it's fine to break the rules – go out drinking after dark. It's your neck in the noose, not mine. I heard you leave the House and what's the betting other men did too? You don't need me to get you sacked. You're writing your own exit.'

Flushed with drink, Mountjoy was not prepared to take this sitting down. He took a step towards the shrouded witness and began to growl. 'Now see here. If one syllable of what goes on tonight should reach the ears of anyone – even one of your closest chums – your life in Abbey House will not be worth a single sou. Head of House or not, my friend, I swear that you'll regret it.'

'You threatening me?'

'I'm warning you. So, let's say nothing more about it.'

Unmanned, though the threat was vague, Ainslie stood his ground. 'You're warning me? That's rich, I must say. Mountjoy, I am warning you. You're running out of credit here. I'm warning you to take more care. Be very, *very* careful.'

Hidden in the shadows, I recoiled at his words. But for now, the confrontation seemed to be exhausted. Tension slackened; like two rutting stags, the men withdrew as if prepared to charge again at some unstated hour.

All the sense of *joie de vivre* had gone. When Ainslie disappeared, mutters of departure drifted through the company. As I stood, my limbs grew heavy; blood drained from my head and I sank down towards the deck. I half remember being dragged, half carried, back along the path and retching in a bush beside the Gym.

Faces loomed out of the dark. I tried to speak. I wanted to let Mountjoy know his sister was a topping girl and what a lucky chap he was, while others tried to gag me. They pulled me past a gardener's cottage, curtains drawn and shuttered. What a weight I must have been! And how was anyone to lug me back to bed without arousing every sleeping monitor?

Later, I was told that Jonny, at the risk to life and limb, had clambered through a window, opened up the courtyard door and, with Mountjoy, heaved the lifeless sack of me upstairs and into Mountjoy's study, dumping me onto the sofa.

We had got away with it – or so it seemed to me. Waking in the half light of an early birdsong morning, I rose and felt a flash of lightning crack across my skull. I lay back. From the window came the distant Abbey chimes. I counted five and closed my eyes, hoping I might sleep it off. A throbbing pulse was beating through my temple.

Next thing I was conscious of was Mountjoy tugging at my shoulder. 'Wallace – up,' he whispered. 'Look, it's nearly nine o'clock. Time for you to move, old chap. Or you'll be late for Abbey.' In his hand a glass of effervescing liquid. 'Come on, have some Enos.'

With knotted tie and crumpled suit, I found the Abbey choristers and mimed my way through hymns and psalms, like someone in a London fog, feeling green and ghastly. The great fan vaulting in the roof appeared a haze of scribbled scrawls, fireworks, mad and meaningless, a pattern without shape or order.

'Charles, you don't look well.' My mother eyed me up and down, as we stood in the sun by the Great West Door. 'Have you been sick?'

'It must have been something I ate last night,' I mumbled.

Lunch was out of the question. 'Well, you had better go and lie down. Should I have a word with Matron?'

Matron was off duty, I assured her. But I would be fine, if I could sleep off the effects of dinner. In truth I'd eaten nothing since the cricket tea on Upper Meadow.

Mother's train was leaving in the early afternoon. I made a weak apology for spoiling her last morning and thanked her for her gallantry in coming down alone.

'I would not have missed it for the world. And you were splendid. Never did a better footman brave the open stage.'

'I forgot to tell you, Mountjoy's asked me down to Connaught Hall after the end of term. They're putting on a show, some sort of Shakespeare Festival.'

She winced. 'We'll have to ask your father. I am not convinced that spending more time with that boy is good for you.'

'But,' I said, 'his mother, Lady Mountjoy, has invited me.'

'Let's see what your father says. I think you must be careful.'

I kissed her on the cheek, all green and sickly as I was, guilty at abandoning her, guilty at concealing why I wasn't fit for purpose – and having just a vague suspicion she was in the right and that for all his charm and swagger, comradeship with Mountjoy and his friends was not the best for me.

I watched her turn and make her way across the Abbey Close, a small, neat figure, dressed in navy blue. Despite our talk, the netted pillbox hat gave her a jaunty air, a dark blue dot that disappeared behind the Alms House wall.

As she disappeared, it seemed that all those memories of childhood were disappearing too. Somewhere, the thread that bound the old familiar patterns had been cut. Now, my path would be the one I chose.

Bilious and groggy though I was, I turned back to the House, feeling oddly confident and free. I would be sixteen in September. Life was waiting round the corner of these sandstone walls. Bill had said 'Be very careful.' So, indeed, had Mother. What did either of them know of life and its enchantment?

Chapter Seven

News that Mountjoy had been sacked came as a bolt of lightning. Stevenson raced into Day Room after lunch one day.

'Please Wallace, Bill wants Mountjoy. But he can't be found. Bill says it's urgent.'

Memories of his great escape from justice meant that Stevenson revered me as a guardian. His stiffened collar was askew; the ink-stained tie was shredded. But he stood up to attention like a private on parade.

'Why should I know where Mountjoy is?'

'I thought that you and Mountjoy – '

'What?'

'I thought that you might know. But, well – ' he trailed off. 'I see you don't.'

'You'd better look elsewhere,' I made a move to read the headline on the paper. '*Dock workers on Strike. Communists behind the move*'.

Pale faced with excitement, as if he were to blame for Mountjoy's disappearance, Stevenson was not to be deterred.

'I've checked his study – looked upstairs and hunted in the changing rooms. I've tried the other studies too.'

'You'd better say he can't be found. He's probably having an early net if there's a match this afternoon.'

'Thanks, Wallace. Yes – I'll do that.' With a click of heels, he bustled off.

Exam time. Boys in the Remove were writing School Certificates. Not that this had much effect upon the sporting calendar. Twice a week, a match was played upon the green lawns of the Upper. A few swots still lingered in the Lower Library – but those who never did a stroke saw little point in sweating now.

I did not give a thought to Mountjoy until after tea. But during prep, a rumour ran that Bill would speak to us at Prayers. Bill rarely spoke in public. All the business of the House was done via the prefects. Bill would only intervene in dire emergency. Even in the greatest sporting triumphs, of which there were many, he would leave the table thumping to his precious Bloods.

At Prayers, we knelt against the wooden benches of the Hall, hands across our faces, muttering the '*Pater Noster*'. Then, with a rumble of heavy boots, we raised our heads and sat, while Bill stood waiting by the door.

'I have to tell you something very serious has happened. One of our number will not be returning to the School.'

Eyes looked anxiously about. I glanced at Ainslie, who sat, head down, cleaning glasses with a rag.

'The person in question is Mountjoy.' A gasp ran round the hall. 'Mountjoy. He was found this afternoon in a sort of public house on the other side of Town. I'm told that he was wearing rough clothes, in an effort to disguise. Investigations tell us this was not the first time in which he – ' and here Bill raised his voice a notch – 'in which he *and other persons* have defied the rules. He seems to have made a regular habit of dressing up and slipping out at night. Mountjoy was spotted by a member of the public after midnight, walking through the Conduit in the Square.

'The Headmaster has asked his parents to withdraw him from the School. Mountjoy left this afternoon.'

Bill paused for breath. This was the longest speech he had delivered during all my years at School.

'There have been other incidents, involving other miscreants. They may be in this very room. When they are caught, they will be punished too.'

Red faced with the effort of delivering so many words, Bill gazed at the Honours Board, then at the rows of gleaming silver on the mantelpiece, before abruptly turning to the door which thudded close behind him.

There was a sickened silence – followed by a burst of noise and universal outrage. Mountjoy! How on earth – how dare they? Mountjoy was the talisman, the rock on which our future hung. What of the Rugby Three Cock – or the First House Cricket Trophy? Who would steer this drifting bark during the months to come?

More than that – we wondered who the other culprits were. I was certain Parsons, Mountjoy's chum and confidant, was with him on those escapades. And Jonny Tait? How many more of us were now in danger?

Ainslie must have grassed to Bill – or dropped a heavy hint that Mountjoy had been on the loose. Had he spotted me, that awful night after the play? A mental note of who was in the cast was all he needed to get the lot of us dispatched for home. The future Head of Abbey House was deep in conversation with another of his cronies. Had he got the goods on me? I thought of Mountjoy's drunken boast 'If what went on tonight reaches the ears of anyone at all, your life will not be worth a sou.'

But had he spilt the beans – or was he merely watching from the wings? He must have known a lot more than I thought. With Mountjoy gone, the age of Ainslie seemed to stretch more bleakly and triumphantly than ever. I was trapped. The fear of revelation meant that any sign of mutiny could bring the future crashing round my ears.

During the days that followed, Mountjoy's absence left a yawning gap. The final weeks were desolate. The hours discussing Eliot and Baudelaire had vanished and each afternoon was duller than the last.

I hid the book of Keats's poems deep inside my locker, like the relic of another age.

One Sunday afternoon, when we were bound to leave the House, I wandered up to Big School, where a mere three weeks before, we took the audience by storm. Big School was an empty barn. Portraits of Headmasters dead and gone looked down, like ancestors. Motes of dust were dancing in the sun. I clambered down the narrow stairs that led beneath the stage. The Green Room was deserted, every costume packed and stowed away; the mirrors and the make-up gone, together with the laughter and applause. A piece of cotton wool had fallen from a bench beside the door. I caught a whiff of Leichner Number Five.

Mounting the wooden stairs again, I wandered out across the stage, gazing at the empty seats and benches in the gallery. Silence. In the rafters that had echoed to applause, all was now as still as stone. Nothing could recall the memory.

I called up to the lighting desk.

'A handbag?'

'Embag!' rattled round the walls.

And then, as if to challenge all the sleeping demons, I began to sing the ballad which had ruined all our fortune. It was as if that memory could not be bottled up and that it must break out again before that watchful audience.

'O I am a bachelor, I live with my son
And I work on the weaver's trade

And the only, only thing that I ever did wrong
Was to woo a fair young maid.'

Headmasters, dressed in red and black, with medals pinned across their chests, were so attentive that their very silence begged for an encore.

'I wooed her in the summer time
And in the winter too
And the only, only thing that I ever did wrong
Was to shield her from the foggy, foggy dew.

I stopped to let the echoes of the last note drift away and bowed to the empty house. The grim Headmasters had been entertained, despite their silence.

But someone else was clapping. For a moment, in a dream, it seemed the pale portraits were applauding after all. Then at the top of the gallery, silhouetted by the light, a single figure could be seen, applauding steadily.

Bashfully, I headed for the wings.

'Hey, don't go yet, old thing. My, my! Like Kathleen Ferrier. Hang about. I'm coming down.'

He disappeared into the sunlight, before reappearing through the double doors that lay below.

'Can't repeat the past, old chap.'

'Why, Jonny Tait! What brings you here?'

'I might ask you that. By the way, my real name's not Jonny. That's a nickname. I was christened 'Stephen.''

'Oh?'

'But no-one knows. What's your first name?'

'It's Charles.'

'Like cats, we guard an inscrutable name. School does that for you, I fear.'

He settled on a metal chair and stretched his feet on the bar in front.

'The Party's over now. And what will poor Charlie do then, poor thing?'

'I'm not sure what you mean by 'party'.'

'Well – the play for starters. Yes, we partied well and truly. Left them calling out for more. Then the after-party party, which got slightly out of hand. After which, another party, as they say in Chancery, 'another party' upped and left the scene. That party's over now and done with. No false exit there.'

I nodded.

'You'll get used to it. The world is full of fickle friends.'

'Actually,' I said, 'he *was* a friend. Perhaps you don't believe it.'

Jonny grinned. 'In time, you'll realise, we walk alone. The friends that we desire are dreams and fables.'

'That's a little harsh.'

Peaceful though it was to sit beneath those gilded portraits, I knew that I should not be there, chatting with a sixth former. After what had happened, I knew that I should be careful.

'He's a good sort, Mountjoy. He'll take care of Number One,' said Jonny. 'As for you, I know it's hard to wrestle with the afterlife, that is, when the scenery's come down.'

'It takes some getting used to.'

'Nonsense. Why, it's not the end. Just a wee bend in the river. Look, you're still afloat, old boy. Only, the view is different. You've moved away, but on you go. Not a lot of point in loitering.

'Mountjoy's gone, but somebody like you will take his place. Play your cards right and your name will soon be on that study door. It will be your turn to play the prince.'

The thought of taking Mountjoy's place depressed me more than I could say. I'd never match his charm or his panache upon the cricket field. I'd be a third-rate copy, like an understudy fluffing lines.

'You know just as well as I do, everybody's on the stage,' said Jonny. 'No-one's ever out of costume. CCF and Chapel, wearing boaters in the Town; who's allowed a tassel on his cap? One day sweeping sawdust, then the next, you top the bill. Some day, you'll be up there, like the man on the trapeze.

'Look at me,' said Jonny. 'You think my life's been a bed of roses? What's it like to be a swot who takes no interest in sport? How did I survive each day? My first year here was Hell. Cold baths, CCF and fagging. I was a wimp. I'm still a wimp, but a bigger wimp than I used to be. Scrawny, hairless; couldn't tackle, couldn't even run. 'Spaccy! – 'Baldy! Spaccy! Cretin!' Life as a fag in the School House Day Room was the stuff of nightmares. Twice I tried to run away. But somehow I survived.'

He marched up and down the aisle now to vent his fury.

'So – you became a character. If you can't beat them, make them laugh. Look at me, you say, look at me. Watch me act the clown. Laugh at the way I walk and talk. I'll be the organ grinder's monkey in exchange for being left alone.'

Jonny waved towards the steely portraits. 'Yes, they know the drill. Mortarboards make wonderful accessories on stage. Life's a show – and public school prepares you for the other acts. Teaches you to carry on until the final curtain.'

'Don't you think that we might all be heading for the exit?' I said. 'Don't you think that *you-know-who* is going to blab about us?'

'What – that speccy sprog? He wouldn't lift a little finger. He's got no authority. Anyway, he's not a prefect yet.'

Jonny was right. Since Mountjoy left, Ainslie had worn a hunted look. Whenever we passed in the corridor, his eyes avoided mine. One of the men in the Lower Sixth told me just how bitterly they felt about the loss of Mountjoy. I was not alone in seeing Ainslie underneath it all. Other unseen hands had drenched his mattress twice that week. No-one had owned up to it. At tea, he often sat alone.

'I shall be gone in ten days' time,' said Jonny. 'All that wild applause will be a distant dream. Chin up, Charlie – when I get to Oxford, it will start again. Pick yourself up and dust yourself down and don the mask again.'

'I believe that some things last,' I said. 'At least with memories.'

'Yes – there may be memories. But things dissolve. Experiences melt like ice in a glass of gin. Maybe things that shape us, things we've done and things we've left undone, maybe little nuggets of the past remain with you. We change them and reorder them with memory, false memory – but who is to say they're right or wrong? My memory is mine. Things morph into the memory – and haunt you in a thousand ways.'

We sat in silence now and felt it drifting slowly back. Cheating and deceiving though these memories might be, moments in the Green Room and the swelling roar of laughter, I sealed them in a solid box, relics of a better time, hoarding them like brittle shreds of parchment from the daylight.

Life went on, as Jonny had predicted. We were still afloat, but the days were drained of colour. Yet another window closed.

It was cloudy, damp July and summer seemed long gone. The Cricket Trophy came and went, leaving a gap on the mantel piece. One grey afternoon, we had been skittled out by Hill House, our total score a wretched thirty runs. Parsons, who had taken Mountjoy's place as Captain scored a duck. We followed meekly to the crease and quickly out again.

Our fielding was dismal; someone dropped an easy catch; the bowling was half-hearted, and the spirit gone beyond recall. Beaten by ten wickets – and by Hill House. It was a disgrace.

Merriman, my co-mate, hurled his cricket bag across the floor.

'What are we to do? We're good as done for in the Three Cock now. No-one seems to care at all.'

We sat on the rough benches. Clouds were scudding overhead and spots of rain were promising another heavy downpour.

Next term we would move to studies – far beyond the Day Room. Free of regulations and responsibilities. Pasted on the leavers' doors were crude advertisements – a bookcase, armchairs, rugs and curtains; on one door, a 'Georgian escritoire, twenty pounds.' There were offers of books for 'cabbed' translations, a set of 'Loeb from Virgil'; Liddel and Scott's Greek dictionaries and 'six unopened baked bean tins'.

But funds were low at the end of term and even a battered armchair seemed beyond the scope of Merriman and me.

'Cheer up, Wallace. Eight weeks off – and we'll be in the Colts next term. We'll build the old House up again and show them what we're made of.'

Merriman was off to fish in Perthshire, weeks of flowing streams and misty mountains on the Tay. I was bound for Alverstoke and the pebbled beach of Southsea. One door closed; the future was a narrow, tapered passageway, leading on towards a gloomy bend.

The fag who brought the post at breakfast thrust a creamy envelope at me. It was addressed to 'Wallace, Abbey House, The Abbey School.' No initial heralded my name. The handwriting in bright green ink was florid and italic. The back of the envelope bore a crest, an armoured hand in the shape of a fist.

'Aren't you going to open it?' said Merriman. 'It looks important. Bet you've been invited to a ball.'

I stole up to the Reading Room, where one lone fag was dusting shelves. Most of the books were ancient, being published thirty years ago. Some had lost their spines and very few of them were read.

I tugged the creamy envelope, careful not to tear the crest. Inside, lay another one addressed to 'Mrs Wallace', together with a single sheet of paper.

Dear Wallace,

Please forgive me, I don't know your Christian name. We had the pleasure of meeting you at tea on Commemoration Day.

Christopher has said that he invited you to join us for the Shakespeare Festival, which we are holding in July. No doubt news has reached you about Christopher's withdrawal. These ups and downs have put all our arrangements out of kilter, so that it is only now that I have had a chance to write. Could you spare a week or two out of your summer holiday, to visit us down here at Connaught Hall?

No doubt you have many things already booked throughout the summer. If so, I completely understand.

I enclose a letter to your mother, begging her permission. Christopher, I need hardly say, has been reminding me for days. His father will not speak to him and he is in the doghouse. But it's time to mend our bridges; we must look towards the future. After his disgrace, you would cheer Christopher tremendously.

Do please write and let me know and pass my compliments on to your mother,

Yours very sincerely,
Madeleine Mountjoy

Merriman was right. It was an Invitation to the Ball. The Coach was waiting and the footman standing at the door.

Part Two
The Rose Garden

Chapter Eight

So began that curious affair with Connaught Hall, whose lakes and lawns still wander through my dreams.

Late July. I'd booked a ticket down from Waterloo Clutching a battered suitcase I had lifted from the loft, and stumbled out across the station yard.

'You're for the Hall?' the driver said.

I nodded meekly.

'Hop in then.'

I climbed aboard the Austin Twelve, whose seat soaked up the sun like blotting paper.

'You're the third today. It's lucky I was here. There's not a bus until well after three.

Connaught Station is no more, thanks to Doctor Beeching. But even on that summer's day, it was more like a cattle halt. Flies buzzed round the empty churns and posters for abandoned trains.

'Is it far?' I asked and wondered whether my two hot half-crowns would be enough to pay the fare and bring me back again.

'Couple of miles,' the driver said, cradling the wheel in butcher's arms.

We trailed through pine woods where the sunlight danced between the trees. Now we were skirting drystone walls and banks of rhododendron. Suddenly, the car swung right, beneath an iron gateway, past a lodge and up a gravel drive. On either side, a leafy forest of bamboo was rustling. We rounded yet another bend and there before us lay the Hall.

Decked with mullion windows and gables like the ace of spades, Connaught Hall had been rebuilt at the height of Imperial power. Sporting a mass of grand ideals, ransacked from other times, it offered large Renaissance doors and spiral chimneys framed from Tudor times. Every sandstone window had been shaped in different ways, with three Dutch gables at the front and two on either side.

Nothing spoke of elegance, but there remained a confident assertion that its roots were full of money.

In front of the house was a gravel yard, lined with scented roses and a lawn that stretched towards the fringes of a lake.

I paid the driver one of my half crowns.

'What time for the return?'

'I won't be coming back, I'm staying.'

'Ah. So, you're an actor, then? You strike me as young 'un. Most of them I've brought today are fogies. She's auditioning, you see. They're acting in a play.'

I turned and walked towards the Hall.

Coming from sunlight into shade, what struck me was a sense of cool, like a temple underground. It smelt of earth and sweet refreshing springs. Heads of lifeless animals peered grotesquely from the walls, shadowed buck, a warthog and a bear below the bannisters.

Family portraits interspersed these creatures, fading photographs of elephants, mahouts and bamboo bearers. Jet black faces clustered round a podgy looking sahib, whose white topee and pompous posture underlined his role in the charade. At his feet were sprawled three giant tigers.

Suddenly, a scrawny maid appeared from down a corridor. In her hands, a teaspoon and a towel.

'Hello – good afternoon.'

'My name is Wallace, Charlie Wallace.'

'Come for Lady Mountjoy? Please wait here.'

Then, with a shriek of metal runners, blinds were snapped and sunshine spilt across the tiled floor, dazzling the spiders, daddy long legses and flies that hung amid the horns. A tiger skin lay spread across the floor.

'Who is it, Maud?' a voice demanded.

'Please ma'am, it's another gentleman.'

'Well, show him in, there's a good girl.'

I was ushered through a great oak door into an airy room that seemed awash with images. Nervous as I was about my first appearance at the Hall, it took some time to realise the room was walled with mirrors, so what appeared to be a crowded gallery was more a series of reflections stretching on *ad infinitum*. Through the window lay a lawn, a flower bed of fading roses, then a pinewood and a wicket gate.

This had been the Ballroom in the days before the War. Bright Young Things in beads and headbands, flattened chests and bobbed hair took the floor with boys in sharp bowties and patent leather shoes. Now the dancing was no more, the polished boards were blank and bare. But in the corner of the room, behind a wide oak table sat a figure whom I recognised.

Clad in a green and turquoise tea gown, Lady Mountjoy peered through spectacles suspended from a chain.

'Remind me,' she began. 'You're – '

'Wallace,'

'Ah – of course.' A half smile briefly spread across her features. What had seemed intimidating now gave way to what I took for warmth. 'Wallace, you're the other friend of Christopher's, of course, you are.'

I smiled back. 'It's jolly kind of you to have invited me.' I wondered who the 'other' friend might be.

'Your mother wrote. She seemed uncertain, but I reassured her. You will be in safe hands here. It's good of you to join our troupe.'

Mother had opposed my spending two weeks of the summer with a friend who had disgraced himself and been expelled from School. But thanks to the glacial speed of the post from distant Singapore and lacking my father's authority, she was beaten down by my passionate pleas and a volley of crested envelopes, containing screeds of inky green.

'So – you have come to join the play. Do you know *As You like It?*

'I've read it.'

'But you've never seen it?'

'No, we never study Shakespeare. Only Xenophon and Cicero.'

'Still, you act?'

I nodded nervously.

'So, let's begin with something simple. Here's a passage from the play.' She opened a pale blue cloth-bound volume. 'Here, begin. The Good Duke in the Forest. Let us hear you read.'

Something from the long day's journey and the train from Waterloo, the lack of lunch, the rapid play of light and shade within the Hall caused the letters on the page to dance before my eyes. The sentences looked meaningless, I rarely stammer, but I stammered then. Standing in the Ballroom with the jangling chains of Madeleine, I felt like the son of the Royalist in the painting '*When Did You Last See Your Father?*'

'Now my co-mates and brothers in exile,

Hath not old custom made this life
Sweeter than that of painted pomp?'

I had barely mangled a couple of lines before she stopped me in my tracks.

'Look, poppet, there's a question mark. You've heard of a rhetorical question? And 'Co-mates' not 'comets', please! I thought you said you'd read the play.'

I tried again with no improvement, while she drummed her fingers on the table. 'Thank-you Charles. That's splendid, splendid,' shuffling the papers. 'Let me see.'

A vision passed before me of the taxi being summoned, of being frog marched through the Hall and out across the drive; the journey home, the evening train, to greet my mother with the words – 'There's been a terrible mistake. They thought that I could act. I can't. They've sent me home to Alverstoke.'

Silence reigned. Outside, the pinewood looked as black as pitch.

Then a frosty smile broke across her countenance.

'Now I remember. Christopher has told me you're a singer. How would like to sing to me?'

I swallowed. 'What would you like me to sing?'

'*Oh, for the Wings of a Dove*', perhaps?'

'I'd like to, if I knew it. I could sing '*Pie Jesu*', but my voice is getting low.'

'Well, sing anything you like.'

So, I began the tale – remembering that barren stage, where three weeks earlier I'd sung to lifeless portraits in Big School. A ballad of regret for all the happiness I'd briefly known, for happiness, which now seemed destined to be dashed away.

'Oh, I am a bachelor, I live with my son
And I work on the weaver's trade.'

On through all that sad and sorry saga of the Foggy Dew. My voice was even lower now, more like a crooning pigeon than a treble from the Abbey School. I prayed it would not crumble as I sang the sad lament. I sang as if my life depended on those moments of remorse and finished with a cadence full of pity and regret. The room returned; the crowded hall of mirrors glared implacably. But Madeleine was smiling.

'Thank-you Charlie. That will do. I'm not sure the material you choose is very suitable. But all the same, your voice is sweet. There is a part. A singer. Amiens.'

She rang a little silver bell. The flaky maid appeared as if by magic at the door.

Take Mr Wallace's luggage up and show him out to the veranda.'

'Yes, ma'am. There's another gentleman who's waiting in the hall.'

'Very well.' A sigh. 'I'll see him. Then I'll join the rest for tea.'

The girl nodded towards a figure hidden in the shadows. From the darkened doorway came another face I recognised.

'Charlie Wallace!'

'Jonny Tait!'

'Lady Mountjoy, please excuse us. Charlie, what a topping treat!'

Madeleine's demeanour, which had flickered on and off, like clouds across an April sky, suddenly seemed supercharged with sunshine.

'Jonny Tait! How wonderful.'

I was led across the hall and down into the dining room, whose tall French Windows opened on a line of balustrades.

Jonny Tait. Of course, I should have guessed he'd been invited. Waves of warm relief at having scrambled through the interview were tempered by the thought that Jonny – Jonny was the real thing. An actor, properly invited, and a friend of Christopher. A tiny stab of jealousy cooled the blazing afternoon, as if a cloud had drifted past the sun. Was I not friends with Christopher? And had he not invited me that starlit evening of Commem? Who was I then? An alto, who sang dodgy ballads passably in tune. And this chap Amiens – was Madeleine displeased to see me? Was I an encumbrance, like an extra guest at dinner?

I frowned and hesitated as we stepped onto the terrace. Still, I had arrived, I had a berth at Connaught Hall. On the lawn, a peacock shrieked and fanned its feathered tail.

At one end of the terrace was a white conservatory, beside which lay a flight of steps that led into the rose garden, its burnt straw brick contrasting oddly with its grey stone neighbour.

Beside the gate, a boy lay on a heap of new mown cuttings, fast asleep, one brown arm on his neck. A maze of box trees stood among the rose beds and a knot garden, with plants of marjoram and thyme. Craggy fruit hung from the walls, espalier pears and plums. In a semi-circle, by a fishpond, posed as for a painting, Christopher and Isobel were sitting side by side, together with a scrawny girl in khaki overalls and a fellow with a panama, whom I had never seen before.

Millie, dear, that scrawny girl was you, although I barely noticed. You were a blur at seventeen, with flaming hair and freckles. Did I spot those crooked teeth, that pleasant, eager, anxious smile, that healthy look of Land Girls, bronzed with August sun? I don't remember. I was bound for Christopher in summer flannels and a school cravat. Round his waist, a First School Colours tie.

Next to him sat Isobel, dressed in a plain white pleated skirt and gazing at the fish below the surface of the pond. Now, I realised the path did not lead on towards them. It jagged and doubled back towards the gate; it wound along the walls with glimpses of the silent foursome. Now it turned again and dashed back to the sleeping sentinel and came to ground in a *cul de sac* at the foot of an ancient pear.

The sun was warm, the gravel hard; the back of my shirt was a river of sweat, while all the time the figures by the pond were like a mirage.

Then, almost impossibly – for box trees do not come and go – a gap showed in the leafy maze and I marched hesitantly through.

'Charlie!'

'Hello Mountjoy.'

'So – you made it here. That's splendid.'

The party rose in unison, strangers gazing quizzically.

'Yes – thanks for the invite.'

He shook me warmly by the hand. 'So – you have met Isobel. And, this is Timmy. He's my cousin. Maybe you've heard of the family firm, 'Shoemakers to Royalty' in Burlington Arcade?'

Timmy grinned and flapped a panama.

'And this is Millie. Millie's our stage manager. Her mother runs a stable up the road.'

I could barely keep my eyes away from Isobel.

How can I describe perfection? Light and clear as Ariel, her blond hair in a band, she seemed to hold the stillness of the garden in a spell.

I felt a pang of envy, as the cousin Timmy placed a paw along her shoulder and the party settled down. Christopher, still smiling, played the host.

'We'll meet the other folk at tea. You heard that Jonny's coming?'

'Yes,' I forced a smile. 'I saw him. He's arrived, he's talking to your mother in the Ball Room.'

Tea was taken underneath a cypress, by the pine wood, thin cut bread and butter and some weak, insipid tea. Jonny joined us, fresh from his audition. Christopher seemed quite elated. 'Golly, but it's good to see you. Mother told me earlier you said you couldn't come.'

'Well, it's quite a saga. But a sudden change of heart. Parents voted to retreat to Caldey Island. So, I was alone.'

'That is simply topping news.' The shock of his expulsion seemed to have had no effect at all.

'Life's been jolly dull since I got home. The Pater's in a sulk and Mother's flapping with her preparations for the play. As for me, there's just a spot of National Service to be done. I guess I'll be in uniform when all of this over.'

'Where's the Pater?' Jonny asked.

'Where he always is these days, somewhere in the Bamboo Jungle, down behind the wood. Spends his time constructing dams and shooting anything that moves.'

As he spoke, a shot rang from the woodland and a cloud of rooks went chorusing into the azure sky.

'So, who is in this starry cast – besides ourselves and Charlie here?'

'Friends of Mother's. Actors and actresses who are resting. That chap there, with the moustache, he's an old flame of Mama's. Plays the Good Duke *and* the Bad. Mother says they toured the North in 1929, then a season at the Vic just before the War. Father isn't overjoyed to have this tyro on his patch, even though he's clearly past his prime.'

'Beware, my Lord of jealousy.'

'Exactly. Still, the Family have bagged the best parts for themselves. Isobel is Rosalind – and I'm her beau, Orlando. My part's frankly very dull. I don't get many laughs. Isobel's got all the speeches. You're the Melancholy Jacques, you've got all the famous lines and Timmy, here, is Touchstone. He's the Clown.'

'What about young Charlie here?'

'Oh, I can't remember. Charlie, what part have you got?'

'Me? I'm Amiens.'

'You're who?'

'I'm Amiens,' I answered, blushing.

'Who in this wide world is Amiens?'

I gulped. 'She didn't say.'

'Ah,' said Jonny. 'I remember, you're the chap who sings.'

'You mean I don't have proper lines?'

'To speak? A few – I can't remember.'

'Not another Silent Footman? That is tough. I'm sure the Mater wouldn't ask you here to play a mute.'

'But she told me you had pestered her to let me come.'

'Did I? Then we must make sure your journey's really worth it. Chin up, Charlie. We shall make an actor of you yet.'

'Who,' asked Jonny 'is that skulking fellow by the tree?' Nodding at the cypress, where a boy in rough brown overalls was handing out the cups and saucers. He looked out of place amid that sunny flannelled company, solid as a rock, with short brown pudding-basin hair and arms as thick as any blacksmith's boy.

'That is Josh, the gardener's lad.'

'He doesn't seem that pleased with life.'

'Josh? He's shy, just give him time.'

I recognised him as the chap asleep beside the gate. He scowled at us and looked away.

'So, not an actor then? Perhaps he's better with a lawn mower?'

'Possibly, but Mother's rather pushed to fill the minor roles. Thanks to her persistence, Josh is going to make his debut.'

'Acting?'

'Yes.'

'You must be joking!'

'Well, she's cut most of his lines.'

'And he is…?'

'Charles, the Wrestler. There's a monumental fight.'

A light mist hovered on the ground; a silver moon hung high above. Dark parade ground calls of 'Rajah!' echoed from the velvet lawns. At the whirr of the dinner gong, I presented myself in a dining room that glistered bright with silver and the gilded frames of Mountjoys.

Madeleine had changed into a purple evening gown. Behind her came a tall, thin lady with a frosty smile.

'Her sister-in-law, Elizabeth Mountjoy. Unmarried aunt.' Jonny declared. 'Jilted by a Guardsman. Keep a steady eye on her.'

Next to Madeleine, sat Geoffrey Challenor, her former beau; the matinee idol's crystal smile looked seedy with approaching age.

The Brigadier marched slowly in.

'Anyone seen Rajah?'

I found myself at the table end, seated between Cousin Timmy and Millie, the girl with flaming hair. You looked as if you'd pinched and scrubbed and bustled through the farmlands, a healthy take-me-as-you-find-me country girl who smelt of pasture. Yes, you seemed a lot more worldly than a boy like me. Leaving School at fourteen, you had worked your passage as a Land Girl. 'Decent work, but sodding lonely,' digging vast potato fields on bleak midwinter afternoons. But they'd taught you how to smoke and swear like any trooper. 'Mum taught Isobel to ride,' you told me. 'So, they asked me if I'd help erect the scenery.'

'You know the Mountjoy family?'

'I spent summer with that Christopher down on the hay fields. Then he said he'd help around the stables, mucking out. He's a little charmer, that one. We got on OK.'

So, you chattered gaily on, though I was barely listening. Had my thoughts been less distracted, life might have been different. What with the journey and the heat, I felt lightheaded, as I drank a thimble full of wine. It was as if I'd been suspended high above the panels and the portraits in their sombre rows, cut off from the conversation, like a moth inside the damask pelmet, drawn but set apart from all the noisy chatter.

At Connaught Hall, Austerity appeared a thing unknown, shed once, like an empty skin. The candles were brighter, the carpets thicker, the steaks (the steaks, by God!) were richer than anything I'd known. The wine was redder wine, the strawberries sweeter; silver glistened like so many candles and there, in the midst, sat Christopher and Isobel, burnished like the Gemini.

Shakespeare was right, old men forget. But memories of certain nights remain indelible. On that first night, it seemed this couple radiated light. Watching them amidst the babbling gossip of the table, they glowed the way a chiaroscuro painting glows with light, casting shadows onto other figures watching in the wings. Isobel had sea blue eyes that sparkled in the candlelight and warmed her cheekbones to a gentle rose. The starched white cloths and gleaming silver, crested glass and old decanters played a fugue of spangled light that danced above their heads, while scarlet soldiers smiled from gilded frames. She wore a long white evening gown; her shoulders and her neck were bare.

I did not sleep a lot that night. The moon shone through the window of my garret in the rooftop. It was perhaps the least important of the many bedrooms. Here, I guessed, the furniture had come to end its useful days. The jug on the washstand was cracked, the motto reading '—me, Sw-et Home'. The carpet was a victim both of moth and possibly of mice; the iron bed and horsehair mattress had seen better days.

But discomfort did not dampen my excitement with a world so different to the one I knew. The drabness and routine of School, the flatness of returning home to find my friends had moved away had been replaced by an enchanted garden and by Isobel.

I sat beside the windowsill and fingered through the script, looking out for Amiens, whoever he may be. I found a jolly ditty on the pleasures of a country life. '*Under the Greenwood Tree*,' it ran '*who loves to lie with me?*' Idle life with nothing to complain of but the weather.

And then a final chorus line, which checked me in my reverie. '*Most friendship is feigning, most loving mere folly.*'

'*Feigning,*' as the notes below the grubby page explained, meant '*Pretence, to make a show of... sham*'.

I stopped and pondered. Was I really welcome at the Hall? Were Madeleine's warm letters simply written down as formulae? Or was I just a substitute, an after-thought for Jonny Tait, in case he did not come? Was I just an understudy, there to swell the scene? Who would treat a favoured friend to bare boards and a mothy mattress? Wasn't Jonny's welcome so much warmer than my own?

From that window, high above the lawn, the scene was bathed in silver, as if from a searchlight hidden somewhere in the grounds. Glossy pewter helmets of the rhododendrons shimmered; the greenhouses and poplar trees glowed surreal grey. The lake was a sheet of polished steel.

As I closed the book, a figure came in view and crossed the lawn, making its way towards the wood. All I could distinguish in the darkness was a charcoal back and the long silhouette of a gun.

Chapter Nine

'Feigning. To pretend, to make a show of, sham, pretence…'

The words revolved around my brain. But how to know who feigns and who does not? What were the signs? Did mothers feign? Did Christopher?

'Making a show' – I thought of Jonny Tait. 'How many parts you play,' he said. 'You're never out of costume.'

Jonny was an actor and the actors' craft was feigning. Jonny could put on a show. And I was here by invitation from those people who were skilled at feigning, knowing when to smile and when to laugh and when to make a show. Who then could be trusted to be true?

And Isobel. Did she know about feigning, putting on a show? If she did, her Rosalind would be a thing to wonder at. Every eye would follow her. But actors – surely 'acting' must be more than just pretending? 'Now is the time to act!' was a call to arms.

I longed to be an actor. Not a sidekick, not a singing footman! Christopher had said 'We'll make an actor of you yet.' But first of all, I had to know the feigner and the fake.

The stable clock was striking seven, as I rose and slipped downstairs and out across the lawn. No-one about. Above me glowed the promise of a perfect day. If I was going to be an actor, I must know my way around the stage.

Beyond the gravel drive, the track ran on for fifty yards or more, before dividing into three, beside the stable yard. One path led towards the pinewood copse, then choked itself in weeds. To my right, a small plantation offered moss and winding ways. Before me lay a pebbled ford. A child in torn blue shorts was building dams from turf and dandelion. His legs were flaked with dry brown skin, some sort of eczema, and at my tread he whistled to a lurcher lying on the bank.

A figure stepped out. It was Josh, the sleeping warder from the garden. He stood, naked to the waist, with close cropped hair and wary eyes.

'Can you tell me where this path ends up?' I said.

'What's that to you?'

'Not much.'

'As far as Wi'm's.'

'Who's Wi'm?'

'My Dad. And you don't want him.'

He gazed at me with level eyes.

'You mean it's private?'

'If it isn't Wi'm you're after.'

'Where is Wi'm?'

'What's that to you?'

'There is no path beyond the ford?'

'Not if you don't want Wi'm.'

Rehearsals took place on the outdoor stage, south of the kitchen garden, in a natural amphitheatre, flanked by wings of rhododendron. Steps had been cut in the sloping turf for an auditorium; the stage rose gently up towards a giant beech tree at the back. On one side of the leafy stage, a giant banner fluttered, bearing a gold and scarlet crest, underneath which it proclaimed, 'The Connaught Shakespeare Festival.'

For Madeleine's bold plan was in the Spirit of the Age. Festivals were ripening, like strawberries in June. Culture in the countryside was all the rage that year. The great composer Britten staged events in Aldeburgh, where, with the scent of ripening corn and call of snipe across the Broads, he played new works to a knowing crowd, who came from Town in open cars and picked their way through reeds and mud and spoke of crested warblers. Meanwhile, another jamboree was launched across the Border in Edinburgh, with royal patronage.

In later years, much ink was spilt about the goings on at Connaught. Boasting firsts like Julian Slade's *Dancing on the Green* and Rattigan's *Bridge into Moonlight*, Connaught began in a minor way in 1949, years before its national fame and long before the famous egg-shaped stage.

All of that is history – but on that festive morning, my thoughts were on the present and its strange complexities.

Wi'm the gardener, stood on a sloping bank, erecting an arbour. Bull-necked and cloth capped, his face the colour of good vintage wine, he lugged the strips of evergreen, to weave a mesh of chicken wire and pine, while flame haired Millie supervised. Christopher was helping too. He offered me a friendly nod and whispered something into Millie's ear that made her laugh.

Dressed in a purple jumpsuit, Madeleine began the morning call. Among the cast, another cousin, Emily, was Celia, the bosom friend of Rosalind. She was a pleasant, easy girl, well used to playing second fiddle. Yet another member of the Mountjoy clan was Gwilym. Gwilym was Orlando's wicked brother, Oliver. The rest of the cast were a motley gang of ex-professionals and amateurs, whom I had met the night before. These included Geoffrey, Madeleine's old beau, who ambled round to greet us, like the heart throb he had been so long ago.

'Delighted to meet you, Charlie,' he drawled. 'Just keep an eye on Madeleine. Flatter her and you'll be fine, m'boy What part are you?'

'I'm Amiens.'

He made a face. 'The singer?'

'Yes.'

'Good show. Well, I'm the Duke. Or rather Dukes. I'm doubling the Good and Bad. One scene wicked, next one good. Quick changes in the shrubbery, I'm told.'

'Good morning, all,' said Madeleine. 'We're going to block the show. Christopher and Gwilym, would you kindly take the stage. Fighting, music, dance can wait. Scene by scene, we'll do the moves and then we'll talk of character.'

I had lied to Madeleine when I said I had read the play. Hastily scanning a worn-out copy, bagged from a bookstore back in Gosport, I had found the story hard to grasp. But watching early day manoeuvres on the leafy turf, I was spellbound, as each scene unfurled. In many ways, it felt just like those early summer afternoons in Big School, leaning back on metal chairs that had seen better days.

Here was an orphan boy, Orlando, treated like a slave at the hands of a bullying elder brother. Here was another bully, Charles, the Wrestler, whom he overthrows. Then a wicked Duke expels Orlando from his home. The good Duke travels to the Forest, where he lives like Robin Hood, surrounded by his Merry Men.

Much of this I found familiar as a fairy tale. When the boy meets Rosalind, (played of course by Isobel), he falls in love and writes her poems, which he pins onto the trees. I understood Orlando well. And what I liked about this story was the way the Forest seemed so friendly and hospitable. There was food for everyone and nobody was starving. And though they talked of snow and wind, the sun was shining warmly down. Life beneath the Greenwood Tree was so much better than the Town. Shepherds drifted in and out and fell in love from time to time, even though a chap called Jacques (Jonny Tait) would try to spoil the fun.

'I like this place,' says Rosalind 'and willingly could waste my time in it.' On that morning in July, Connaught, with its woods and lakes, its peacocks and its rose garden seemed a perfect place to waste the time.

'I wasted time', as Richard says, and *'now doth Time waste me'.*

But now there came a sticking point – and here I grew confused. For Rosalind escapes from Court, disguised as a man. Things now move from bad to worse, when she encounters brave Orlando. Each of them, you realise, has eyes for one another. But instead of a happy ending halfway through Act Three, Shakespeare has them playing games to act out their disguise. Rosalind declares that though she's actually a boy, she will *pretend* she's Rosalind providing that Orlando woos her, chats her up and learns the art of love – as if (*as if!*) she were the real Rosalind.

And so, what follows is a game of make believe and feigning. Orlando feigns to woo a boy who makes believe that he's a girl, when all the time *she* is a girl (except – *except!* – in Shakespeare's time the parts for girls were played by boys). Millie, do you follow this? Because in these enlightened times when boys and girls are urged to *choose* their gender, Shakespeare played that game four hundred years ago.

So, Isobel and Christopher played Rosalind and brave Orlando. Isobel wore slacks and strutted in a mannish way, lecturing her friend and brother in the ways of love, speaking speeches trippingly as if all acting were a lark and natural as breathing. I may have said that there was something devilish beneath the guise of the demure Madonna, something wild that flashed across her eyes, as Rosalind declared 'I'll speak to him, like a saucy lackey.'

As for Christopher, I knew that he could do no wrong. His acting, too, was natural. Their scenes were like a private conversation and the audience were eavesdroppers to watch events unfold. Again, I felt a stab of envy. Something lifelike in the way these two performed together made me wonder where the border lay between the faithful and the fake. Both the cousins Emily and Timothy looked out of place, embarrassed to be on that stage at all. They fluffed their lines and fidgeted and looked about them all the time, longing for each wordy scene to end.

I was not the only one to sit upon that grassy bank, watching this pair exercise their charms. Offstage, Timmy watched with open mouth, a flush across his cheeks, a sullen furrow playing on his brow. Elizabeth, the single aunt, was also witness to the scene, casting an approving eye and throwing a disdainful glance towards the rest of us as if to say 'That's how it's done. Do it better if you can,' while in the corner of the stage, another figure stood in silence, narrow eyed and brooding. It was Josh the gardener's boy.

Watching the romantic games of Rosalind, I felt a strange anxiety – that in this world of Greenwood Trees and sunshine, danger lurked.

We broke off for elevenses – for cordial and gingerbread. Christopher sat down with Jonny Tait. I watched them laughing, while Isobel retreated to the safety of her aunt.

Cousin Timmy turned to me. 'They're not half good,' he grunted. 'They'll act us off the stage. I'd better mug some lines.'

'I haven't many lines to learn,' I said.

'Well, good for you. I'll sneak out for a spot of swotting. Will you test me in an hour's time?'

I was not due to sing until the afternoon. I wandered off. Isobel and Christopher disturbed me with their laddish games.

I passed a narrow passageway of dark green rhododendron towards a path, which led across the west flank of the Hall and found the hut by accident, a mile beyond the shallow ford. There was no-one to guard the road. The track was rougher; moss and ragwort nosed profusely through the stones. On my left, the Bamboo Jungle glowed in an unfriendly way. Further down the hill, I reached the cottage, where Wi'm lived.

Yellow paint peeled from the woodwork. Windowpanes were cracked and dirty; smoke rose from the chimney; gutters rusted; hens pecked in the mud. Somewhere, deep inside, a child was crying, rhythmical and low.

Outside, sheets of rusty iron lay in a wilderness; a goat gazed from a paddock by a hutch of rabbits and a woman in a petticoat was bending to a wicker basket. Then at the end of a row of sheds, a pigsty, housing three gigantic pigs.

I've never been fond of pigs; the smell, the lack of hair, the fat, pink skin; the strength and power – but more than that, the eyes, the all too human eyes that sum you up in knowing ways. For it is you, they seem to say, you that lose your dignity, when the throat is cut and the flesh is scoured and the carcass hangs on the butcher's hook. This the pig appears to know and he will fight you if he can, hot and bloody, fleshy pink and wise.

One of the pigs, an old red boar in a separate pen of ragged iron, glared at me. He stank of whey and rotting vegetation. As children peer from farmyard gates, I watched this pig with a tinge of fear. The eyes stared back at me, so hostile, knowing, unafraid. For full ten seconds, he held my gaze, until I looked away, half ashamed, as if I had been watching people in a zoo.

The path now snaked back on itself and lost direction in the wood, meandering through firs, until it finally expired. The wind had died and now the wood was still.

Outside, in the garden, we had felt the heat of summer, but here was a shroud of dusty gloom. The air was chilly, I'd lost my way and brown shade stretched on every side.

Fifty yards on was a patch of green. On either side, a wall of brambles rising to the sky.

Nettles clawed my ankles, then a clearing full of giant weeds, beyond which stood a wooden hut, with dirty windows and a door. The roof was made of thatch, the panes intact, the woodwork creosoted. Spiders trailed silver curtains from the sloping eaves and Queen Ann's lace and sorrel nodded idly round the walls.

No one was in sight. I padded over dewy grasses, dodging shafts of sunlight, stopping now and then to listen. A spider's web on the dirty pane, a boot mark on the lawn. I tried the door. The latch flew up. The hinges swung back freely. They were newly oiled and the air inside had a spicy scent, as from a well-kept larder. In spite of the daddy long legses, the cracked panes and the cobweb rafters, it was clear the place was used; a clean swept floor, two chairs, a table and a bookshelf on a crate. There was an old green sofa too, from which the stuffing poured like mushrooms on a grassy meadow.

I found a basin and utensils and a cupboard stocked with jam and tea. At the far end lay a mattress with a mothy eiderdown. It was as clean and well prepared as any secret hideaway.

I wandered round the half-lit room, flicking through the dog-eared books. Some of the spines had fallen away, but the titles took you back to childhood,

Kidnapped and *King Arthur's Knight's – The Tale of Lancelot,* a faded *Treasure Island.* I opened the stained brown cover and read the inscription in a bold italic hand.

'To Christopher, wishing you every happiness. Christmas 1941
Fondest love, Elizabeth'

Something in the air outside warned me to be still. For now the birds were silent, as if someone else was on the prowl. Then I noticed it, a parcel hidden underneath the shelf, wrapped in newsprint, nozzled like a can. It must have weighed a good four stone. Was it an ancient souvenir?

Quietly as I could, I pulled the paper wrapping back. The dull glow of dark metal met my gaze, the heavy, conical dead weight of what looked to be a war time bomb.

A child of war, I knew these things – and of the risk they posed. Four years after peace was signed, they lay in wait for the unwary. Dropped too far from a target zone to land in mud or fields of hay, the prize of ragged children in the woods or rat-infested bomb sites, few months passed without a lethal gift from the Luftwaffe raising its head for the Bomb Squad to defuse.

Perhaps the target zone had been in Portsmouth or in Alverstoke, where we lay shivering as children in the garden shelter. Or was it just a passing whim to terrify the peasantry? Somehow it remained intact, a parcel of destruction.

But someone had discovered it and wrapped it up with loving care and bore it back to the creosote hut to fester for a rainy day. Strangely awesome in the dark, this trunk of steel was biding time. Sweating slightly, half expecting to be blown to smithereens, I wrapped it up and placed it in the hiding place again.

Timmy was pacing up and down behind the auditorium, clutching a copy of the play and stopping now and then to beat his temples with an open palm.

'Where've you been? It's nearly lunch. I thought you'd disappeared for good.'

'Sorry. Just a little walk.'

'You said you'd test me on my words.'

'I'm ready now, if you are.'

'It's like carving granite, but I've learnt a page or two. Come on.'

Wi'm was now erecting a marquee, helped by a surly Josh.

Christopher had said that Timmy was to play the clown, But the more I read of Touchstone's lines, the less clown-like they seemed to be. Everybody in the play was either in disguise or feigning. Timmy had a speech about the whole effect of telling Lies. But as for comedy and clowning, Shakespeare, would do well to learn a thing or two from Oscar Wilde.

He battled on with all the desperation of a drowning man, till finally he sank down on his knees.

'A waste of time,' he moaned. 'It might as well be Sanskrit.'

'Have another go, tonight.' I gave him back the book. 'It's not your fault you've only started. What's the bet the others have been practising for weeks?'

'Damn nice girl, whatever.'

'Mm.'

'We've known each other since – I can't remember.'

'Lucky you.'

'And even though she is my cousin and, as they say, 'My Intended –''

'She's your what?'

'She's My Intended.'

'But' I said, 'you're cousins.'

'Nothing wrong with that, old boy. Cousins marry all the time. Soon as I come down from Oxford, couple of years from now, Isobel will be nineteen. That's when they say we'll be hitched.'

'Who is 'they'?'

He waved a regal hand. 'Them aunts – Elizabeth and Madeleine, Mama. Good thing Isobel will still be on the youngish side. Won't have done a Season, won't have met the competition. Best for her to settle down at once, that's what they say.'

'And what is Isobel's opinion?'

Timmy winced. 'I've no idea. Anyway, there's years to go.'

'Two years.'

'You're right. It won't be long.'

Shocked to learn that Isobel's was stamped and sorted like a Pasha bride, I was amused by Timmy's air of confidence.

'How well do you know her, then?'

'I told you – we are cousins. Cousins understand each other. Instinct, if you like. She's been at school in Switzerland at some young ladies' college. I haven't seen her all that much. But when I join the firm, we'll settle down as right as rain.'

To have such simple views, was that a recipe for happiness, assuming that the road was straight and true? It seemed a million miles away from feigning and despite my fears, I felt a sneaking admiration for this blinkered optimism.

'So, you'll marry and live happy ever after, like the fairy stories?'

Timmy frowned. Perhaps he thought that he was being joshed.

'Yes,' he said. 'She knows as well as I do that she's My Intended.' Flapping a cream panama, he sauntered back towards the Hall.

'Teatime – and a halt was called. 'Tonight,' said Madeleine, 'there'll be a madrigal or two. And Father's reading Malory. I hope you'll all be there. It will be fun.'

We drifted off. I climbed the stairs towards my lonely garret, pondering encounters of the day. Beyond the severed headed game which crowded out the stairwell, the first-floor panelling showed coats of arms and mottos from the past. *'Semper Eadem,'* – 'Ever Constant' – *'Nisi Dominus Frustra'* – 'Without God, we strive in vain.' Blue and scarlet gauntlets seemed to rise out of the shadows. Gilded crowns of laurels loomed, as if the passage led towards some long-forgotten tournament.

Oh, to be a knight-at-arms and slay the chubby dragon – not, I sadly realised, as if the damsel cared.

Near the stairway came the sound of raucous male laughter and a voice I recognised.

'Chekov never thought of that. Look, honestly, you're quite absurd.' The lisping tone was Jonny Tait. I turned and knocked. For full five seconds, there was silence, followed by a clatter. Then a voice called 'Who goes there?'

'A friend.'

'Stand and unfold yourself.'

The door swung open. Christopher and Jonny stood like naughty children, hands behind their backs. The air was yellow with tobacco smoke, the window swung without a latch.

'Caught red handed!' Jonny beamed. 'Instant rustication. Come, come in. There's brandy and cigars.'

'Mother disapproves, you know,' said Christopher. 'She reckons smoking stunts your growth.'

'Like masturbation.' Jonny added gaily.

They must have been drinking long before the break for tea.

'Sit down, sit down,' said Christopher. 'Cigar? A glass of brandy?'

I shook my head. 'Cigars will make you sick?'

'I'm sure they will. Remember when I tried a cigarette?'

Jonny looked a little bashful. 'And of course, you have to keep a clear head for the madrigals.'

'Nobody's asked me to sing.

'I'm certain that they will.'

'Christopher was talking about guns,' Jonny explained. 'You see in *Uncle Vanya* – do you know the play by any chance?

'I don't.'

'No matter. Listen, there's a gun, which comes on in Act Three. Now, anyone with any sense will know that once a gun appears, it has to serve a purpose in the play. Ibsen does it all the time. Guns on stage must have their uses. If there is a gun, it must be used.'

'Only,' added Christopher, 'in Chekov it may fail to work. Like so much else in Chekov, even guns can disappoint.'

'Well, not always. Guns are props – they have to serve a purpose.'

Jonny looked at me again. 'I don't think Charlie's interested. What have you been up to then? You've not had much to do.'

'Oh, this and that. I talked with Timmy. Wandered round the place a bit.'

'Find anything interesting?'

'Not really. Didn't get that far. I bumped into the gardener's boy. He wasn't very welcoming.'

'Josh?' said Christopher. 'He's fine. He's just a little shy.'

'Of course,' said Jonny, stabbing a cigar butt in an ashtray. 'But you know him pretty well. Much, much better than we do. Didn't Madeleine remark that you two were inseparable?'

There was a pause. Did Christopher look just a little shady?

'Not a bit.' His eyes glued to the carpet. 'We were little boys – running round on the estate with pointed sticks and catching minnows. Then – you know how things pan out. With school and that – you drift away – you find yourself a different crowd. We weren't exactly friends.'

'How 'not exactly?'' Jonny mused. 'You spent a lot of time together. Doesn't that in some way make you friends?'

'Not at all. There's lots of people whom I've had to spend the time with, people whom I'd never count as friends. Boarding School has that effect. You learn the art of toleration.'

'You don't count him as a friend?'

'I told you.'

'Playmates?'

'Jonny, he was there – it was a while ago.'

'Well, it's the wrestling scene tomorrow. Have you been rehearsing that?'

'You'll have to wait and see.'

I realised this was the first time that I'd been with Christopher, my so-called friend, since I arrived. He and Jonny, on the other hand, had been inseparable, except when either of them took the stage. There was *camraderie* between them. As for me – they were two grown up people with cigars and I was tagged along, in case – in case of what? In case they both grew tired of one another? Was that why the garden boy had glowered with malevolence, because he wasn't counted as a friend?

'*Beware, my lord, of jealousy.*' I had not read *Othello* yet.

'Talking of guns,' said Jonny Tait. 'Your father's always firing off.'

Christopher frowned. 'He can't stand plays. Or literature. Especially Shakespeare. As for Culture, when he hears the word, he acts like Hermann Goering.'

'All the same, he's not the only one to own a gun. Tell us more about your friendship with the garden boy.'

Christopher was silent. Then he grinned – 'You think my sister's good? Isn't she just Rosalind down to her very ankles?'

'Makes a very pretty boy,' said Jonny, screwing up his eyes. 'Makes me very envious to watch you two performing.'

'What do you think, Charlie boy? Better than your lads in drag? Eat your heart out Gwendolen. Our Isobel's the real thing.'

'Except, *except*,' said Jonny 'that she's *not* the real thing. Shakespeare's Rosalind, (you know this better than me, Christopher) would have been a boy in drag, back in Shakespeare's day. Boys played all the female parts. No-one put a girl up on the stage. Then, like Viola in *Twelfth Night*, Shakespeare plays the story backwards. 'His' or 'her' supposed disguise becomes a chance for lads to flirt. Three full acts of flirting between two boys on the stage, one of whom pretends to be a girl pretending she's a boy. Lots of coming on and kissing; even mock-up marriages. Quite enough for our Lord Chamberlain to get a lather up. Then, when they have had their fun, Shakespeare writes the big finale. 'Rosalind' puts on a dress and everyone is safe again. No-one gets arrested for improperly soliciting. Anyway, it's Shakespeare, so we think of it as holy writ.'

Jonny sniffed his brandy. 'Put this play in modern dress and Oscar Wilde's as mild as milk.' He paused and looked out at the sky. 'You know that sonnet that begins '*A woman's face with Nature's own hand painted?*''

' – *Hast thou, the master-mistress of my passion,*' Christopher intoned.

'Written to a boy, perhaps an actor in the troupe. Possibly a Rosalind, a Celia or Viola. But then, after the Restoration, Nell Gwynn occupied the stage and all the pretty boys were unemployed. They'd never act again.'

Dim rays of a rosy sun were lighting up the clouds. Somewhere down beyond the lake, a dog was yapping noisily.

'As for Millie?' Jonnny said, smirking at his brandy.

'As for Millie – what?'

'Oh, just a shot into the dark.' He paused and eyed us. 'I don't think that she's an actress – what do you think, Charlie?'

No-one spoke. I cleared my throat. 'I'd better dress for dinner.'

Christopher looked up and said 'It's very good to see you, Charlie. Gosh, I'm awfully glad you're staying on.'

He looked as if he meant it. Christopher was just as fine an actor as his sister. Just as skilful in the art of feigning and pretend. I toddled off towards my garret, musing on the mournful songs that I was due to sing of friendship and the frailty of love.

Chapter Ten

A line of chairs had been arranged along the lake, beside the reeds. Veiled in a mosquito net, which hung around her like a shroud, Madeleine strolled arm in arm with the Brigadier, who chewed a large cheroot. Behind her, like a bloodhound, came the watchful Geoffrey.

How we English love *al fresco* entertainment in the summer, longing as we do for balmy nights and swallow skies. In spite of weak mulled wine and chilblains, evenings spent out in the open promise something rich and rare, a moment seized and treasured, but tonight, the air was warm and even rugs were not required.

A rustle of applause announced the entertainment would begin. Shadows could be seen against the sky. A heavy silence followed, lasting more than half a minute. As at a Christmas party, when a lull falls on the guests, children in frocks and paper hats are suddenly quite still. The cake has been forgotten and a boy with a half-eaten sausage stares; the tinsel tree looks quite forlorn beside the whispered conference in the hall. A guest has failed to come, a vacuum that no games can fill. Now, amongst the line of chairs, there grew a sense that something might be wrong. The silhouettes across the water stood as still as stone.

A heron rose, a clumsy paper shape that soared and clattered. Then, as if from out the lake itself, a voice rose like a fountain. Now it floated through the trees, a strange lament in language written centuries ago.

'Come when I call – or tarry when I come.
If you be deaf, I must prove dumb.'

As the notes climbed through the air, I knew that it was Isobel. Something in the semi-darkness and the stillness of the night caused reality to soften.

Something like a tidal wave of sound engulfed the senses, swept away the landmarks, left me shipwrecked on the currents of the night.

Her voice seemed quite unearthly, high and pure as liquid silver, fashioning a world of dreams where anything was possible.

'Stay awhile, my heavenly joy
I come with wings of love
When envious eyes Time shall remove.'

She curtsied in the dusk; there was a stunned and mute applause. She made her way to a vacant chair directly next to mine. Wi'm had enhanced the intimacy of the event by cramming every chair close to its neighbour, so that I was sitting knee to knee with Isobel. She wore the same white chiffon dress that I had seen the night before, a dazzling low-cut gown, that left the shoulders bare. Never in my short life had I sat so close beside a girl; flesh and blood beside me, smelling of Chanel and summer wine.

The Brigadier sprang to his feet, an acorn of a man. His voice was throaty, deep; it sounded like a farmer grinding barley. Perfectly erect in evening dress, he stood with head held high.

'An extract from *Morte d'Arthur* by Sir Thomas Malory:

'Then, Sir Launcelot began to resort unto Queen Guinevere and forgot the promise and the perfection that he made in his quest and ever his thoughts were privily on the Queen....'

Of the rest of the evening, I remember little, though I have the programme still, a sheet of faded carbon, frayed and greasy at the ends. *April is in My Mistress's Face,* followed by *The Silver Swan* and *Never Weather Beaten Sail,* a gauze of sound that floated on the air. We sat cocooned, our knees just touching, telegraphing in a secret code.

There was no embrace, of course, no palm to palm, or whispers in the dark. No murmured voices, sweet and low, but if there was a moment, now, I knew that it was mine. The steady beat of pulse on pulse, of thigh and arm on arm. That fine, taut frame that must respond to each note in the poring dark; she did not flinch or quaver at the warmth upon her legs and arm.

If it were now to die – the numbing pain of dark desire. The madrigals passed swiftly by. I woke up to the scatter of applause.

The party rose and my companion smiled, stood and made her way to join her aunt beside the lake. Wi'm began to stack the chairs, aided, more or less, by Josh, who hovered by the family engaged in warm congratulations for all the performers.

Daylight had gone. Above the elms, a band of crimson hung. Geese whirred high above the lake and then from way beyond the pines there came a distant, muffled roar, like an explosion, somewhere far away, beyond the road to Petersfield. Momentarily, the chatter ceased, then rooks began to caw. We listened. There was nothing more. The scar of sunset healed into night.

Next morning, after the madrigals, I looked for a sign from Isobel. None came. Time had indeed removed; a veil shrouded her. At breakfast, she looked wrapped in thought, like one attempting some obscure, imponderable formula. When cousin Timmy tried to draw her into conversation, she cut him off. He coloured up and choked upon his toast.

'Charlie,' said Madeleine, crossing the Hall. 'I want you to work with Gwylim today. You can use the Ballroom and he'll take you through some of the songs. Naturally, the string quartet will join you when we dress rehearse.'

Gwylim had dark curly hair, dancing eyes and a cheerful grin. Small and wiry, he resembled none of the other Mountjoys. As I crossed the threshold of the many mirrored ballroom, the kaleidoscopic figures and reflections of an elf perched at an upright piano came in view. He strummed the *'The Lover and his Lass'*.

'Come in, come in. You're Charlie, yes? Let's have a shuftie at these songs. Madeleine says you're a singer. But you didn't sing last night?'

'I wasn't asked.'

He stared at me. 'Well anyway, let's hear you now. Let's have a go at *'Under the Greenwood Tree.'* Gwylim played a merry introduction and we set off at a tempo, which I struggled to maintain. Halfway through the song, he stopped and swivelled on the piano stool.

'Something wrong?' One eyebrow arching quizzically.

'No,' I said, 'it's just a bit too fast to follow.'

'It should be a jolly song. *'Who loves to lie with me – and tune his merry note.'*

'Look,' Arne repeats it: 'merry, *merry* note.' It's not funereal.'

'Yes,' I said. 'But yet he *'loves to lie'*. And later on, he says that friendship is a fraud and love is folly.'

''Lying!' Oh, you chump. The fellow's lying on the ground! He's sunbathing and eating fruit. And pleased as punch about it all. As for the later songs, they're saying, Look, it's great – we're free. We live in the woods with the wind and rain. And nobody is lying. People back at home may lie – but here the weather's what it is. And if it rains or if snows, yet all the same it's honest rain. And if it freezes, still it's honest snow.'

'So why does Rosalind go on pretending she's a boy?'

'For safety. So that nobody can take advantage in the wood.'

'I thought you said the wood was honest.'

'Well, it is.'

'So why does she continue with her game of 'let's pretend?''

He shrugged. 'I don't know. Listen, Charlie – when you 'tune your merry note', try to sound as if you mean it. That's what acting's all about. Even if you're feeling sad, you have to make it sound as if you're not.'

'You mean I must pretend?'

He glared at me. 'OK. Pretend.'

I rather took to Gwylim. He was different to the others. Less actorish and showy, he was self-assured without the need to let the others know.

From time to time, he summoned me to practice in the Ballroom. There, he strummed a tune and took me through the vocal score. 'You're coming on,' he said one day. 'You're settling towards a tenor. In a month or two, your voice will be as pure as driven snow.'

'Great,' I said. 'We open in a week.'

'You'll have to busk it somehow. You'll get by, don't force it. Just believe in what you're singing. Act the words, as well singing all the notes.'

'I'll do my best.'

I had in fact been practising, as far away as I could go. I skirted round the lake and warbled to the rushes, trying all the time to keep the cracks and octave slides at bay.

'Try this one. The hunting song. It's just a filler. It begins –

'What shall he have that killed the deer?
His leather skin and horns to wear.''

He played the march. 'Now sing along. We'll do it line by line.'

The tune was simple, but the words were baffling. The chorus ran

'The horn, the horn, the lusty horn,
Is not a thing to laugh to scorn.'

I stopped. 'I'm sorry Gwylim. I'm not sure that I can act that one. It doesn't make a lot of sense.'

He grinned. 'Yes, it's a bit obscure. The horn, you see, is what you give your neighbour when his wife is – loose.'

'I'm sorry?'

'When she's – how to put it? – 'wandering' around?''

'You mean she's feeling horny.'

'Charlie – that's a mite indelicate. Remember where you are.''

'I'm sorry.'

'Yes, but in a way, you're right. I guess they've told you something about all the birds and bees. So, if a wife was 'wandering', they thought the reason must be that the husband could not please her. The horn becomes a symbol of fertility, you see.'

I frowned and thought about that conversation in the changing room. 'God, you're a horny bastard.'

'So, the horn will help the husband to be horny?'

Gwylim blushed. 'I wish you wouldn't use that word.'

'I'm sorry – Shakespeare uses it and I don't know another word.'

'The husband's called a 'cuckold'. And he has to wear the horn. They thought it was hilarious.'

'Except, it's not. The chorus says it's *'not a thing to laugh to scorn.''*

'And then *'It was a crest ere though wast born.'* So married life is not the same as *Romeo and Juliet.* He grabbed a copy of the script. 'Somewhere, in another scene, Rosalind says lovers are *'December when they wed'.'*

'I thought the play ends happily?'

'It does. But not for 'ever after'. Lovers wed. The curtain falls. But don't expect a happy marriage following a happy ending. Look no further, just in case you find *'the lusty horn.''*

Outside on the leafy stage, Christopher and Josh had been rehearsing for the wrestling scene, with Rosalind and Celia. Madeleine had scoured the nearby countryside for someone who could help to stage a realistic match. A barrel-chested regimental sergeant major, with a set of whiskers, held the stage. He was explaining a difficult handhold. Christopher, in rugby shorts and jersey, Josh in overalls, eyed each other like a pair of boxers at a weigh-in. Both were sweating slightly in the sun.

'Come now, gentlemen. We'll speed it up,' declares the soldier. 'One, two three – and off you go.'

Josh displays a natural balance, grabs Orlando by the waist and lifts him up; Orlando grapples with the Wrestler, crouched across his back. He breaks the hold, but can't escape, held by the Wrestler's forearm, squeezing all the breath out of him, as Orlando gasps for air. Once again, the hold is broken and the two stand facing one another, panting heavily.

It is realistic, how they bind into each hold. Josh is on Orlando's back again; it seems, he must be thrown. A patterning of blue-white veins stands out across Orlando's arm. The Wrestler's chin is buried in Orlando's shoulder, knees well bent and ready for the throw. But Orlando won't submit. The struggle carries on; the Wrestler pinions Christopher, as if he plans to crush him or to lift him up and hurl him at the crowd.

Back held tight to Josh's chest, Christopher breaks free from the embrace – then with a grunt he finds his feet. Josh hurtles past him, landing with a thud across the mat.

Both are up and ready for the spring. It's looking dangerous. Christopher is slighter, taller, feet well poised, his forehead damp and dark hair tousled by the brawl. Josh is stockier and firmer, resting hands upon his thighs like a close-in fielder.

Suddenly, from upstage, Geoffrey bawls *'Forebear! No more!'* and adds *'How dost thou Charles?'*

'He cannot speak, my Lord.'

But Josh is far from done. He's ready for another round.

'Bear him away,' says Geoffrey. Josh eyes the panting Christopher with something between misery and rage. Orlando wipes his brow and smiles at Rosalind.

He settles down upon the turf beside Gwylim and me. 'What do you think? A decent start?'

'I thought he was going to kill you.'

'Yes – he's quite a toughy, Josh.'

'I hope he's read the script. Though something tells me that he doesn't read a lot.'

'You'd be surprised,' says Christopher. 'He's deep, that one.'

'You seem to know a lot about him.'

'No, we haven't spoken much this year.'

The days at Connaught drifted by, a line of summer nights and sunny afternoons; dazzling, misty dawns, dissolving as the sunlight baked the lawns and turned them into yellow straw.

During breaks between rehearsals, we would bask in deck chairs in the shade. Jonny had unearthed a gramophone, together with a box of pre-War hits. Half heard notes of *Little Sir Echo* and *Then the Angels Sang* floated through the rose gardens and hidden shrubberies. We tried our skills at croquet on the grass below the terrace. Gwilym was an expert, standing nose above the croquet hoop, ricocheting paint-cracked balls down grassy banks, through parterre borders, rattling on flowerpots and scattering opponents.

One of Gwilym's victims was the wretched Cousin Timmy, who grew so desperate at watching balls dispatched to every corner, that one afternoon, he swung his mallet like a golfer, sending the ball skywards, like a fizzing hand grenade, to crash some way beyond the hoops. It landed on a glass frame with a shattering commotion that drove the rooks out of their nests and up into the sky.

Timmy threw his mallet down and stomped off in despair.

'What's eating him?' said Gwilym. 'Unrequited love or indigestion?'

I was left to find the missile, nestled in a bed of straw, beside a thick-veined cucumber. Stretching my hand through jagged shards, I wiped a stain of green away and ambled back towards the field of play.

But if Timmy's croquet had been blighted, so was mine. A crystal wall enveloped Isobel, a veil she threw around herself whenever off the stage. Elizabeth, the bitter looking, disappointed aunt, would suddenly materialise and spirit her away. There was no chance of conversation. I began to wonder if the madrigals had been a dream.

I trusted Gwilym, maybe more than I had trusted Jonny. Jonny could be cynical and wearisome at times. Gwilym played a straighter bat – or so it seemed to me. One morning in the Ballroom, I said 'Gwylim, what do you think of Isobel?'

He flicked through pages of the score, as if he wasn't listening, then stopped and swivelled round the piano stool to look at me.

'Isobel, my cousin? Well, I've known her all my life. She's quite a feisty character. But you can see that, can't you?'

I blushed. 'I wondered. She seems rather shy.'

'I wouldn't count on that. She's quite a star of course. She must be like her mother was at seventeen.'

'Was Madeleine a star?'

'She would have been. But then her family whisked her from the limelight. She was married off before her time. I gather she was radiant, the way she held an audience. But mind you, there were rumours that the company she kept was rather fast.'

I pondered, baffled. Rather fast?

'Would you say Isobel was fast?'

'I rather hope she's not. But all the same, when she Comes Out next year, she'll have a stack of fellows queuing up to dance with her.'

'So, you don't think she's fast?'

He looked away and flicked the score. He seemed a little flustered. 'Charlie, if you want to know, I'd keep a proper distance from her. Wait until you're that much older. Don't you think that's wise? Isobel is – ' Gwilym shrugged, as if embarrassed, lost for words. 'Now what about this final song, *'Then is there in heaven.''*

'Mirth in heaven' was to be the climax of the play. The god of marriage, Hymen enters, to the strains of mystic music, as he blesses all the couples, who approach him two by two.

Madeleine had promised me a special silver costume, hired from Maurice Angel up in London. I would appear as if by magic from a hidden passageway, dug beneath a glossy rhododendron bush, to sing a hymn of wedlock and the blessings of the marriage bed. Fighting through the dead leaves and the bracken that concealed the entrance, I told Wi'm my costume would be torn to shreds if there was not a proper path to reach the stage.

Wi'm swore something audible and told his son to deal with it. I liked the idea of bursting on during the final scene. For that single moment, I'd be centre of the stage. All eyes would be on me as I sang the wedding hymn. I was determined this should be the highpoint of the show.

Rehearsals staggered on. That afternoon, we reached the final act. The play, it seemed, had wound itself into a fearful knot. A foolish shepherd, Silvius, has fallen for a shepherdess, called Phebe, who in turn has lost her heart to Rosalind. Orlando's reaching breaking point. He's tired of playing games with 'him', or 'her' disguised as 'Ganymede'; or with the 'her' he thinks of as a 'him'. Or has he seen through her disguise and knows that Ganymede is Rosalind?

The foursome meet and caterwaul. The Shepherd speaks about his love, of sighs and tears, of passion, faith and mournful adoration, while Phebe says the same and then Orlando echoes them.

'And so am I for Phebe.'
'And so am I for Ganymede.'
'And so am I for Rosalind.'

'And so am I for no woman,' says Rosalind – or Ganymede – or Shakespeare's adolescent boy.

Unconsciously, I mouthed the lines, until I noticed Jonny Tait had squatted down beside me.

'Forgive me.' Jonny smiled. 'Shakespeare knows the human heart. What has he been through himself? How does he know what it's like to love something impossible – and yet to go on loving?

'And I, for Rosalind,' he murmured. 'Well, you're not alone. Half the cast have got their eye on her.'

I blushed and swallowed. 'Is it really obvious?' I said.

'Don't worry, it will pass. There's lots of chaps find her adorable. People call it 'calf love'. It's a crush, I bet it's not your last.'

We sat in silence while the scene moved on. 'It's hopeless,' Jonny added. 'But that's part of the attraction. Hopelessness, the sheer impossibility of winning through. It's Launcelot and Guinevere – the adoration from afar. Ideal and impossible. What does Troilus say? *'Imaginary relish is so sweet.''* He paused and kicked the turf.

'And so are you for Isobel.

'And so is Josh for you know who.

'And Geoffrey for Madeleine –

'And I, as you no doubt suspect…. It seems to me that everybody's after something else, in search of the impossible.'

He broke off as the scene continued and the actors wandered off.

'These shepherds and these shepherdesses hail from antiquity. Back in the days of Ancient Greece, the poets wrote about the mountains of Arcadia, where shepherds played their pipes and sat upon the rocks and fell in love. It was the Golden World, a sort of chaste, enchanted Eden. Shepherds fell in love with shepherdesses and with shepherds too. Shakespeare's just translated them and moved the scene to Arden, where books are in the running brooks and there is good in everything.'

'So,' I said, 'you think it's just a crush?'

'For you or me? Each to his goal. Well, maybe I am wrong. Maybe, years from now you will remember Isobel. Sigmund Freud believed that we return to that first love, like criminals returning to the scene of crime. *'On reviendra toujours à ses premières amours.'*

'So how does it all end?' I asked.

'For Shakespeare? Love and happiness. A neat reversal back to wedlock. Everybody gets a slice of Happy Ever After. That's the way of fiction. But for us, it's not so easy. There are too many loose ends.'

'Jonny, you once said 'The world is full of fickle friends.' Did you really mean it or were you just putting on a show?'

'Maybe both. I am a cynic. That's my character, you know. The Melancholy Jacques, with a steel pin for your balloon. Stopping you from getting airborne and reminding everyone that in good time, the party will be over.'

'Has Jacques ever been in love?'

'I think he must have been. Nobody could be so bitter, if they were not disappointed. That's what makes him angry about all the fantasy.'

Madeleine had other things upon her mind, beside the roller-coaster loves and longings of her cast. Despite the constant presence of the ever-zealous Geoffrey and the fact that her stage manager was frequently in tears, more important matters were at stake. A wagon load of posters was distributed to local shops, along with sacks of coloured hand bills. But stubbornly, the ticket sales for 'Connaught's Shakespeare Festival' had stalled. A promised flood became a trickle, then a drought and Madeleine announced one morning that rehearsals were suspended, whilst we publicised the show in nearby Farningham.

At half-past one, a rusting, dark blue charabanc drew up outside the Hall. Some costumes had been finished. Others were not yet begun. Christopher and

Isobel looked radiant in Lincoln Green and cinammon, with doublet, hose and shining leather boots. Geoffrey wore a velvet cloak and Timmy, clothed in red and yellow motley, looked as wretched as a Merry Man could be.

At the front sat Madeleine, dressed in deep maroon, with ornamental pearls like Queen Elizabeth at the Armada. I had been delayed within the bowels of the basement by an anxious wardrobe mistress, keen to dress me up in cast-offs, so I nearly missed the bus. I found an empty seat beside the prim Elizabeth.

'Nothing to wear?' she said severely.

'Nothing that fits me, I'm afraid.'

She turned towards the window, as we hurtled down the drive. I noticed Josh, the garden boy, did not appear to be on board.

Then finally, she turned to me. 'So, you're a friend of Christopher?' I nodded. 'Then perhaps you might explain what happened back at School.'

'You mean...?'

'Why he was asked to leave.'

'Ah, well,' I said, 'he drank and as you know, that's not allowed.'

'That's all? He drank? And nothing more? And that's a sackable offence?'

'Well, I don't know, I'm junior.'

'But there was nothing else at all? Madeleine suggested that there'd been some sort of scandal. Did you know about it?'

'Not at all.'

'But then you said that you were friends? He must have told you something. Though you seem a good deal younger than that fellow Jonny Tait. I really don't approve of him. He's far too louche. He's dangerous – and clever.'

Elizabeth was silent for a moment, then she cleared her throat. 'And so, you're not a *special* friend? And yet you've been invited here.'

The dull roar of the engine drowned the words from any listeners. Elizabeth persisted. 'So, you think that it was just the drink? I worry about Christopher. There's something dangerous about him. As with all that family, they don't think of the consequences. Madeleine was just like that and I'm afraid he has her genes. Luckily for Madeleine, my brother steadied her a bit. But there's a streak that leads them into every kind of trouble. Isobel is safe, they've tucked her off to Switzerland. She's learning how to walk into a room and how to act the lady. As for Christopher, he doesn't choose his friends with care. I'm sure they must have led him quite astray.'

The thought of leading Christopher astray struck me as comical. But now Elizabeth was in her stride.

'As for this theatrical adventure, I need hardly tell you that my brother's far from keen. He disapproves of theatre. But Madeleine has always had her way. And Christopher is simply indiscriminate – as you should know. You won't believe the riffraff that he brings into the Hall. Utterly unsuitable companions. It's the current fad for Socialist equality. 'Jack's as good as his master.' Well, it stands to reason, Jack is *not*! Otherwise, the master would be Jack.'

With a snort she turned away. The bus rolled into Farningham. Christopher brushed past my shoulder as we scrambled down the steps. 'Auntie grilling you, I wonder? Did you spill the beans?'

'Not a word of me,' I said. 'Besides, I have no beans to spill.'

'Good man.' He winked. 'You ask no questions and you get no lies.'

It was a Wednesday afternoon. The High Street was deserted. True, an old photographer, extracted from the weekly rag, was summoned to take photographs of Isobel and Geoffrey. But there was no-one to accost with pockets full of handbills and it was an aimless company that wandered down the cobbled streets, past the green and blue jars of the locked and shuttered pharmacy and empty shelves of the bakery. Blinds were drawn down at the barber's and the butcher's trays were bare.

As late night revelers greet the dawn, with soiled skirts and limp carnations, so our pageant ghosted through the silent streets of Farningham, below the ruined castle, past the iron grills of hardware shops.

Even Madeleine appeared to have her spirits dashed. We loitered by the rusting arches of the Jubilee bandstand.

'Nothing doing here,' said Geoffrey.

'No, indeed,' said Madeleine. 'We'll gather at the coach in half an hour.'

Christopher and Jonny disappeared, no doubt to the find the nearest pub. I went to look for them and found a nest of passageways. Footsteps echoed on the stones. But the next street was as empty as the low tide on the bay. I hurried past the sun-baked blinds, the fire escapes and mottled roofs. The earth seemed to have swallowed them completely.

Above my head a painted sign announced 'The Lilac Tea House'. On the door, a faded sign assured me it was open.

'I'd like some tea and cakes,' I said, wondering if my last half-crown would be enough to buy a stamp as well, so that I could write to Mother begging for more loot.

The waitress was a pale child in printed dress and canvas shoes, as if the sun had bleached her blood away. Tables jostled shyly beneath ancient prints of hunting scenes and faded flower cloths that had seen better days.

Outside, in a bucket, the geraniums were wilting. A black cat stretched across a bench. Nothing else was stirring on this steamy afternoon, until the bell began to jangle and the cat shot from her perch. I looked up. There was Isobel.

My instinct was to be invisible, as if I was not there. I drew my chair to face the yard.

'Charlie! I thought you'd disappeared.'

'I tried. I can't find Christopher.'

'He's probably in trouble then. Do you suppose he's drinking?'

'I don't know. Your aunt assumes that I know every move he makes.

'If Daddy finds he's drinking, there'll be hell to pay. He's stopping Christopher's allowance if he's caught again.'

'I gather Daddy's not a fan of other things he's up to.'

'You're right. 'A good spell in the Guards is what you need' he always says. They were rattled by what happened in the summer term. Wrecked his chance of Oxford. Now the Army seems the next best thing. We're all a little fretful.'

Why, I wondered, do we talk of Christopher, instead of you?

'I'm sure he'll cope,' I said. 'He always does. Even at School, nothing seemed to keep him down. He always came out smiling. I wonder, does your aunt know where you are?'

She grinned. 'I've given her the slip.'

She ordered tea, refused to let me pay for it and dropped a lump of sugar in the cup. We were alone. No witnesses, except the cat and someone in another room, a running tap and sounds of washing up.

I sat, uncertain what to do. This Ganymede in Lincoln Green, this 'boy', this girl in belt and boots, completely took my breath away.

'Are you enjoying it?'

'You mean rehearsals, staying at the Hall?

'Are people being nice to you?'

'Oh yes – they're jolly kind.'

'It must be rather difficult – I mean you're so much younger.'

'Not at all. I'm used to it,' I lied. I couldn't keep my eyes off her. She sat so calmly, toying with the teaspoon, as if everything was natural and we were easy friends.

'I don't think everybody's happy. Timmy looks quite downcast.'

'Timmy?'

'Yes – '

'What's wrong with him?'

I swallowed. 'Well, he says you're his Intended.'

Isobel threw back her head and gave a shout of laughter, so loud that the table rocked.

'Timmy! He's a fool. He's such a joker. Always has been.'

'It didn't sound a joke to me.'

She stopped and gazed directly at me. 'Timmy is so pompous. Christopher and I, we used to tease him. Just because his family owns half of Lincolnshire.'

'I didn't know.'

'Last winter, he was staying here and Christopher had written him a jokey Valentine. It was anonymous, of course. Unfortunately, Christopher had used my pen and notepaper – and Timmy guessed where it had come from – he's a bit naïve...'

She broke off, then began to giggle, holding up a napkin.

'What's the wickedest thing you've done? I bet you've played some tricks. Christopher is always telling me about the pranks at school.'

The picture of a sunless Dayroom flashed across my mind.

'Christopher and I would dare each other to do stupid things – like walking on the parapets or climbing round the chimney stacks. One of our best dares was skinny dipping in the Lake.'

'Skinny dipping?'

'You know, swimming naked, without clothes. You had to sneak behind the reeds so nobody could spot you. Otherwise, there would be trouble. We were nearly caught one time, but nobody found out.'

'Golly,' I said. 'Sounds a lot of fun.'

'Charlie, you'd have loved it. You should try it in the early morning before anyone is up.'

I was baffled by this change of mood. Had I stumbled through the gate into the Secret Garden? Suddenly, the veil had gone and I was gazing at a face that shone with wicked joy. Where was the chaperoned Madonna? Was it just an act?

Was she just as reckless as her brother? Had the mirror cracked into a thousand smithereens, each reflecting yet another possible persona? Was the actor always acting? Could there be a solid core? Who could tell the dancer from the dance?

Isobel stopped laughing. 'But it wasn't always fun. Sometimes, he'd go off with Josh and say he hadn't time for girls, especially his sister. He would tell me to go home.'

'Off with Josh?'

'Yes – they'd go fishing; or make dens deep in the Jungle. Sometimes, I would follow them and spy like a Red Indian. No-one ever knew that I was there.

'Josh and he were close?'

'As thick as thieves. But then, you know my brother. Always friends with anyone. That's what he's like. He never makes distinctions.'

'Yes, I understand.'

'What was the word you used just now? 'Intended'? *Nobody* says that. Bet you copied that from Timmy. He's a fool. But all the same I like him, he's my cousin.' Isobel looked at her empty cup, then back at me. 'I like you too,' she said and grinned. 'And not because you've been a friend to Christopher. I'll tell you what – you look a bit like Christopher did when he was your age.'

The skies had opened, pouring riches.

'Actually, I like you too,' I mumbled, screwing up a napkin. 'Better go. We'll miss the bus.'

'Who cares?'

Who cares? If in that moment, time had stopped, if I had leant across the faded tablecloth and kissed her, then would everything be different? If it were now to die. But I was ankle deep in love.

Something had occurred. I leant back on the leather headrest, as the bus ground up the gravel drive. A meeting of the minds, a *rendez-vous*, a clearing in the forest. Almost a declaration. Nothing now could ever be the same.

As we drew up by the house, she flashed a smile. 'Thank-you for tea,' she said and disappeared into the hall.

Out on the veranda, bats were swooping down like Spitfires, racing crazily against a sky of deepest blue, whirling at the creeper in a frightening parabola. Jonny sat upon a bench. A leather book lay on his lap, as he declaimed the lines,

'A splendour falls on castle walls
And snowy summits old in story.

Then a breeze along the gravel path blew in a tiny cloud of ivory against the blue. The ladies on the terrace called for cardigans and shawls, as Jonny, tumbler in hand, addressed the growing dark.

'Oh, love they die in yon rich sky
They faint on hill or field or river
Our echoes roll from soul to soul
And grow forever and forever.'

Below us, in the Rose Garden, a figure waited in the fading light. A gust, another curling cloud. And all next day, it rained.

Chapter Eleven

Dawn broke in a purple bruise. No skinny dipping today. No brilliant sheen of glass; the lake was dull and muddy grey. Dark clouds hung like giant balloons. By nine o'clock, the first raindrops were thudding on the panes.

After yesterday's hiatus, Madeleine was keen to press ahead. We moved into the Billiard Room, a lofty barrel-vaulted dungeon, crammed with cases of dead foxes, otters, weasels and a mink, which stared forlornly through the glass.

Isobel appeared when called, then disappeared into her room. Christopher, too, looked withdrawn. Everyone seemed curiously tense, as if for an exam. When cues were missed or actors dried, Madeleine would drum her fingers. Only Jonny seemed at ease, lisping through the 'Seven Ages', as the minutes trickled by.

But something of the splendour of the night before remained, locked up in the memory, a thread of gold dust, which the gurgling drainpipes failed to wash away.

Jonny's speech of 'mewling infants', schoolboys with their 'shining faces', lovers sighing woefully like overheated furnaces proved the main distraction. To each age a character – the bearded soldier, justices and old men in the portraits of the panelled dining room could tell as much. As for the whining schoolboy, I had left that Age behind, transformed to the pining lover. Isobel had said as much. 'I like you too,' as Rosalind or Ganymede might say 'Come woo me, woo me.'

The Billiard room was not ideal, for space was at a premium. The giant table made it nigh impossible to move around. Madeleine was not at ease and in the end, she lost her rag. Seizing Millie's prompt book, just as Geoffrey stumbled on a cue, she shouted 'Learn the bloody lines. You call yourself an actor?' and hurled the book onto the floor, then stormed out of the room.

Geoffrey smiled wanly, shrugged and picked up the offending book. 'I think the weather's clearing,' he said, gazing at the scudding clouds. 'Let's wait and then continue out of doors?'

Lunch was served, cold beef and bowls of yellow junket pudding. The prospect of an afternoon spent cooped up in my attic room did not inspire. I donned a mac and strode out in the rain.

Crossing the Hall, I almost struck the Brigadier, who burst out of the Ballroom, eyeballs all ablaze, shocked and haggard, followed by a banshee yell from Madeleine. He gazed at me, as if I were a stranger, blinked and strode towards the stairs. Later, I remembered that throughout my stay at Connaught Hall, this had been our sole encounter.

Skirting the reeds of the mournful lake, I followed a path that curved and dipped into a copse of rhododendron. Sodden branches brushed my face; the moss path squelched unevenly, when from close behind me came the sound of rifle fire. From a path, just parallel to mine and lined with dog roses, Josh and Christopher appeared. Josh wore brown cloth trousers and a cap; beneath his arm, a gun. Neither spoke. They disappeared along the path of dog rose, followed by the faithful lurcher.

'Sometimes, I would follow them and spy like a Red Indian,' Isobel had said. I wondered if she followed now. I struck across to the other path. In no time I was soaking wet, as a cascade of drumming rain began. Not only that, low lying branches seemed to beat me back. They lashed and sprang, as if the wood were suddenly inspired with rage. Twigs and tendrils intertwined into a mesh of fury.

Blinded by the rain, I missed the path they took and struggled deep in nettles. Inch-thick brambles clawed my face. I blundered wildly through the thickets; bracken dug into my boots and needles stabbed my trousers. Strange hands pawed my streaming hair and snatched away a borrowed trilby. Now, I struggled violently, head down, crashing like a crab. I shoved against the undergrowth that would not let me by.

Then suddenly it parted. I had found the path again. Above my head a canopy of green lent some protection. My hands were watery and red and bleeding from the brambles. I gazed, as through a screen of broken glass and peered around.

The path was like a rabbit run that curved and disappeared. Briar and bracken fought me every foot. Whenever the canopy overhead revealed the light of day, it felt as if I walked beneath a towering waterfall. And when I paused to think about the way, I had a sense of being followed.

I had lost direction now; my only hope was that this path would lead back to a field, a gravel drive, a shelter, something human. Now it plunged deep down, the vegetation grew less green; the canopy began to alter; no more pines, the trees were taller, wider girthed and loftier. Now, instead of brambles, there were leaves as large as soup plates. The ground below was soft and dark with peat and bulbous roots of trees that spread their bony fingers. I came upon thick clusters of green moss and rocks and blanched white grasses, fanning gaunt leaves high above and blotting out the light. Pathways beckoned left and right, down cheap inviting alleyways, while underfoot, the leaf mould sank through centuries of decay.

And everywhere the silence clung, like an extra layer of skin. Somewhere high above, a woodcock screamed, but still the path meandered ever downward through the Bamboo Jungle.

Deep amidst the roots and rotting tendrils of the wood, another path ran parallel to mine. It was concealed by bamboos, bristling with sea green lances. Suddenly, I heard a cry.

I stood stock still. To meet even a dog would come as some relief. But if you can sweat in a catacomb of moss and drenched with rainwater, I was surely sweating then. For ten yards down, the pathways merged and still the sound continued.

There was a blur of white, a yellow face distorted by the shadows. Then a shape collided with me. It was Isobel.

She wore a loose knit tennis sweater under an open raincoat. The buttons were undone. She wore no hat; her hair was streaming. Leaf mould covered her hands and face and mud had stained the pristine jersey.

Shocked, we stared at one another. Then, 'Are you all right?' I murmured.

She was shaking violently. 'What is it?' I asked. She shook her head and pointed up the path.

I took her in my arms. I held her. There, her soft breast upon mine.

'Darling, darling Isobel.'

Words unspoken, given air at last and breathing now. There, for ever. 'Darling, darling'

I can smell the damp, dark leaf mould and her soft, wet hair.

Now the sobs were more controlled. I raised her head to see her face. 'What is it you're frightened of?'

There was no need to speak. A rustle of leaves and the bamboo lances parted. Wi'm's gigantic boar stood there, twitching his nose and grunting.

The pig stood face to face with us, pink ears cocked and trotters firm. He raised his snout and eyed us, snuffling, winking piggy eyes. I was not prepared for the size of those massive shoulders and bulging thighs, the coarse pink skin. It had been hounding, following with mocking grunts, making little rushes, driving her towards the swamp.

Now it pawed the earth and tossed its head, as if to acknowledge me. Wrenching a stem from the nearest bush, I murmured 'Slowly up this path. I'll keep the thing at bay.' The bamboo cut my skin.

And so, we started, struggling up along the path, armed with a bamboo banner. It would have been hard for the brute to charge, for the ground was steep and slippery. I yelled 'Go on, go on,' as with one hand I drove the exhausted Isobel, whilst with the other, I thrust a jagged lance towards the beast. Soft earth stained our arms and backs each time we fell and when we stopped, the animal would make a little charge. Our feet and hands were caked with mud; at times, we hardly moved at all; at other times, I carried her.

Branches grazed our backs and necks; the light grew slowly brighter. Reeds and roots on either side gave way to dark green shrubbery. And gradually, the path began to flatten out, the gap grew wider. Then a branch of rhododendron brushed across my head.

The creature stopped. It waited, snorted, rubbed its back against the bush. And then it turned and trotted down the slope towards the Jungle.

Now only rhododendrons wove their roots across the way. The rain had stopped and wild grey clouds were scudding overhead, as we broke through the top of the wood and a curtain of pink azaleas. We stood there on the sodden lawn and caught the scent of roses.

On the veranda, wrapped in a black raincoat stood Elizabeth. A jet-black cormorant that peered across a stormy sea.

'Isobel, dearest – are you ill? Just look at your clothes. And Charles – where have you been?'

'She's had a fall. One of the pigs escaped in the Bamboo Jungle. Gave your niece a scare.'

Isobel was deathly pale as we helped her into the Hall. There, in a flurry of smelling salts, hot baths and towels, she was ushered away, like some rare vase that calls for expert care.

That was the last I saw of her that day. I felt depressed and cold. I squeezed the water from my boots and stinking socks and sat down in the shuttered hall, surrounded by the heads of slaughtered game. I felt exhausted. What on earth, I wondered, was I doing here, hanging round, with nothing much to do; here and there a song to sing and everyone about their business, most of which I failed to understand?

Even at the darkest times, I rarely felt homesick at School. This was something different, for clearly, I was out of place, invited on a false passport to what I thought was Paradise. 'Calf love', Jonny called it. I had looked it up the night before. '*Temporary infatuation of an adolescent';* and in brackets *'(Immature)'*. Slumped across the horsehair armchair in a corner of the hall, I tried to live that moment in the Jungle, feel her skin and hair. I knew that it was hopeless. Fifteen years, and callow as a calf, I never had a prayer. My stomach ached. I longed to be at home.

'Charlie?' It was Gwylim, a dark smudge amid the shade. 'You OK?'

'I'm fine,' 1 said.

'I hear you've played the hero, rescuing a maiden in distress.'

'Not exactly. Some fool drove Wi'm's boar out through the wood. It's not a pretty sight.'

'But still, you've scored a Brownie point or two.'

He settled on the window ledge. 'How are things? It seems to me the weather's upset everyone. Madeleine is in a rage, Tim's in a sulk and that young chit called Millie, the stage manager, turns up red-eyed every damn rehearsal. Says she's got a tummy bug and keeps on rushing off to vomit. If she wants to vomit, why on earth ain't she at home? We could well be heading for a car crash.

'People say she's very young. Young and inexperienced. Needs someone to buck her up. SMs get the rubbish jobs and very little thanks. Then there's other lunatics – what do you think of the garden boy?'

'Josh?'

'The Wrestler – yes, the garden boy. Bit of an odd choice, I'd say, casting him in Shakespeare. I wouldn't risk him in my team, even if you paid me.'

Late that night, I wandered under driving clouds and gusts of rain, past the awnings of a large marquee that tugged upon its guy ropes like an anchored schooner; past the soughing beech trees and an old, abandoned swing. From a distance came the mournful whistle of a train. I sat upon a counterpane of leaves beside the empty stage.

To and fro, between the tangled branches, a dim light was burning from a room that once had been the Nursery. Then a figure leant out in the dark and gazed across the lawn. A mop of curly dark brown hair that did not look like Isobel. Only the chime of the stable clock and the hoot of an owl disturbed the night. I climbed the stairs and must have slept till scudding clouds gave way to dawn.

When sorrows come, they come not single spies, but in battalions. That morning witnessed scenes of desecration round the Hall. The guy ropes on the big marquee had come adrift the night before. Somebody had cut them with a knife. They were not frayed but sliced clean through to leave the canvas billowing.

Nearby were signs of further vandalism on the lawn. One entire bed of roses lay beheaded on the path, scarlet petals bleeding. Nor was that the end of it. All four croquet mallets had been ritually dismembered. Handles smashed, they lay like cripples in their narrow box.

Nonetheless, the weather had improved and with it, tempers. Madeleine seemed unmoved by the news of the destruction. 'Wi'm can deal with it,' she said and ordered Millie off to tell him. Then, with Geoffrey beaming by her side, she murmured 'Thank-you Charlie. I believe you saved the day.'

The garden paths were running brooks, the lawn was like a spongy sea, but as the minutes ticked away, the ground grew firmer and by midday came a burst of sunshine.

Only Christopher looked out of sorts. He did not laugh or smile or share a joke with Jonny. He looked peaky and unkempt. Normally the life and soul of any gathering, he sat apart and when onstage seemed hardly to be bothering.

'Wake up Christopher,' bawled Madeleine. 'You're like a zombie. Come on darling, try to look as if you mean it. You're in love!'

'Sorry, Ma. I'm just a little weary.'

'You've had two days off. What have you got to be tired about?'

When the scene was over, Christopher avoided Jonny Tait, choosing instead a wicker chair close to where I sat.

'Hello, Charlie. God, I'm feeling awful. Must have caught a chill.'

'Were you out in all that rain?'

'Not me. Spent the day upstairs. Ma was in a dreadful mood. Thought I'd hunker down until the storm had passed away.'

'Is it always like this?'

'Always, every single show. Tied in knots – and when it's over, she'll be wreathed in smiles and planning what to do next year. Crazy, but she's always done it. Just can't let the theatre go.'

Christopher was shaken by a heavy bout of sneezing. He blew his nose and turned to me. 'You don't look all that hot yourself. You OK? I'm sorry that I haven't been the perfect host. All the same, I think you're fine. And Mother's really pleased with you. Said this morning that you'd helped a lot, I don't know why.'

'Thanks.'

'Now listen, this is something serious I want to ask you.'

'What about?'

'I'll tell you. And I'm saying this because I like you, Charlie, as a friend.'

'Go on.'

'Confidential.'

'Yes?'

'My parents. Well – it's pretty clearclear that Mother's having problems, as no doubt you've realised. Long before they married, she'd been in a spot of bother and they say that Geoffrey was involved. None of Father's family approved when they got married. But the Old Man, he adores her; he'd do anything for Mother.

'Now with Geoffrey on the prowl, it seems that things are getting rocky. Frankly, I can't stand the way that fellow carries on. But the reckoning will have to wait until the show is done.'

'And what then? Pistols at dawn?''

'Father hates to make a scene. As you know, we don't get on. But I'd hate him to be hurt. Charlie, I just don't know what to do.'

This was a different Christopher to the careless chap, I thought I knew. I'd never known the mask to slip so far.

'What about you, then?'

He frowned. 'I don't know what you mean.'

'Don't you think you might be hurt?'

'By whom?'

'Well – possibly by Josh?'

'Josh? You mean the Garden boy?'

I'd overstepped the mark. He bit his lip – then broke into a smile. 'Oh, hurt? You mean the wrestling? There's no chance of that, old boy.'

118

'I didn't mean – '

'Look, I am an actor. And you saw us in rehearsal. Wrestling isn't dangerous. That's what acting's all about. Making people think that what you do is genuine. Then you bow and walk away. And do the same tomorrow – and tomorrow – making people think that what you do on stage is real.'

Christopher knew what I meant, but he refused to go there. So, I tried another tack.

'But can you trust your feelings then? When are actors genuine? If they're always acting, is there anything that's real?'

'When they're not pretending and not putting on a shown – '

'Yes, but how is one to tell?'

'You have to trust them, I suppose.'

'Well, suppose that someone says to you 'Well, honestly, I like you.' Maybe he or she is feigning, that's another word for lying. How do you know whether they are 'putting on a show'?'

'If I liked them, I could tell.' He smiled. 'I think you'll make an actor. All you really need is practice and a bit of time.'

Christopher had lied to me – though I suppose he rarely told the truth, that time or later. Friend or not, I felt excluded. Neither of us told the other what they knew or didn't know.

One hot afternoon, some days before, I'd struck along the path that led towards the creosoted den. There, I found the apple crates, the bookcases and eiderdown just as neatly set out as before. The firebomb lay carefully wrapped in *The Daily Chronicle,* its brassy nozzle gleaming in the glow of afternoon.

I held this deadly creature with a sense of fear and fascination, knowing if I dropped it, it could blow my head away, pound the blue enamel dish to dust, the Coronation mug, the worn bone handled knife, carved in a tiny sickle shape.

Time no longer was a friend. The garden wall could only last a day.

And what about you, Millie, dear – Land Girl dressed in overalls? Maid-of-all work, busy backstage, manufacturer of props and leafy scenery? It was quite a change from Mother's stables, working at the Hall; but no doubt just as back-breaking, the endless hours of labour that you put into that stage. Still, as I discovered, it was not your back that broke that summer.

Hearts were breaking everywhere, not only yours and mine. But neither of us knew the others' secrets or the pain. What if we had told each other everything we knew? Would it have been different in the end?

Climbing to my garret, while the others changed for dinner (I possessed no evening dress beyond a collared shirt and tie), I found a scrap of paper on the pillow and a message written in a neat round hand.

'Come. I'm in the Nursery' and signed with a letter 'I.'

With no idea where Isobel might be, I skirted down the stairs and crept along the corridor, tapping on a white oak door, which led into a bathroom. There was a view towards the Lake, where Josh was walking by himself, a gun beneath his arm.

A door closed further on – I turned and glimpsed a figure on the stairs, a mop of curly, dark brown hair amid the shadows of the Hall. I tried that other door; I knocked and turned the handle to what must have been the Nursery. And Isobel was there.

The whitewashed walls looked dull and grey in the late afternoon. There was an iron bed, a rocking horse and a wicker chair, a washstand and a patchwork quilt and on the mantelpiece a china doll. Isobel sat in the alcove with her cheek against the windowpane.

'May I come in?'

She did not move, her silhouette against the sky.

'I'm sorry, you're unhappy. Is there something I can do?'

I stood beside the iron bed. Her cheeks were streaked with silver.

'You're worried about Christopher?'

She started. 'How do you know?'

A rifle shot from somewhere in the Jungle echoed and the rooks wheeled up, lamenting through the trees.

'He has a gun,' said Isobel. 'there's nothing you can do.'

'Josh?' She nodded.

'Josh is crazy. All the same – '

She stared at me. 'You know what's going on?'

I sat down on the iron bed. 'I think I understand.'

'Josh adores him, don't you see? And now he's lost him and your friend – '

'Jonny, yes?' I said again.

'When Christopher's at home, you see the change. Josh starts to live. His eyes, the way they sparkle when he's here. They used to hunt and fish together; Josh has taught him everything. There was a place down in the woods, where they would camp. I know he's odd, but what if he does something dreadful?'

'Josh? He wouldn't. Honestly, it's not what people do.'

'You think so? Charlie, you don't know him. Josh is like a tinder box. Since Christopher came home last term, there's been some awful rows. Father said that he should go straight off to National Service. Later, if he stuck it out, the army would be his career. Josh then told his father Wi'm that he was going too. Not that Josh would get to Sandhurst; he told Wi'm that he would be a squaddie in the Guards.

'That made Father furious. He said Christopher should give up mixing with that sort of person. Officers should not be seen consorting with the garden boy.'

'Christopher and Josh are close?'

'I'm scared that it could ruin him.'

'Your mother?'

'Doesn't want to know.'

'You really think that Josh would dream of shooting anyone?'

'I don't know what to think,' she said.

I gazed across the croquet lawn. The thought that Josh would take a pot at Christopher or anyone was ludicrous. But all the same, I'd seen the wreckage of the night before.

Christopher knew how to draw affection like a sponge. He had the knack of turning clay to gold. Christopher could brighten up the drizzle of an afternoon with just a word, a friendly smile. I knew the magic formula. I had been captured, after all. And in my callow way I knew a little about jealousy. But as for bitterness and blame, they were beyond my understanding. Failed friendships I could cope with, not with anger and revenge.

From outside, another shot and rooks began to caw. I waited, swallowed, summoned up my strength and whispered 'Isobel.'

She did not stir. I tried again. 'I love you, Isobel.'

'Even more than Christopher?'

'Oh yes, much more than Christopher.'

She nodded. 'Charlie, yes. I know.'

'Come. We'll go together. We can find him; we can settle this.'

Gliding down the service stairs, along the darkened corridors that led towards the kitchens and the laundry, we were infiltrators, spies in foreign territory, silent and invisible as air. Past the kitchen garden, past the beech tree on the lawn – 'I'll go,' I said. 'You follow after thirty. I'll be on the path.'

'It's chilly.'

'Take my jacket. Quickly, wrap it round your shoulders.'

Mist was rising from the lake, as we worked to the bramble patch. There was a smell of mint and garlic as we reached the clearing, set about with Queen Ann's lace. Mud stains marked the door. She pressed the latch. We were alone. No sign of Josh or Christopher. We stood in shadows, wrapped in silence. There was the knife and the souvenir mug and the blue moth-eaten eiderdown.

My shoes were soaking wet with dew. She gazed around. 'You know this place?' I whispered.

She shook her head and then began to tremble, as I came towards her, took her arm and then like an impulsive diver plunging from a cliff, I kissed her on the lips, upon her eyes and mouth. I clasped my arms around her as she stumbled. We were kneeling now and pressed together in a desperate embrace.

Then in a blur of fumbled clothing, something more possessed us. Blindworms in the dark and driven on by something far beyond our longing and desire, beyond the need to cling and clasp, we fell onto the mattress and 1 felt the texture of her skin – the silken softness of a thigh, a mouth and breasts like flowers giving up their scent to die; I put my hand between her legs and felt a moist attraction like a breathing sea anemone. I felt that I was going to burst, my cock, my penis throbbing with a frenzy of its own. And with a thrust between her thighs, a little cry of ecstasy, in agony and wonder as if life were being sucked away – so on and on, a strange ecstatic thrusting, until suddenly a dam was burst, an orgasm that surged and poured out in a flood.

Seventy years on, I wonder – did it happen? Just like that? I was fifteen – or sixteen nearly. Memory plays wicked tricks. I wondered, even afterwards, if I had dreamt it all – pieced the truth together from a skein of random accidents. Solid truth can chop and change – even when you know it in your heart.

There are such uncertainties of who said what to whom and where, but there are certainties as well. Something of the core remains; and though we change, reorder them, they have their own reality. With time, I grew convinced that I had not imagined what occurred.

Exhausted, we lay back, amazed and listened to the world outside. A ringdove called out from the woods and Isobel lay in my arms. Her pale frock was crumpled and her eyes were stained with tears.

Something stirred outside. A clatter as the light poured in. The door burst open and I gazed into the barrel of a gun.

It rested on the ground, a foot away from where we lay. I gazed at two dark goblin eyes. Isobel was still as stone. Cold sweat ran along my back.

He smiled, revealing hard white teeth and gave a narrow laugh. Then, grinning in a silly way, he hitched his trousers with a shrug and slammed the door. His mocking laughter echoed through the wood.

Chapter Twelve

Clouds were drifting freely, when I closed the wooden door. Mist was creeping through the trees; our feet grew sodden with the dew. I had checked the box, where tea and jam and stale bread were stored. No-one had disturbed the parcel, wrapped in *The Daily Chronicle.*

'Josh won't tell?'

She shook her head. ''Not unless he's desperate.'

'He's looking pretty desperate to me. When shall I see you?'

'Dinner time.'

'But after that?'

I tried to kiss her, fumbled it, her body frail as reeds. Was it already fading, like those petals on the lawn?

'Don't catch cold. Look, keep my jacket. You can give it back tomorrow.'

'Yes, OK, I'll see you soon.'

But Isobel was not at dinner. We were told she had a headache and was lying down. There was a gap in the seating plan, which nobody had filled. Down at the table end, I kept my eyes on those around me. Millie, pale, morose and picking at her dinner, pushed her plate away, as Timmy scraped each morsel, like a man condemned.

But it was not easy to ignore the throaty laughter that echoed further up the room. Madeleine was beaming at a photograph of Geoffrey, headlined in the local rag. It read '*Matinee Idol Tops the Bill in Rural Romp.*'

I caught the eye of Jonny Tait, some places up from me. Christopher and he were whispering like two conspirators. Jonny gave a knowing wink in Madeleine's direction, while Gwilym's words came back to me. *'The horn, the horn, the lusty horn.'*

Sitting alone, the Brigadier looked sick and deathly pale.

I slipped out to the terrace, where the clouds were racing to and fro.

Something quite momentous had occurred. The scene had shifted. No more Whining Schoolboy or the Sighing Lover, I was now an actor, a performer, what-you-will. I had what it takes to play the man.

The secret was between us. Actors know the art of feigning. I could play the innocent as well as anyone. Proud of what had happened, was I guilty or ashamed? Not one bit. I felt sublime, delirious. I'd done the deed or so I dearly thought. The wonder of it made me long to be more daring still, to climb the ivy at her window, steal the night away. My heart kicked at the very thought of it.

As for Josh – those dark eyes gleaming down the barrel of a gun, mocking laughter, as he strode away – had he learnt of fading friendship, old familiarity grown chilly and companionship transformed into a formal nod?

Class was something that had not concerned me before now. The world was evenly divided between officers and men, the wardroom and the other ranks, who swung on hammocks in the hold. Socialism had not made its mark. There was one eccentric beak, who taught History and told us about Lenin and the brotherhood of man. But the gap between the servants and the ones they served remained.

The milkman called, the collier, the gardener and the chimney sweep; one met without any real insight on their lives. They lived in two roomed cottages, with outside toilets, open fires. We passed the time politely, as they waited by the kitchen door to pocket up a bill or heave the coal sacks to the cellar. No doubt we were patronising, but they rarely bridled. Fate had thrown the dice. The poor must cope with it alone.

But what if someone crossed the bridge and tasted all the sweetness – and then felt the bitterness of being exiled from the party? If you prick us, do we bleed and if you wrong us, do we not revenge?

A fitful night. From time to time, I woke to see those goblin eyes. In the half grey light of dawn, I had a dream of broken glass and woke to find the casement window banging. The catch had snapped and now the frame was pounding on the sill.

Outside lay a gusty morning, dark clouds rolling anxiously; damp confetti rose petals lay scattered on the lawn.

Somebody was bathing in the lake. A grey, distorted figure. Now it vanished. There it was –before it disappeared again.

My thoughts were on other things, on Isobel, the buried hut. The need to speak with Isobel, the need to thrash it out with Josh. If I was a performer, it was time for taking action.

Dressing at some speed, I made my way down to the hall. Jonny was already up and halfway through *The Telegraph,* when there came a heavy thudding from the outside door. Wi'm stood in the porchway, breathing heavily and in his arms a sodden bundle, streaming pools of water.

'Gimme a hand.'

We heaved the object through the heavy door and on into the drawing room, where puddles gathered on the carpet.

Millie. It was Millie on the sofa, like a sack of clay. Her lips were blue. That flaming hair was doused in mud and slime. And what a weight – a sagging, lumpy weight, all stained with grass and reeds, her blue blouse marbling her arms. Oh, you were no Ophelia. You clutched no willow bough, no clothes spread wide and mermaid like to bear you up above the flood. Nothing so fantastic. You were gross as dirt and dung.

Then Christopher burst through the door and took command. He rolled you on the carpet, knelt astride and pumped the water from your lungs.

A distant cough, a chuckle and the frail sound of vomiting; bile, ooze, saliva, mud and water retched in fountains; sobs and eructations soaking through the woollen carpeting, as Millie struggled inch by groaning shudder to be born.

Just as it was over, just as life began to stagger back and Millie was once more arranged in comfort on the sofa, a tartan rug appeared from nowhere, towels from the laundry room, and Christopher was on his knees beside the sofa, drying hands and wiping mud from off her face and neck and sodden dungarees. He spoke to her in soothing tones. 'Now, Millie. Easy does it. Steady now, you'll be OK.'

Madeleine appeared, white as a sheet, in a long dressing gown, all pink and padded at the sides.

'Why, Christopher – what's going on? Look what's happened to the carpet.'

Christopher ignored her. He was still addressing Millie. 'Well done, lovey. You're OK now. Take a big breath – now another.' Millie retched into a towel. 'Mother, can you ring the doctor. Millie nearly drowned.'

Men have died from time to time and worms have eaten them. But not for love. And not for Millie, comrade of my later life. Land girl in the dusky fields, smouldering with passion, did you leap or lose your footing? Was it chance or something more, an impulse for the infinite? What if Wi'm had not been passing by?

Christopher was at your side throughout that murky morning, Christopher, who dried your tears and rubbed your forehead, soothed your sorrows; ordered towels and warming drink, steady as a rock in a typhoon. How was it that every incident should feature Christopher? Like planets round the sun, he seemed to magnetise our orbits, soaking up affection with a grin.

Millie, did *you* blossom in the warmth of Christopher's regard, only to be cast aside, as others had before you?

When the doctor came, the rest of us were banished from the room. He spent an hour with you, then later, closeted with Madeleine. After that, a Land Rover drew up outside the porch. Your mother, summoned from the stables, hurried in to join the fray. Later still, the doctor and the Land Rover departed, along with Millie, in whose wake a trail of mud stains marked the grey mosaics of the hall.

Jonny settled down again. I drifted to the dining room, where breakfast had been cleared away and maids were flicking linen cloths in readiness for lunch.

'Never fear,' said Jonny. 'We shall feed you up before tonight. Can't have the Wedding Singer's tummy rumbling through the dress rehearsal.'

'Will she be OK?' I said.

'Millie? Yes, I guess she will. Nasty shock to slip like that. Those banks around the lake are dodgy after all that rain.'

'You think it was an accident?'

'Of course, what else?' His voice was loud and boomed around the shadowed walls. 'Fancy a breath of air,' said Jonny. 'Take a turn along the drive?'

I followed him across the gravel, as a pale sun glimmered though the clouds.

'Can't be seen to gossip,' Jonny said, '"The Walls Have Ears' – 'Careless Talk' and all that rot.'

'What do you mean?'

'You must have noticed. Millie's hardly been herself during the past few days.'

'So?' I said.

'So, what's her trouble?'

'Well – a crush on Christopher?'

'Bullseye, Charlie. Hit the nail.'

'That doesn't mean she – '

127

'No, it doesn't. Listen.' Jonny pursed his lips and whistled a familiar tune, one which I had heard before and which he knew I'd recognise. 'You know the second verse,' he said. '*She laid her head upon my bed/She said, 'what shall I do?''*

I swallowed – 'You mean Christopher – '

'*Just to keep her from the foggy, foggy dew.'* Actions have their consequences. As we found at school. As Christopher, for all his charm, is often slow to understand. He doesn't take precautions and it's landing him in trouble.'

'So, Millie is in trouble – and you say because of Christopher?'

'A decent way of putting it. Which only goes to show how much damage charm can do.'

'You mean that she was – '

'Yes – in trouble.'

'Gosh,' I said. 'What happens now?'

'Well, you know the family. They'll try batten down the hatches, try to stop the news from leaking out. I doubt Madeleine would entertain a shotgun marriage. Millie might be whisked away to a quiet retreat or a fancy clinic. They're never short of cash or influence.'

'Did he tell you yesterday? Is that why he was glum?'

'Pretty much. His Father's had a few shocks from the son and heir. Doubt if he can weather many more.'

We walked along in silence while I registered what he had told me. Christopher and Millie?

'After that?' I said.

'The Show goes on, as it did before. That's Madeleine and that is Connaught Hall.'

Actions have their consequences. Any fool could tell you that. But Christopher had seemingly defied the laws of gravity. Hitherto, he had avoided all the consequences. Now that he was rumbled, was he crashing down in flames?

The shock of seeing Millie stretched out on the sofa, made me shiver. There were consequences with a vengeance for the girl.

'Poor Millie.'

'Yes, poor Millie.'

'Will she keep it?'

'I don't know.'

'And Christopher?'

'Dear boy, a year from now he'll think it just a scrape. The sort of thing a lad gets into before settling down.'

'You mean he's not in love with her.'

'That's not a word he's ever used.' He stopped. 'You don't look all that good. You feeling peaky? Have some lunch.'

'No thanks. I'll skip it. I'm a little tired of eating junket.'

'Get some rest. And Charlie boy, the word is 'Mum' for what I told you.'

'You can trust me, Jonny.'

'Yes – I really hope I can.'

I sat by the lake and tried to get my head around it all. These were consequences that I'd never thought about before. I had been a mere spectator, who could set a scene, a filler in, as Gwylim put it. Not a central character. No-one gives attendant lords a second's thought when Rosalind and brave Orlando come on to the stage. Would my actions yesterday be 'just a scrape' a year from now?

'*He doesn't take precautions.*' I knew nothing of precautions. Having swum beyond my depth, I drifted with the tide. But the sight of Millie, sprawled and dirty as a lump of clay, flashed across my retina and would not go away.

As I reached the Hall, a voice called 'Charlie, have you just a moment?' It was Madeleine, appearing from behind the grizzly bear.

She was in her sanctuary, the refuge, where she planned and plotted. Madeleine sat in a sea of paper, broken fountain pens, inkwells, handbills, half read books, a giant desk with sliding lid, from which a further avalanche of crested paper was cascading onto tables, chairs and on the floor.

'Come in, Charlie. Do sit down, if you can find a chair.'

I scraped a pile of papers from a wooden piano stool. Above the desk, a silver frame and photograph bore the inscription 'Fondest love to Madeleine' and signed 'Frank Benson, Manager.'

'Charlie, I'll come to the point. I want to speak of Isobel.'

A hot flush caught me unawares. What if we'd been rumbled?

'Isobel is delicate. She knows little of the world. But neither, I suppose, do you. She is a girl of sentiment and I suspect she may have formed a strong attachment, let us say, for you.'

I started to reply. She raised a hand. 'No, let me finish, please. Yes, it is ridiculous, I know. You're far too young. I realise you've better things to do. But Isobel's a dark horse and she doesn't give a lot away. How do I know? A mother's intuition. One day Isobel will have a beau, perhaps her cousin, or a friend of Christopher. That is for the future. All the same, I shouldn't like to think of you, a guest at Connaught, finding yourself compromised or made a fool of by my daughter.'

Madeleine gave me a look, as if expecting a reply. I realised the interview had still some way to run.

'Only – ' She paused, theatrically. 'We found an article of clothing hidden in her room. Your jacket, isn't it? Look. On the collar 'CJ Wallace'. That *is* you? I've no idea how it was found with her belongings. Did you lend it to her? No, that isn't very likely. Still, I'm sure you wouldn't wish to cause embarrassment – to Isobel – or Christopher. Or me.'

Madeleine sat back and peered at me across the bureau. Her smile was less friendly than before. 'It's been good to welcome you to join the cast of *As You like It*. So, let's hope the next few days pass off without a hitch.'

She turned towards the window. 'Shakespeare in a summer garden. What could be more charming? Shakespeare brings the best out of the English. Comedies that end in marriage – people like that sort of thing. 'Journeys end in lovers meeting.' Neater than a tragedy with all those corpses at the curtain call.'

The conversation ended. I was ushered out into the hall. The veiled threat of exile hung unspoken in the air. As we left, I murmured 'I hope Millie's going to be OK?'

Madeleine screwed up her face. 'The silly girl. She's been here long enough to know about the lake. Those banks are treacherous. Ridiculous to walk alone. I've ordered Wi'm to fence them off.' She paused. 'But thank-you Charlie. I'm so glad we understand each other.'

There were no rehearsals on the stage that afternoon. The Dress Rehearsal would begin at eight. The cast were told to rest in preparation for the show. I wondered if I might creep in unnoticed to the Nursery, but Aunt Elizabeth was standing guard beside the door.

The hut was empty as a shell. The package wrapped in newspaper had vanished – with the eiderdown, the books and knives, the plates and mug – all gone and not a crumb of bread or apple core remained. The place was just a simple hut for storing Wi'm's machinery. Dust motes dancing through the cobwebs were the sole inhabitants. It was as if the rest had been a dream.

Josh was in his shirt sleeves, putting benches round the theatre. The old brown lurcher rested on the bank to snap at flies.

'Josh,' I said. 'I need a word.' He looked away. 'I need to talk.'

Those queer, dark eyes swung round and glared. 'You bogger off. You leave me be.'

'Please. Just a minute. I can help. It's something about Christopher.'

He flinched and hesitated. 'Honestly,' I said, 'it won't take long.'

Wi'm swore and asked him if he planned to stand about all day. And then Josh murmured 'Wait beside the holly tree. I'll be along,' and heaved another bench into the line.

The holly bush was one of those scooped out affairs, which gardeners use for storing rakes and wheelbarrows, compost heaps and rusting iron. A narrow path led past the kitchen garden to a wild patch, where arrowroot and darnel grew. The stink of decomposing grass and vegetation made me retch.

When Josh appeared, he nodded and we moved inside the holly tree, where sallow, greenish light danced on his face.

We eyed each another. He was taller, stockier than me. I knew that if he hit me, I'd be gone without a fight.

'Thanks,' I said.

'For what?'

'For coming here.' He shrugged and waited. 'Look,' I said, 'I'm sorry that you've been upset by everything.'

A sullen child, he wouldn't meet my gaze.

'Christopher's your friend, I know. And in a way, he's mine as well. But there are others. Everybody wants a piece of Christopher. You've known him longer than the rest and so I guess you understand. You wouldn't want him hurt, would you – or allow him to be harmed?'

A gleam of anger lit those eyes. He swore and took a breath and looked away.

'I know you feel he's let you down. I wish you were the only one. A lot of other people think so too. But Christopher can't help himself. He's made like that. It doesn't mean he likes you less or cares for other people more than you. That friend of his, that Jonny Tait – you think that he's a steady chum? Christopher won't bother with him after this week's over. I doubt if he will see me either. As for Millie – well, it won't surprise me if they never meet again. That's the way it is with him. He'll join the army, go away. And that's the last I'll see of him. But you'll be here when he returns. You'll see him like we never will. Surely that's worth waiting for? You wouldn't spoil a friendship doing something that would ruin it?'

Part of me was lying, feigning, telling only half of it. I never meant to part with Connaught Hall. But there was still a core of truth. For surely that was Christopher. The Midas touch that turned to gold and quickly back to clay.

'Who's getting hurt?' said Josh.

'You've got a gun.'

He laughed. 'You think I'd use it?'

'People have been known to.'

'Hah! In story books and films.'

'You've also got –' I paused. 'You've got a bomb. You know it's dangerous.' He glared in accusation. 'Now you've moved it somewhere else. Josh, that bomb is dangerous. It could destroy us all.'

'So?'

'It's lethal – do you want to blow us all to smithereens?

'I can take care of it.'

'So, tell me what you plan to do?'

'Mind your own business.'

'Look,' I said, 'I promise not to tell a soul. But swear that you'll get rid of it. Or there'll be a disaster. Josh, it's serious. Ask William or the Brigadier. They can call the Bomb Disposal Squad and it'll be OK.'

Josh looked through the branches.

'Think I'd use that gun as well?'

'People do, you know.'

He smiled. 'I've thought of it. I've thought somehow – but what's the use of that? They lift you up and kick you in the dirt. *That* fuckin' hurts. Who wouldn't want to hurt them? Yes, I've wanted to. To hurt them – make them feel what it's really like. I've thought, yes, I can show you. What's the use? Some folk don't notice what they do, they never learn.'

'You'll deal with the parcel then?'

He sighed. 'I like to keep it with me. Like I know it's dangerous. These people, yeah, they've got it all, they've got their friends and parties. I've got summat that could blow them into little crumbs of dirt. I've got summat – I'm as good as them.'

Sweat was pouring down my back.

'Just promise me you'll deal with it.'

I waited. Then he shrugged and whispered 'Yes. I will – OK.'

'Thank-you, Josh. And thanks for keeping quiet about Isobel.'

He started to say something, changed his mind and walked away.

Chapter Thirteen

The Dress Rehearsal took place on a warm and sultry evening. Madeleine was right, we thought. What could be better than the Bard in summer? A background of azaleas and peacocks strutting on the lawn, dying sunlight, piano music, voices raised in laughter.

So, we fleet it carelessly, as in the Golden World. Books were in the running brooks and there was good in everything. '*Under the Greenwood Tree*', I sang, my husky tenor warbling through rhododendrons leaves. Rosalind and Ganymede, Orlando and the Wrestler. Good Duke, Bad Duke dabbling with Shepherds, Silvius and Phebe; Clowns and Coronets united in celestial harmony.

So, Isobel in Lincoln Green, the boyish girl who plays at love, the Ganymede who makes the spirit sing: '*What would you say to me now, if I were your very, very Rosalind?*'

Oh, Rosalind, I'd kiss before I spoke.

Now it is dark. A spotlight shines, making grasses greener, every shadow sharper than a tree. A light breeze stirs the bushes and a scent of wine drifts from the tents. Bats go spinning round the eaves and in the darkened shadows, Geoffrey fondles Madeleine.

This is the whispering hour, when base male bawds keep sentinel. Lines and definitions fade and ambiguities arise; bushes become bogeymen and cats see through the green baize door. Fools pursue their fantasy and so it ripens hour by hour. The clock ticks and the darkness deepens. Men have died from time to time, but this is comedy.

Watch the rustics, as they gambol – Audrey with her bleating goats, Touchstone with his cap and bells. Even the planets are coupling. Orlando shall have Rosalind and all shall be well.

At the end of the play, as God of Marriage, clad in a suit of silver, I burst out from my bush to sing great Hymen's wedding hymn of joy. Music plays, the Heavens smile. '*Wedding is great Juno's crown.*' Celebrations, Epilogue and mild applause from Madeleine, who cries enthusiastically 'Well done, well done. We have a show!'

Would that life were just as simple. On that evening of July, the early stars were glimmering. It seemed as if our wishes might come true. Journeys end in lovers meeting. Why should there be consequences?

Next morning, I was in the orchard, hard behind the rose garden. Plums had fallen in the grass for bees and wasps to gorge on. I waited on a fallen log and heard the stable clock strike twelve.

I'd waited for a hopeful sign, but coming into breakfast late, Isobel had thrust a piece of paper in my hand. Another childish note, in careful, rounded lettering, a scrap torn from a writing book of French irregular verbs.

Meet you in the orchard at 11.30.
Don't be late.

The only letter I possess, wafered by the years. Can I bear to touch it now and smell the sieve of time?

Finally, she came. She wore a white frock and a sunhat. Slowly walking through the grass, stopping now and then to pick a plum.

She sat beside me on the log and neither of us said a word. We listened to the blackbirds singing joyfully above us. Then Isobel said 'Charlie, look, it's over.'

'What?' I gave a start. 'You mean – '

'I mean with us, it's over.'

'How can it be over? Why, it's only just begun.'

'That's why we should finish now. Before it all goes wrong.'

'For God's sake, how can it go wrong? If you mean Josh, I've dealt with him. He'll never spill the beans. He's promised me, he'll settle things with Christopher as well. He's fond of him, he understands.'

She looked at me, dumbfounded. 'What on earth has Josh to do with it?'

'I thought you said –'

'He doesn't matter. Josh! I mean we can't go on.'

'Isobel,' I said 'I love you. Don't you understand?'

She looked away and stroked the plum, smoothed it on her cotton dress. Her bottom lip was quivering.

'You're far too young. You must know that. You're just fifteen, for heaven's sake.'

'I'm not. At least, I won't be soon. I'm not a child anymore.'

'What do you suggest then? Run away? Seek my father in the Forest of Arden? Charlie, this is not a game, it's not a play.'

'Your mother ran away.'

She gave a laugh. 'To act. She was an actress.'

'Just a girlish fling?'

She threw the plum stone in the grass and turned away to bite her lip.

'It's over now. How could we carry on? By post? By secret meetings? Romeo and Juliet? Oh goodness, Charlie, you are very young. Look, I've thought about it all. When Christopher and Millie – '

'What's it got to do with them?'

'You heard what happened. Such a shock, an awful shock. I thought, Poor Millie, oh, poor Millie. Then I thought – it could be me – or us, if we were stupid. It could be us two, Charlie. Tell me, what would we do then?'

It was my turn to laugh. 'You think – with us…?'

'It's possible.'

'OK, it's possible. But then you take precautions.' Sounding just as if I knew about those mysteries.

'By the end of this weekend, this play, this show, it will be over.'

'Not for us. We'll write. We'll meet. Look Isobel, how can you bear it?'

'Charlie, you are very kind. You're very sweet. I'm fond of you. I don't know why; I was so stupid – yesterday. What happened in the hut was nothing.'

'Nothing! Nothing? Isobel, you know what happened, don't pretend. It's not a show. It's not a play. I love you – don't you understand?'

She turned away. This gamin boy, this devilish Rosalind; this girl/boy I'd been dazzled by, this Ganymede, the playful, witty, know-all with a wicked smile – the person whom I thought I knew – dissolved before my eyes. A girl, a lovely, gorgeous girl, someone, a creature I adored and did not understand.

I blurted 'Is it Timmy then? Is that what it's about? Is Timmy, your Intended? Has your aunt been cooking up a story? Well, it's nonsense, if you ask me. Why listen to them?'

Isobel looked quite bewildered. 'Charlie, don't you understand? It isn't Josh – it isn't Timmy, least of all, it isn't Timmy – Timmy's just irrelevant – it's you and me – I mean it *can't* be you and me. And as for love! I don't know what it means – but honestly, we can't go on – '

'Why?' I shouted. 'Why?'

'It's crazy. Anyone with half a brain can tell you that. I'm fond of you. But what you tried to do last night – I couldn't face the consequences.'

'What do you mean 'I tried'?'

'You tried to – make me – '

'Tried to? God! We did it! You and me. Don't you deny what happened. You and me, you let me. What? You think I dreamt it all? Isobel, I love you.'

'Don't say that – don't say it. Stop it.'

'Things have happened, things you know that we can't wash away.'

'Oh, stop it, Charlie. Stop it.' Tears were streaming down her cheeks. 'How can you do this to me?'

I took her arm. I kissed her cheeks, her wet, damp lips. I kissed her hair, her lovely hair. 'I love you, Isobel.' I kissed her hands and face. 'I love the way you walk, the way you move. I love the sparkle in your eyes. I love your voice, the way you laugh. I love to hear you sing. And every night, I dream of you – no, listen, please – '

But she was up and on her feet and running to the rose garden.

'Isobel!

She turned to wave. Then off she ran across the lawn, her hair blown back and ribbons streaming.

High on the balustrade, her aunt Elizabeth was gazing down. I shouted 'Isobel!'

She turned to raise her hand, as if her eyes were dazzled by the sun. There was the sound of a closing door and the quiet click of a croquet ball.

When I wake at night, I wonder if indeed I dreamt it all, that Connaught was a fantasy. I wonder too if dreams console us for the coming end. Lying in the dark, we reminisce about the brambles that have choked us and the paths that we have missed.

I was on the cusp of life, a man – and now a boy again, plunging in a well of darkness. First love, last love. '*On revient toujours a ses premiers amours.*'

The hot sun glowed, impervious. I lay down on the grass and closed my eyes.

After some minutes – or an hour, I had no sense of time – a voice called 'Charlie.'

I ignored it, feigning sleep. 'Charlie, wake up. Or you'll get sunstroke. Make yourself quite ill.'

Christopher. The guardian with tarnished wings.

I did not want to speak or listen. But I slowly rubbed my eyes.

'Sit up, come into the shade.'

We hunkered down beside a plum tree.

'You look down. I guess I know what's up. It's Isobel. She's given you the push.

'You know?'

'She hasn't told me – well, not much. Look, Charlie, everybody has a crush upon my sister. She has that effect on everyone. It's happened many times. She likes you. But you're very young.'

'I wish you wouldn't say that.'

'Sorry, chum. But she's an innocent. She leads men on and then she has to back out suddenly. It's not her fault. You know what girls are like.'

'I wish I did,' I said. 'I wish I understood a tiny particle of them.'

'You've had a knock, but chin up, Charlie. See it through till Saturday. The show goes on – you're feeling down, but actors just keep plugging on.'

I felt that I'd been here before – the Deep Heat of the changing room and Mountjoy: 'You're a trooper, Wallace. You won't let us down.'

How much had she told him? Did they share their sordid secrets, peer into each other's souls? Had he brushed away the 'little incidents' of yesterday, like crumbs across a picnic table? Bitter though my situation was, to sit back on a tree, beside this damaged elder brother was a consolation. Far more damaged than I'd been, he rose up like a cork, in spite of fate, in spite of all the consequence that followed him.

Did he ever feel remorse? Or was it all a show, acting as if all were true until the curtain fell and then you wiped the make-up off and hurried rapidly away?

I forced a smile. 'And how are you?' I said.

'Things have been better. But there's no point in my complaining.'

'Millie?'

'Ah.' He cleared his throat. 'Old Millie will be fine. What *was* she doing, silly girl?'

'You mean…?'

He looked a little sheepish. 'Charlie, someone's spreading rumours. Don't believe what other people say.'

'I heard that you and Millie had been – '

'Sweethearts? In a way. I may have been a little careless, giving her to understand that I was smitten, if you like. I didn't mean to lead her on.'

Like Isobel, I thought. Sister and brother, two peas in a pod.

He shrugged. 'You know what girls are like.'

'I've told you; I don't understand. I wish I knew what they were like.' But I was past pretending now. And there was no-one else to ask. I said 'You mean to say that you and Millie didn't.'

'What?'

I couldn't find the words. I blushed. 'I thought you must have – '

'Fucked?'

I stopped, embarrassed beyond measure.

'Fucked?' he said again. 'Yes, Charlie, if you want to know, we fucked each other in the Spring. You want to know what fucking is? The hayloft in the Riding Centre. Millie wanted it and so did I. And if you really want to know, it's not the first time either. I'm not proud and Father's mad. So now you know. I didn't mean to tell you, as you're far too young. I didn't want to bother you. But if you know what fucking is, well that's what we got up to and it's caused a racket and I'm sorry.'

Suddenly, he stopped and kicked a tree root viciously.

'Thanks,' I said. 'I'm sorry too. Will Millie be OK?'

'Of course, she will. And after all, it's me that's in the soup. After this show's over, I'll be off to join the Guards.'

The buoyancy had gone. He bit his lip, as Isobel had done. A spoilt child discovering the world is not his friend.

'Thank-you,' I said, 'for telling me. And yes, I know what fucking is.'

He shrugged. 'OK, you're not naïve. But as for me, I've blown it. Still, I guess I might recover. Maybe when you reach my age, you won't behave in such a stupid way.'

I longed to say that I knew something about girls as well, wanted to come clean and say, I've reached the state of manhood too. I know exactly what it means to fuck. And that I ached for love. But there was a gap a mile wide between us. Had he ever loved? Did Christopher, for all his charm, love anyone beside himself? He had been kind and generous and worn his charm with easy grace. But had he loved, as I did with an aching love for Isobel – as Millie must have ached for him – for all his glowing charm? No, the secret must remain with Isobel and me.

The buoyancy was gone. He looked becalmed and hurt – and young.

Despite my own bleak mood, there was no time for turning back. I took another plunge. 'I spoke to Josh,' I said.

'Ah, dear old Josh. He's such a chum.'

'You said that you were never friends.'

'Well, that was not exactly true. I said that we were buddies, in the way that young lads are, long before they get to meeting girls. We had a den back in the woods and yes, we got up to some larks – skylarking, just schoolboy stuff. It wasn't ever serious. We messed about, as kids do – and then, well – you walk away.'

'Did Josh just walk away?'

'I don't know what you mean.'

'He seems to be more serious, more fiery.' I waited. Then I said, 'I know about the bomb.'

Christopher looked startled and a nervous smile flickered.

'Like the gun in Chekov? If it's on the stage, it must be used?'

'For Heaven's sake, you don't mean that?'

'Of course, I don't. Yes – Josh is quite a wild thing. That's why he's fun. But you can't still be friends for life. It doesn't work that way.'

'You don't think he is dangerous?'

'What makes you think…?'

'Well, Isobel – ' I paused. 'She thinks he could do something dangerous and rash.'

'Charlie – you said you've talked with him. Well, thank-you. You're a brick. Now, for the next day or two, I think it best we both forget that Josh and Isobel and Millie may have caused us complications. Look, I hate to say this of my sister, but she isn't worth it.'

Mountjoy's words were like a stab. and seeing my reaction, he lent round, his face an inch away from mine.

'She isn't worth it, Charlie. Nor am I. I think you know that now. Let us hope that some day 'you will meet someone who's worth the time.'

We sat in silence, listening to the rooks beyond the Jungle. Then he stood up, slowly turned and offered me a hand.

'Good old Charlie. Like I said, forget the rest. We're in a show. For two days, think about the show. That's all that matters now.'

'Christopher,' I said. 'What do you think he's done with it?'

'With what?'

'The bomb.'

'I honestly don't know.'

He pulled me to my feet. 'I'm glad you're here,' said Christopher. 'I knew you wouldn't ever let us down.' The old school confidence was back. 'So, let's enjoy our last two days of freedom while we can.'

Late afternoon at Connaught Hall, the level light across the lawn and peacocks screaming through the air.

A trail of limousines crawls up the dusty gravel drive to where W'im in a clean white shirt directs them into line. Hampers on the lawn and picnic baskets crammed with chicken salad, starched white cloths and cold white wine, chink of glasses, merriment, the buzz of conversation. All of Surrey seems to have converged to witness Madeleine's triumphant Festival. The flag flies from the makeshift mast, emblazoned with the Connaught Arms. A string quartet is playing Schubert by the entrance to the stage. Rhododendrons and azaleas glow in the late afternoon. And from the corners of the lake a gentle breeze is murmuring.

Actors troop across the lawn behind the great marquee, to huddle in the leafy lanes that lead onto the stage, waiting to declaim the lines, which they have honed for days. Shakespeare's *As You Like It*, freshly minted for this summer's evening. Old words, now made new by actors, putting on a show.

Everything is written down; only the 'how' is indistinct, casual, accidental, yet in many ways irrelevant. Everybody knows the outcome. There are steps to improvise, a cue turned late, a slight delay, a line stressed in a different way. A violent reaction to a piece of news – yes, that was good. But how you telegraphed it, signalled it towards the gallery. Though the emphasis may vary, still the words are not delayed. Plot lines follow like a train and Pat! comes the catastrophe, whatever happens in between.

First night nerves, adrenalin – the buzz amid the waiting guests, as Madeleine appears to give her audience a welcome. Breathless hush, a gentle cough, the murmur of the violins and Christopher's Orlando, strides from right behind the towering beech tree, headlong to the centre of the stage.

'As I remember, Adam, it was upon this fashion bequeathed me by will, but poor a thousand crowns.'

Gwilym plays the wicked brother with a dark affected sneer – planning with the Wrestler how to finish off the brave Orlando. Then the Wrestling – and Josh, who looks a little cowed, allows his friend to take the practised holds in a convincing way. Josh is thrown and carried off the stage to mild applause.

Now is the time for Rosalind to greet Orlando with the words *'Sir, you have wrestled well, and overthrown more than your enemies.'* The lovers are both exiled – one disguised at *'all points as a man.'* And so, we leave the fractious Court and Wicked Duke for liberty. We come now to the Forest, where no flattery is found.

'Here shall he see no enemy', I warble from the bank. The string quartet keeps easy time. I start a little nervously, but move into the swing of things, daring anyone to mock my reedy tenor tones.

Jonny Tait emerges from a leafy bower, to intone the famous 'Seven Ages'. He speaks the lines laconically, as if composing every scene. The audience is spellbound, as he moves from Age to Age, from Mewling Infant to the Schoolboy, then the Lover, Soldier, Justice and the Sixth Age, when his manly voice begins to crack. But Jonny's *coup de grace* occurs when Adam staggers on, dead with hunger and fatigue. The old man shows what must await us all in *'Second childishness – sans teeth, sans eyes, sans everything.'* It sends a chill across the night.

Much as I try to end the Act with a rousing chorus of *'Heigh-ho, the holly,'* something of the sting of Jonny's words sticks in the memory. It leaves the audience subdued; the Interval applause is muted.

Crowded in the cast marquee, we bolster one another. 'Fine show,' whispers Geoffrey, swigging brandy from a flask.

Isobel is hemmed in by her mother and her aunt. I cannot reach her. Christopher appears aglow with energy and friendliness; here, a complimentary word and there a pat upon the shoulder, rousing troops to greet the second half. 'They're loving it,' he beams at me. 'Hey, well done, Timmy. Gwilym boy, I thought that you would knock me out just then. And Josh – good show. Terrific fight.' A smile bestowed like sunshine, bringing summer buds to bloom.

I find Josh standing close to me and watching Christopher. The burning anger of the past has fizzled out and died away.

I mutter 'Josh, thanks for your help. I'm grateful to you. Just one thing. Where did you put the shell?'

He frowns. 'Oh, that, it's safe.'

'Where is it?'

'Over by the bushes there.'

He beckons, peering in the dark. 'It's hidden safe.' He points towards the blurry rhododendrons. 'Not a soul to see it there.'

I am flabbergasted. 'In those bushes – God! You must be mad! That's just where I enter in the final act! Beside the passage. Josh, you can't have – Look, I might collide with it when I come in the dark.'

I look around for Christopher, but Madeleine is bawling 'Second Half, Beginners please' and Christopher is off to scribble verses on the trees.

'Josh, you have to move it. Take it somewhere far away. It could blow us all to blazes. Honestly, I beg you, go!'

Sensing urgency and panic in the poring dark, the fear that I might stumble on the shell and blow us to the moon, he takes a step back. 'Go!' I say. 'You've nothing more to do on stage. Don't breathe a word. But if you have to, we can stop the show.'

Yes, I think he understands the urgency, the life or death. 'Be careful though. Be very, *very* careful what you do.'

He nods and disappears. A trumpet plays and Rosalind and brave Orlando take the stage again – for poems carved on every tree and laughter, heartache suffering, disguise and unrequited love, weaving a world of counterfeit, a web of mirthful make believe, where everything that breathes is working to a happy end.

'O coz, coz, coz, my pretty little coz, that thou didst know how many fathoms deep I am in love!' she cries. Or he cries. For this Rosalind is 'Ganymede', the boy.

Disguised! How many counterfeits, disguises has she seen? How many feigning friendships has she undertaken in the past? How well she acts and counterfeits, how well she feigns to play the part.

I have heard of your paintings too, well enough.

And I, how many fathoms deep am I, in love, with Rosalind? With Isobel. Am I alone in never counterfeiting what I feel?

He must have followed my instructions, in a bid to move the shell. It needed careful lifting from its bed of moss and bracken, crawling through the roots and leaves along that narrow passageway. The ground is all uneven and the pitfalls wait for the unwary. Feet sink into yawning gaps; a pile of twigs may hide a hollow in the forest floor.

The bomb explodes in a thunderclap. An orange curtain fills the sky and hot wind blows the beech trees black. Rhododendrons burst in all their bones and bleeding sinews. Gaunt stark skeletons of flame come licking round the theatre. And everywhere is burning light and yellow leaves and falling timber.

Scarlet mouths scream silently, as wood and forest blaze into extinction. Deaf amid the tumult, I am running, running, helplessly, running through the fir cones and the crackling of branches. Gasping, breathless, hopelessly; knowing nothing can be done to stop the flames that pour across a shattered frame.

Fragments from the fire hang in charred black twigs and broken branches, as a new day filters through. Later, they were shovelling the mangled flesh and scattered clothing. The sole of a boot, a piece of shirt, not a lot to recognise. A disk from the collar of a mongrel dog, a piece of broken crockery, while smoke still hangs in wistful patches round the theatre's edge, like morning following the Blitz. Stubs of ash and silver birch point angry fingers at the sky.

When sorrows come, they come not single spies....

Somewhere in that morning mist, the news emerges that the Brigadier has placed a gun inside his mouth and blown his brains away.

Part Three
The Wheel

Chapter Fourteen

'Duck, Wallace! Duck!'

A boot shot past my head and landed with a thud, knocking down the coal scuttle and scattering the papers. Merriman stood grinning, ear to ear. 'Get your nose out of that book, you shirker. Miss another practice and they'll drop you like a lead balloon.'

I sighed and put the book down and poked the embers of the fire.

'Just because I'm not a sweaty bastard, Merriman. Hey, there's other things in life.'

'Like reading books? You'll get boss-eyed. If Bill gets wind that you've been cutting practices – '

'To hell with Bill. You need a shower. You stink the place out. Look, you're spreading muck across the carpet. I didn't pay good money out to watch you spread the dirt.'

He aimed the other boot. I ducked. 'You shit! You'll take my head off.' I tackled him. He lost his balance, sprawling on the armchair.

'Crazy bastard! Lunatic! You need to take some exercise, work out your frustrations.'

Autumn term. The evenings drawing in. Outside, raucous laughter drifted from the tuckshop, fellows singing bawdy rugby songs. The study was a hovel, an escape route and a sanctuary. From the passage, cries of 'Fag!' echoed up the stairway, followed by a thud of feet, the race not to be last. The smell of toast came wafting from the prefect's private kitchen and a steady thump of the boot room door, as Colts came in from training.

Liberated from the Day Room with its rules and its regulations, we were in the Lower Sixth. Much of life had changed, but much of it remained the same. Cold baths, collar studs and corps boots, regular inspections. We were middlemen and we were neither gods nor scum.

I had returned with a hole in the heart and a creeping sense of emptiness. The prospect of resuming school was grim.

We studied Plato, Socrates and Xenophon in Greek. Xenophon's ten thousand soldiers wandering through Asia Minor proved a gloomy tedium in which the time stood still. I'd check my wristwatch, half convinced the hands had ceased to move, as grey-haired masters rambled on about the Medes and Persians.

Plato, on the other hand, arrested the attention.

'Think of it,' said Mel, the beak who taught us Hardy in the Third Form. 'What we see around us are the shadows on a wall, shadows dimly lit by firelight in a hollow cave. Everything we see is imitation of the real world. Man is like a savage who has never ventured from the cave, never seen the colours of the sunset or the smell of rain. Never felt the warmth of daylight or the chill of early dawn. Yet, this savage thinks that what he sees, these shadows on the wall, shapes that flicker, are the real thing. He knows nothing of the world outside. He thinks reality's an insubstantial quivering of shadows. Pretty dull, you think. Now pay attention, Merriman.'

'I'm hanging on your every word, Sir.'

'Well, suppose our caveman ventures out into the real world, suddenly discovers that the sun is blazing like a fire, feels the wind upon his face and tastes the fruit upon the trees, wouldn't he be staggered by the beauty of Creation?'

'I think he'd abandon life inside his stinking cave, Sir.'

'That's exactly what he'd like to do. He's a philosopher. The man who has discovered the Essential, the Ideal. Fifth Essence of being, the Quintessence, if you like. And if he goes back to the cave, what do you think he'll see?'

'Not a lot – not if he's just been dazzled by the sun. I reckon he goes blundering about in all that shadow play, at least until his eyes get used to being in the dark again.'

'Exactly. Our philosopher has learnt that everything we see is just an imitation of the Real World beyond. Every table is a copy of the Perfect Table, every chair an imitation of the Perfect Chair.'

'Right, Sir, what's a Perfect Chair? My study chair is horrible.'

'Every chair has qualities possessed by every other chair. Some are comfy, some are not and some have arms and some do not. But what they have in common is a purpose. They're for sitting on. That's the function of a Chair. We might call it 'Chair-fulness.' Why? Because they imitate the *Idea* of a Chair. Or if you like, the Ideal Chair, the Chair beyond the Cave.

'And if that's true of chairs and tables, then it must apply as well to other abstract things, things like Beauty, Truth and Justice. All of us have some idea of what is right and wrong. Each of us has some idea of Justice, even if the things we see are wretched imitations.'

'Such as beatings, Sir? Or hanging. Then there's fagging, Sir. Do you think fagging's right or wrong?'

'The Greeks had slaves. The word is '*doulos*.''

'That's not Justice, is it Sir?

'Maybe not – and so you have a notion of what Justice is – or should be – rather than this imitation that we see at School. Plato is attempting to define what Justice means. Our attempts are woeful imitations, Merriman.'

'Which makes me a philosopher?'

'I wouldn't count on that. As for Beauty, close your eyes and think of something beautiful. Don't snigger. I won't ask you what it is. All the same, I'll bet we know what Beauty is or what it can be. Most of us have some idea or some Ideal we dream about. Many thought Helen of Troy came closest to perfection. But even she was no more than a copy of that one Idea.

'Now, back to *The Republic.* Pay attention, Wallace, please.'

I focused on the text, although my thoughts were miles away. 'Close your eyes and think of Beauty'. There was that familiar face – the light boned figure, parted lips, a neck like porcelain. A smile as brilliant as the sun and eyes of cornflower blue.

'She's not worth it.' Christopher had lied.

I had wandered from the Cave, found what lay beyond the shadows. I had known the Real World and lived with the Ideal. Now that I was back again to blunder through the chilly mornings, CCF parades and Latin prose, the world of silver lakes and lawns and blossoming azaleas felt more solid and more real than the grit beneath my feet, so that I barely knew if I was dreaming or awake.

I had left the Hall next morning. After the disaster. The lawn was a chaos of fire engines, white ambulances and police.

No-one slept. The company lay shrouded randomly in blankets. Most were still in costume, sprawled across the hall, awaiting news. Dawn seeped in between the shutters, as a well-known silhouette slid across the tiles, like a ghost.

'Charlie, you awake?'

149

'Of course. What's happening outside?'

'Chaos. But so far as we can tell, there's no-one missing. Only Josh. What happened? Where on earth could he have been? What was the fellow up to? Anyway, they've put the fire out. Could have been a massacre.'

'So, what's the news about your father?'

'God, it's awful. Mother's with him now. The doctor's been. He died at once. He must have slipped – an accident. I can't tell you how desperate things are.'

Silent forms lay slumped among the shadows of the Hall, underneath the grizzly bear, the kudu and impala. And Christopher, the darkest of them all.

After a while, he said 'Charlie, I need to be moving on. Quite a lot to do, what with the fire and the Police. I guess they'll ask a lot of questions about Josh – and other things. And Father too. I haven't slept and Mother's in an awful state. Don't you think you ought to run along?'

'You mean go home?'

'It might be better for you. There'll be lots and lots of questions. I don't want you tied up in this. It might be very difficult.'

'I see. And Isobel?'

'She's with her aunt.'

'I wonder, can I speak with her?'

'You'd better not. She's had a shock. But then of course we all have. Look, I'll call a taxi. There's a train that leaves at nine.'

Later, as I watched the mullion windows disappear, a wave of nausea struck me. I threw up across the leather seat.

'That'll be a half crown extra,' said the driver. 'You been drinking? Look, you've messed my car up good and proper for the day.'

Christopher had said he'd speak to Madeleine of my departure – though it seemed a feather weight amid the general turmoil. I had removed the silver sequined costume, placed it on the bed and packed my suitcase, clambered down the servant's stairs and out towards the holly tree where Josh and I had met and where the morning mist and smoking branches drifted in a fog.

I remember almost nothing of the journey home, catching the ferry from Portsmouth Harbour over into Gosport. I had not warned my mother of my unforeseen return. How could I? I had not a single penny left to spend. I do recall the pale look of shock upon her face, as I stood wanly by the window of the red front door, fumbling, incoherent explanations about my return. Yet how glad she was – or seemed to be – to see me home again.

Re-entry to the normal world, the humdrum world of what they call reality, was difficult. I told her almost nothing about what had happened at the Hall. After all, what could I say? And where could I begin?

'There was an accident, a fire. They had to call the whole thing off.'

No newspapers would carry tales of such a trifling event. It would not feature in a column of *The Daily Telegraph*. I settled down to watch the last few weeks of summer trail by and it was term again and trunks 'To Be Delivered in Advance'.

But something else was bugging me, some physical impediment. I thought the shock of the explosion might wear off in time. Yet every day, it felt as if the world were made of cotton wool, or that I held a cowrie shell and heard the crash of breakers. Now and then, a ringing echo seemed to clang inside my head. I failed to hear my mother calling from another room.

The shock of the explosion had affected both my ear drums. In crowded corridors and halls, the noise became a babble, odd confusion, indistinct. I waited, hoping that the roar would finally subside.

Term began. Always the old excitement – 'Have you seen the study?' 'Such a doss!' 'What set are you for Greek?' 'Will you turn up for trials?' Maybe I had hoped that with the pressure of routine, I would climb back into my former self. It didn't work. It felt as if a beam had shattered, bringing down the whole façade of games and Chapel, rules and prefects, leaving me adrift.

'That's a pretty raddled tome you're reading,' Merriman declared. 'Let's have a butcher's.'

'Not with muddy paws like yours, you won't.'

'What is it?'

'Poetry.'

He laughed. 'Look Wallace, if you waste your time in cutting games and reading mimsy poetry, they'll ostracize you.'

'Who will?'

'Every fellow in the House. Try to show some spirit, man.'

I tried to keep my temper. After all, it was October. Rowing with a study mate would not improve my frame of mind.

'OK,' I said. 'We'll talk about it later – when you've showered.'

After he had gone, I slipped the book into a bottom drawer and hid it with a scarf. The smell of ancient leather, which I'd noticed in the summer, the crackle of the frail leaves, the woodcuts and the blackened font made it feel exotic, something rescued from a wreck.

For that is what it was, the book of poems, with the neat inscription *'Christopher, with love from Isobel'*. It was a talisman, a broken spar from something drowned forever, buried deep beneath the waves. The bookmark lay across the words I had encountered in the summer, words that, when I read them now, were like the letters of a friend.

'No, no, got to Lethe…

Something Christopher had said. You read a passage and you think, yes, that's exactly what I feel – and what this person said and felt a hundred years ago. A figure speaking to you now across a gap of time. Black words on a cold white page, speaking to you in a room. Almost as if Christopher were there.

Mountjoy's absence was the shadow that still hung about the House. He was rarely spoken of, but everyone could feel the loss. From time to time a chap would mutter, 'Mountjoy wouldn't stand for this' or 'Mountjoy would have laughed at that' and old heads nodded sadly. That bright flame had been extinguished. Even Merriman, for all his *bonhomie,* could not ignore it. 'One day,' he assured me 'we will set this place ablaze again.'

I had written once, a clumsy ill-phrased note to Christopher, wondering, without the words, what Isobel was doing now. I thought of the Brigadier, stretched out along a narrow bed, wasted and forgotten in those reckless summer days. Naturally, there had been no reply from Connaught Hall. The battered book of poems had become a rosary, held between my palms to stop the past from slipping far away.

Self-indulgence is, perhaps, the hall mark of the young. No doubt, I was wallowing and difficult to live with. Merriman was tolerant, a better friend than I deserved – and it was largely thanks to Merriman that I survived.

During those long afternoons, when yellow leaves had carpeted the Slopes above the Town, I thought from time to time of Jonny Tait. When we met in Big School, he had spoken of a world replete with triumphs and disasters. Jonny saw it as a carnival, a show. The curtain fell, the revels ended, then you dusted down and travelled on. I wanted something more substantial than a vision that dissolved like ice cubes in a glass of gin. Something more than just another clean slate of a day.

Armed with a newly minted mask, Jonny would be sailing through the Quads and Colleges of Oxford, unburdened by memory or traces of the past.

Meanwhile, in the Abbey House, Ainslie and his fellow cronies occupied Top Table. He was a wretched Head of House. Bureaucratic, boring, like a middle ranking orderly, he fretted over silly details such as lateness into Prayers, the neat state of the Boot Room or the rowdiness at House PT.

'He's killing it,' said Merriman. 'Three days on Call for coughing during Prayers.'

'I thought you coughed for England.'

Through those middle years, I felt a sense of *deja-vu* – as if the routine of the place revolved in some great planisphere, with actions and reactions all identical from day to day. Only the cast appeared to shuffle round the carousel. Everybody viewed events from different angles, now the pit, the circle stalls, the gallery and sometimes on the stage. The whole machinery of school, with rugby in the autumn term, hockey, cricket in the summer seemed eternal and unchanging. When the music stopped, your place was higher than before. You waited for the whirligig to circle round again.

Trudging back towards the House in battle dress one afternoon, we heard an altercation on the path beside the Armoury. Stevenson, the nervous fag, who clicked his heels at each encounter had grown up. He was gung-ho, transformed into a zealot. The creases on his battle dress and blanco-ed spats showed all the zeal and dedication of a sentry on Horse Guard's Parade.

A skinny boy in uniform, a size or three too big for him was cowering by the cabbage patch where Stevenson lambasted him.

'Dross – you're dross! You let the whole battalion down,' he growled. 'You're marching with the same arm and same leg. You're marching like a monkey.'

'Sorry, Stevenson,' he whined. 'I'm trying, honestly.'

'With scum like you, we'll never win the Drill Cup, you're a shambles.'

Merriman broke in between them. 'Leave the kid alone. Wait your turn, young Stevenson, until you're made an NCO.' He cuffed the fourth former, who back away and scowled angrily.

'Little fascist,' Merriman said, trotting after me. 'Stevenson is odds-on favourite to be Head of Dayroom. Pity those poor underlings. He'll be like Genghis Khan.

'Bet you've no idea who that young whipper-snapper was,' I said.

'The new bug? Do you think I should? We never talk to little boys.'

I grinned. 'Well, he'll be grateful. You can be his guardian angel.'

'Pull the other one. Come on, I'll race you to the To'ey.'

Days wore on, but as I sat back with the tenors in the choir, I spotted the kid whom Stevenson tormented, squeezed among the trebles. Curran was his name and so, predictably, they called him 'Curly', with his blond unruly hair that spiralled out like mattress springs. High above us hung the angel with the King Size cigarette.

The carousel moved round and round. I dreamt of smoke and burning trees. I'd often wake up damp and sweating. When I dreamt of Isobel, I cried to dream again.

Once, we read *Macbeth*, a king whose deeds have dreadful consequences. Millie had met consequences, retching on the Wilton carpet. Now I wondered, if I'd face the consequences too.

Isobel was not some vague Ideal. But I had lost her – just as I'd lost contact with the errant brother Christopher. Christopher had been erased from every noticeboard and page, from every list and Latin set. It was as if he'd never been.

One grey afternoon, when we were dumped out of the Three Cock, beaten by a minor Boarding House, a mile away, we wandered homeward, caked in mud, kicking stones in black dejection.

'Two years' time, we'll win that Cup,' said Merriman. 'We'll salvage something. All the silver's disappeared. There's nothing left to fight for. Look at Ainslie in that silky waistcoat. What a popinjay!'

'That could be us in two years' time,' I said.

'If you tread warily. Mustn't get the old heave-ho, like poor old Mountjoy did.' He paused. 'I heard a rumour. Do you think it's true?'

'What sort of rumour?'

'I heard Mountjoy got someone in trouble.'

'Trouble? With a boy?'

'You dafty! No – I heard he'd knocked a girl up, put her in the club. Mountjoy had a girl friend and I hear they had a bit of fun. I wonder, Wallace, do you think it's true?'

'I've no idea. Who told you that?

'Ainslie.'

'Ainslie! Would you trust him?'

'You knew Mountjoy, Wallace. You were friends,' said Merriman. 'Tell me, was that why they sacked him? Not for drinking but for other things?'

'I honestly don't know. I didn't know him all that well.'

'I thought you did. Bill told us he was leading you astray. Mountjoy was a devil, but he must have overstepped the mark.'

'I don't know what you mean.'

'It's funny that you didn't know him. I thought you were bosom buddies.'

'Well, I guess you're wrong. I wouldn't say that we were all that close.'

It was Mel who helped to find a way out of the darkness, Mel, who gave a helping hand as much as Merriman. He prised the subject open on one soggy night in February.

Sex. We rarely spoke of Sex. Sex and teachers never mixed. The subject was taboo. A House of horny teenagers and yet we barely spoke of it. Feeling horny? Take a shower – or run it off, you beastly lush. Bill, of course, saw beastliness around each murky corner. Any mention of arousal bordered close to mutiny.

Mel was not like other beaks, who thought of us as cannon fodder, lining up before the guns of ritual exams. With him, we were human beings, chaps with whom you might converse and when he spoke, it was as if we'd read the books he spoke about and understood what art and music meant.

'This passage is recitative,' he quoted from Euripides. 'You hear the conversation, then the orchestra strikes up 'Pom-pom'– it leads into an aria, as in *Don Giovanni...*'

Sunday nights meant open house to fellows brave enough to climb the stair up to his shabby rooms, a mile west of town. Unlike most societies, he offered only food for thought. But Merriman and I would walk the narrow streets, released from lockups on a dull weekend.

We talked of matters no-one ever talked about in School. Was there a God? How did you know? And what if you were just a thought in someone else's mind? Literature – what made it good or bad? Was Communism worse than Socialism or Utopia?

That night, Mel produced a poem none of us had read before

'Try this one. It's called *The Ecstasy.* '

We sat in horseshoe silence round the fire, as he began.

'Where, like a pillow on a bed
A pregnant bank swelled up, to rest....'

A bedtime story, so it seemed, in which the poet and his lover blend as perfect souls. The poem spoke of perfect love, '*refined*' from all impurity.

Then suddenly, it veered off and with a shock the poet spoke instead of flesh and feeling.

'*But O alas, so long, so far*
'*Our bodies, why do we forebear?*'

If souls are 'mingled', why not bodies too? Aha! A simple trick to get his girlfriend into bed – or have her on the grassy bank, in short to have the thing which many boys can only dream about. Black words on a cold white page across the gap of time.

After it was over, no-one spoke. We did not have the words. The poem dealt with intercourse. Or 'fucking'. That was what I'd called it, lying by the plum tree on that awful day with Christopher. But this was not the time or place. Sunday nights were meant for topics such as Architecture.

'Has anyone got anything to say?' asked Mel. 'You understand the gist of it and what it's all about?'

There followed grunts and shuffling of flimsy Banda pages.

Hardcastle raised a hand. 'I think we know what he is up to, Sir. But why the footwork? Why does he go on about his purity?'

'Why do you think he does?'

'Well, Sir, we know it's a seduction. Yes, I think we get that far. But all this talk of mingled souls. He's not exactly Casa Nova. Anyway, the girl would have lost interest by now.'

'You seem to know a lot about the way girls think,' said Mel.

'He ought to, Sir,' said Merriman. 'He's got three sisters, haven't you?'

'But do you think he's serious?'

'He's trying to justify it all. This stuff about the intermingling – Sir, you don't believe it. We know what he's really after.'

'Well, it's true that John Donne was a famous womaniser.'

'John Donne, Sir? I thought he was priest!'

'He was. But later on. And not, I think, when he was writing this.'

There followed groans and whispers – 'Dirty w***er.'

'Don't you think that he's sincere? A body needs to share the love?'

'That, Sir, is a dodgy thought.'

'Bill would call it beastly, Sir.'

'The Bible says you have to arm yourself against temptation. Save yourself until you're married.'

'Surely, that's his argument,' said Mel. 'He's saying 'Look, we're made for one another. Why delay?''

'Because Sir, you will burn in Hell. Don't you believe the Bible, Sir?'

'Anyway, she might get pregnant.' Merriman joined in. 'I'd warn this girl. I'd say 'You mustn't listen to this wicked man. He's leading you along the garden path.''

He winced – 'You know, last summer term, Sir – I heard that someone here at School – ' He trailed away. The name of Mountjoy hovered in the air. 'Someone got it wrong,' he added. 'Well, it wasn't fun for him – or her – not in the end.'

The conversation faltered. Mel looked round. The others nodded.

'So, you all agree,' said Mel. 'That this is just an argument, written by a hypocrite, pretending to be pure? Does anybody disagree?'

The moral certainties of ten teenagers brought us to a halt. Alone, I put my hand up – and then swiftly pulled it down again.

'Interesting.' Mel rubbed his hands and cleared his throat and gazed around. 'John Donne made a mess of things. He fell in love. The girl was pregnant. Yes – he 'put her in the Club' and he was in disgrace. He was imprisoned by an angry father. But he stuck it out, he loved the girl and yes, he married her. As far as we can tell, they both lived happy ever after.'

Mel was not a latterday John Donne. In Fair Isle pullover and open neck Vyella shirt, he jabbed his pipe before the fire, lost in thought. His hair was thinning. Maybe, he'd experienced that moment on a violet bank when souls were intermingled and the other answered 'No'.

We wandered the deserted streets in silence on our way back home till Merriman declared 'That was an evening to remember. Funny old stick, Mel. You'd think he'd got a point to prove. I doubt my parents would agree. But all the same – perhaps he's right. And maybe things will change.'

'Maybe they have,' I said. 'I'm glad you didn't mention Mountjoy.'

'So am I. It's best to think of Mountjoy as he was. Otherwise, it might have spoilt things.'

Chapter Fifteen

1951

It was Jonny Tait who told me Isobel was married. He floated through the fog of a November afternoon, as I climbed on the London train. Jonny seemed unchanged by his two years up at Christchurch. He called along the platform in those old familiar tones.

'Wallace! What brings you to Oxford? Goodness me, you've grown.'

Jonny had grown too, or rather swelled. His lips were thicker and the cheeks, beneath the Homburg hat were touched with crimson lake.

I glanced at my watch. Five past two. I wondered what the chances were of getting up to London and back to School before the Curtain Up.

'It's the first night of *Hamlet*. I'm Laertes,' I explained.

'Laertes, the Avenger. Lucky boy.'

'*Hamlet,*' Mel had told us, when we gathered at the start of term, 'is all about deception and revenge. A boy returns from university to find his father dead, his mother married and a ghost declaring that the newly married uncle is the murderer. '*Sweep to your revenge,*' the Ghost commands.

'Hamlet delays, pretends he's mad – or has he really lost his wits? – discovers everyone he meets is tainted with deception. Hamlet's uncle is a villain; friends are there to spy on him; even Hamlet's girlfriend has a role in the charade. Who should he believe or trust in this false world of make-believe? – until he meets a troupe of actors who perform a play and demonstrate the truth of things, by acting out a drama.

'Just remember, all of you, that acting *is* pretending. It's a world of make believe – but one you must believe in. Let your imagination fly. You're not just there to speak the lines – you have to ask what drives you on to say the things you say and carry out the actions that you do.'

Hardcastle put up a hand.

'But sir, if everyone is acting, acting out a character, they're *acting people acting parts* where everybody lies. If I'm a King pretending that I'm just a decent fellow and Hamlet's acting that he's mad and practising deception, then nobody can have a clue who they can trust or not.'

'Young Hamlet's in the same position. But there's one thing Hamlet knows. The Ghost has told him on the battlements.'

'But just suppose the Ghost is lying?'

'Hamlet thinks he may have lied. That's why he wants to stage the play. To see if it's an honest Ghost.'

'But Sir, this play that Hamlet stages – you said acting's make believe.'

'And out of make-believe, we *'hold the mirror up to nature.''*

'But Sir!'

'Enough of speculation. Let's begin rehearsals. High on the ghostly battlements, a soldier cries *'Who's there? Stand and unfold yourself.'* In other words, 'Reveal who you are.''

I raised a hand. 'Why doesn't Hamlet sweep to his revenge?'

'He does – but only when provoked and poisoned by a true Avenger. That's you Wallace, young Laertes. Hamlet broods and meditates. Laertes charges in. His father's stabbed, his sister drowned, he doesn't wait for second thoughts. He does the deed. Then Hamlet acts. But each acts in a different way. And now,' he closed the book, 'let every fellow play his part.'

'I doubt if I shall make it back,' I said to Jonny. 'If I don't, then Mel will have to stand and read my lines. But that'll wreck the show.'

'Relax. There's nothing you can do. We shan't go any faster just by fretting at the time.'

I blamed Bill for the whole affair. He hated theatre. That letter from the college had been handed out at breakfast time, but I mislaid it and I'd only opened it the night before. They'd asked me for an interview before I took the main exam. My pleasure quickly drowned in guilt. How could I let Mel down? I had a vital part to play. I banged upon Bill's study door. An odd contraption of bright lights flashed red. The word 'Engaged' was lit. I sat up on the wooden shelf and drummed my feet until the light flashed green.

Bill was deep in Himalayas of grey paperwork.

'Well, you'll have to go,' he murmured as he read the letter.

'Sir, I wondered, would you ring and ask if they could change the date?'

He sniffed and looked as if I must be mad. 'Out of the question. You must go.'

'But, Sir, I'll miss the play.'

'Yes. I'll speak to Mr Melvin and I'll let him know.'

I was dumbfounded. Surely, he could see – the show had to go on. Big School would be packed with almost every ticket sold. Hamlet, dressed in sable black, would meet his father's buried Ghost, go raving mad – or, at the least, put on an antic disposition; stage a play-within-a-play, murder the Lord Polonius and drive Ophelia, his sweetheart to an early grave. And then to meet his Nemesis Laertes, bellowing 'Revenge!'; the frantic sword fight, poisoned chalice, dying gasps of Queen and King; wholesale destruction of the Court. Then *'Goodnight sweet Prince and flights of angels sing thee to thy rest.'*

What would people see instead? A hollow space and no Avenger. Mel on hand, a copy of the text within his paw, or worse, a substitute, a stand-in boy who barely knew the lines. We had rehearsed the sword fight until we could do it in our sleep. We leapt and bound across the boards. The feints and blows, palpable hits and agonizing death throes – it would have been an awesome spectacle.

'Sir – '

'Now Wallace, you have been invited to an interview at one of the most prestigious universities in England. Do not allow yourself to dream of acting foolishly.'

'No, Sir.'

'You must not let these minor matters interfere.'

And so, the whining schoolboy took the train to Waterloo, crossed London in a taxi to arrive in Oxford at midday. A lesser college, short of applications of some quality, was seeking candidates from Magdalen and Balliol. Arriving at the Porter's Lodge, I wandered through a maze of quads and dingy looking courts to find a staircase with a crooked door. There, in a low beamed room, a puzzled don in fraying tweed bombarded me with questions about world affairs. What did I make of China's intervention in Korea? Was I surprised that Mr Churchill had returned to power? Would the Festival of Britain cause a surge of national pride or was it just the dying gasp of an exhausted Empire?

I had boned up on Sophocles and Plato on the journey. The quickfire questions stumped me, for the future of the Prince of Denmark weighed more heavily upon me than the Reds of North Korea.

But as luck would have it, it was Ainslie, who had saved the day. Ainslie, our despised and now departed Head of House. Like many men before him, Ainslie's days of National Service had seen him join the Glosters Regiment. Rumour ran that he was shipped to join the 1st Battalion at the Battle of Imjin, that gruesome conflict of the War. Stephenson, who knew these things and read about them avidly, regaled us with their tales of daring do – how the Glosters had repulsed advancing Chinese hordes and carved their names upon the scrolls of immortality.

Whether awful Ainslie ever saw a hint of action seemed to us unlikely. But it proved a lifeline. I was led back to the Lodge and set off in the drifting fog.

I wondered what the chances were of catching that West Country train, when there amid the clouds of steam and shrieking brakes stood Jonny.

'Ripping luck to see you, Jonny.'

'How are you, old thing?'

'Couldn't be better.'

'And the dear old School? Is that a Prefect's tie?'

Jonny grasped the irony. 'Good gracious me! Cock of the walk? School Prefect and the First XV? I knew you'd turn up trumps, young Wallace. But of course, I'm disappointed.'

'Do you reckon I'm a turncoat?'

'Well, I'm not exactly sure. I never thought of you as one to wear the rebels' livery.

Yes, I squirmed. For it was true. I had caved in and worn the colours, joined the lofty hierarchy. Every Saturday that term, I'd canter from the white pavilion, clad in gold and royal blue before a baying multitude. Bloods. I had become a Blood and worn a tasselled cap to Town, after charging up the wing to chase a high ball, struck by Merriman.

And yes, I wore the waistcoat and the stick to saunter into Town, with fags to clean my boots, to dust the study, light the fire; fellows standing stiffly, as we drifted past the Dayroom. Grubs had turned to butterflies for one short afternoon.

Jonny smiled genially. 'So, you are the Avenger?'

'Laertes never gets revenge.'

'But neither does the Prince. Not until he's forced to take some action. But you're not a one for Danish introspection. You're too energetic, Charlie.'

'There's a chap called Ashcroft.'

'I remember. Moody, sallow faced, he'd be a shoo-in for the part.'

'You ought to see our sword fight. It's terrific. Full of cut and thrust.'

'I'm sure it's very thrilling,' Jonny murmured, looking slightly bored. 'Still, at least you're acting. That's a step towards rebellion. All you need to be a rebel in these strange benighted times is to join a theatre club or learn to play the violin.'

The guard was calling 'Princes Risborough.' Dusk was gathering outside when Jonny said. 'You've heard the news from Connaught?'

'Not a dicky bird. Have you?'

'They say that Christopher's the life and soul of the officers' mess. Christopher, the chocolate soldier. He was bound to cut a dash.'

'Have you seen the family?'

'Not since the fire, no, not at all. But I hear things, read the papers. Look.' He took a crumpled cutting from a leather wallet. In the half light of the carriage, it was hard to read.

'Lady Madeleine Mountjoy is pleased to announce the engagement of her daughter Isobel to T.G. Mountjoy of The Manor, Wokingham ....

'Engaged?'

'Look at the date,' said Jonny. 'It's November – and a good two years ago.'

Flushed and shocked, it felt as if the floor had opened up to show the racing sleepers far below.

Married? To her cousin Timmy?

'But she couldn't stand the fellow.'

'Stranger things have happened. Maybe after the disaster, she was after some security. Timmy's family – if it *was* Timmy that she married – well, they've made their pile. She's married into pots of loot.'

'Isobel's not like that.'

'Are you sure? I thought you said you didn't understand the way girls think. She must have changed her mind.'

I couldn't speak. I just remembered what she said 'It's over now. How could we carry on?'

A boy returns to school to find his former girlfriend married. Scarcely is her father buried than she sashays up the aisle to marry an appalling clown. Frailty, thy name was Isobel.

I lay back on the carriage seat and watched a world of make-believe. Fickle friendship – fickle, fucking feigning.

'Nothing wrong, I hope,' said Jonny folding up the evidence. 'You're not upset? I know you had a *pash* for Isobel. But then you had a thing for Christopher, if I am not mistaken. Hey, what's done is done. We can't go over the old ground. Besides, I bet you've other fish to fry.'

At Waterloo, I rang Mel. 'Sir, I'll do my best to make it back. Count on me, don't worry, I'll be there.'

The engine shuffled slowly down the long unfriendly platform. I tried to settle down again, watching billboards drifting by. All I saw was Isobel, cosseted in Wokingham, a married woman, Timmy's reechy kisses on her cheek.

At Salisbury, we stopped for what felt like eternity. The train had lost a driver. I leaned desperately against the window. At last, we were off again and all was black outside.

Tisbury, Gillingham, Temple Combe. Wiltshire plains gave way to Dorset. All I could see was my own stained reflection in the glass. We were travelling and, it seemed, not travelling at all, locked inside a tiny capsule, shuffling at snail's pace, towards the end of an appalling day.

A boy returns to school to find his girlfriend married to her cousin. Everyone, it seems is feigning, acting in a play. Beaks in gowns, the Bloods in blazers, CCF in combat kit. And Isobel, as insincere as water on a wheel.

Was it then for real, all this rage for Isobel? What if I were feigning too? Acting in the way one is supposed to when betrayed? Tears we shed on stage are real tears – and if our tears are real, how does fiction differ from the stuff of raw reality? Charlie Wallace, bound for School one late November afternoon, comes upon a giddy tale of falsehood and betrayal. Cast as the Avenger, careless of the consequences, he will play the role, the fiction and the dream of passion. *O, from this time forth, my thoughts be bloody or be nothing worth!*

With a jolt, the train had stopped. I leapt out of the carriage, hared the full length of the platform and was outside banging on the window of a taxi. High above, the station clock read seven thirty-two. The show would have begun. Mel would have stood before the velvet curtain to explain that I was absent. Were there sighs of disappointment from the crowded hall? A stand-in boy or Mel himself thrust into the silver doublet? Still, the show goes on; the palace guards set out to meet a Ghost. The Prince in sable black returns to mourn his murdered father.

The taxi stalled, then roared across the gravelled station yard, past the grey Memorial Gardens, where the Abbey loomed out of the fog. Skirting through the Close, we halted with a screech outside the walls of Big School. I tossed two notes towards the driver, slammed the door and hurtled down the stone steps to the Green Room.

'Wallace!' Cries of exultation, 'Wallace, mate, you've done it.' Cries of horror from the stage above *'Look, where it comes again.'* Ghost talk – I'm a ghost myself returning from my exile. Clothes are torn from the poor understudy, waiting with a book, and thrust upon my head. Slops and tights and frilly collars, cloaks and swords all buckled on and we are bounding up the stairs to greet the fanfare of the second scene – the uncle, smooth as syrup, booms *'Though yet of Hamlet our dear brother's death, the memory be green...'*

There is a smatter of applause, as members of the audience take note of young Laertes, who they thought was lost in Oxford. I, for that brief moment, am the centre of attention. Young Laertes – not Prince Hamlet and his thoughts of death.

Now I'm off the scene again. Laertes is dispatched to France, cleared away for Hamlet and the King to hatch their plots. Down here, in the Green Room, with its airless, crowded atmosphere, soldiers in thick jerkins jostle courtiers in Tudor cloaks. The smell of sweat and Leichner Five and Nine is heavy, redolent of other nights and other triumphs. Somewhere in the past I catch the lisping tones of Jonny Tait and Mountjoy's barking laughter.

Up there, on the dusty boards, Hamlet rages on about the Frailty of Women, each word like a bell. *'She married – O most wicked speed....'*

I glance across the room. Beyond me, on a crowded bench sits Curran in a green embroidered dress, but there's no mistaking that familiar shock of blond unruly hair. Curly Curran, he's the chap that Merriman had rescued after army practice years ago. Older now and taller, though his voice has yet to break, Curly has been cast to play Ophelia, my sister.

Curly wears a muslin dress, his tangled hair tied firmly back. The crimson lake upon his lips and eyeliner both emphasise the sharp blue colour of his eyes. I notice how attractive he can be. Blue eyed, parted lips, he could be any teenage girl. He's skittish as a colt. Our eyes meet and despite myself I feel a rush of recognition and a swelling of desire.

Boys have played the part of girls since Shakespeare and beyond. Always slightly diffident, there's something heavyweight about them; you can never quite believe they're girls. How they sit, their mannerisms, constantly remind you that on a different stage, they're wearing rugby boots and tackling in the mud.

Curly blushes, looks away. It's time to go on stage.

Act One, Scene Three. Enter Laertes and Ophelia. Here, Laertes warns his sister to beware of Hamlet's protestations, even though '*perhaps he loves you now.*' We meet on stage before the painted battlements of Elsinore. After the journey home, after the anxious hours, my heart is racing, Mel's advice '*You must believe in what you're saying*' ringing in my ears. Who needs to imagine, when each syllable of warning echoes like an anvil from the heart?

'*Fear it Ophelia, fear it.*' Every word acquires an urgency. For standing in the spotlight is the ghost of Rosalind.

I stumble, fluff my lines. '*Perhaps he loves you now,*' I murmur. '*But you must fear, his will is not his own.*' I seize her by the arm. She looks amazed – this is not how we had rehearsed the scene with Mel, when we were wearing uniform. I mutter darkly '*Fear it, my dear sister.*' When she backs away, I'm staring at the blue eyes of a frightened girl.

We face each other silently and standing toe to toe, we feel each other's breath; we read reflections on each other's pupils. Beads of sweat appear upon Ophelia's upper lip. She looks wide eyed at me, afraid. For in the very torment, tempest, whirlwind of my passion, I have kissed her on the lips.

Kissed. Or was that kiss in my imagination too? Kissed the lips of Isobel, a stranger to me now. I feel the hot breath of her lips, as, with a sudden wrench, Ophelia pulls herself away and remonstrates in angry tones.

I sense a certain restlessness that's creeping through the audience. Is something wrong? Is this what they have come see performed? Where is the Ghost and Hamlet? Who is this Laertes anyway? I greet my father, old Polonius and exit feeling chastened. OK, Hamlet, I'll be back one day.

Curran stomps into the Green Room, slumps into a corner, scowling.

'You OK?'

He glares at me. 'That's not the way we practised it.'

There's nothing ladylike about him now. He's bristling for a fight.

'What's wrong?'

He's two years junior. He knows that he can't take me on. Curly glowers in silence. There's another Ghost scene underway, the Green Room feels empty. I walk over to the corner, calmer now. He looks upset.

'Did I do something wrong?' I murmur.

Curly glares at me. 'I thought that you were going to snog me. Did you?'

'Did I? Curly, that would be a first.'

I pause and take a breath and then we both break into smiles.

'I'm sorry, chum. Carried away. It's been a toughish afternoon.'

I feel the ice begin to thaw. He sits back with his head against the wall.

'I'm worried about Bill. He says I shouldn't spend my free time up with you and Merriman.'

'That's typical of him. Don't worry. Bill hates everything to do with plays.' He makes a face. 'So, Bill thinks I'm corrupting you?' I say. 'Look, you did really well. So, no hard feelings, eh?' I offer him my hand. He takes it.

'Quick,' he says. 'I'm needed back onstage.'

I watch him gather up the dress and walk towards the steps. He turns to flash another grin. There's something devilish about the sparkle of the eyes and something dangerous within the corners of a smile.

Since that autumn afternoon when Merriman had intervened beside the Armoury, where Stevenson was dealing grief, Curly has become an acolyte. Common between Merriman and Curly is their Scottish background. Common between him and me is that we're fond of reading. We ignore the rule declaring year groups never mix and Curly drifts into our study to discuss his latest book. Truth to tell, he's brighter than the two of us combined. He's reading Rimbaud and Verlaine and talks of *Madame Bovary.* His dad's an Oxford don. Which makes me wonder what he's doing here in this benighted school, where sport and army combat are the rage.

But now, I have to wait backstage while scenes awash with cunning plots unfold and long soliloquies on life and death are uttered. There's feigning falsehood everywhere. A play within the play – a fiction, but so striking that the guilty King has by the very cunning of the scene been struck that he has called for lights in mid-performance. Finally, my father is concealed behind a curtain to listen to a conference, where he is stabbed to death.

My turn at last. *Act Four Scene Five*. I bound across the stage. '*That drop of blood that's calm proclaims me bastard!*' I declare. Curly drifts into my view, '*mad as the sea and wind*'. The King, (Hardcastle in a Medieval kirtle) tricks me. I delay – he wraps me in his tainted plot. Now Hamlet is the target for my fury. Now, the scene is set. We arm ourselves for the finale. Rapier against rapier, point to point. The actor playing Hamlet is the sallow Ashcroft from School

House, a decent actor, even though he is no friend of mine. His great success was earlier at School when he was Cecily. But now his pale, careworn face and deepset eyes make him a Prince. He oozes melancholic self-regard.

We've played this swordfight many times. Practised till we're sick of it. A clash, a feint, a slash, as with a sabre; back and forth we go, cavorting round like ballerinas to the gasps of all the Court. I dab and switch direction before Hamlet thrusts across my arm. '*A hit, a palpable hit,*' Osric declares.

Some poisoned interplay takes place with Hardcastle, the King. Then we are at it once again. Young Hamlet strikes a second time, while Gertrude, the unfaithful mother, drains the poisoned cup. And now it is my turn to strike. '*Have at you now!*' I cry, slashing what ought to be his arm, but well-a-day! the Prince has turned and meets the full side of my rapier across his face. A welt appears along his cheek, a streak of white that's turning red and slowly seeping drops of blood. I stand back, mortified and yet elated by the blow. A shadow drifts across his brow, as if he is about to faint. Then like a cheetah from a tree he leaps at me with fury. Now we go pell-mell for one another. Carefully rehearsed moves have been thrown into the winds. Hamlet's full of wild indignation at my recklessness, hell bent on destruction. I give ground and parry, force him back, then summoning my own frustrated anger at the day's events, I launch my counter challenge, full of rage.

'*Part them; they are incensed!*' the cry goes up. We jostle, blow on blow – and finally, when forced apart by four strong lads, we stagger breathlessly and gasp our dying words. The King is dead, the Queen and several courtiers and Ophelia; and Hamlet, dripping gouts of blood, and brave Laertes, the avenger.

Isobel is dead to me – and Christopher and Rosalind. I lie back on the stage and watch the blood soak through the boards.

Chapter Sixteen

Morning came; the roaring in my head was like a tidal wave.

Ashcroft had been carted to the Cottage Hospital in blood stained shirt and leather slops, where six red stitches sewn across his cheek made him piratical.

'So, you think *Hamlet*'s better off without the Prince?' barked Mel. 'You could have murdered him. What in the hell was up with you?'

'I'm sorry, Sir.'

'You bet you are. I've half a mind to have you sacked.'

'How is he, Sir? Will he be fit enough to act tonight?'

'He's shaken up. But he'll be there.'

'At any rate, I made it.'

He grimaced 'What got into you? Besides attacking Ashcroft, what was all that game with Curran?'

After the excitement of the train, I'd barely slept. The headache banged between my temples and my hearing came and went. I waited in the dusty classroom, whilst outside, the Abbey bells were booming out the midday chimes. 'Teamwork... discipline... restraint,' the clichés drifted through my ears. I wanted to throw up and fall asleep.

'Wallace.'

'Sir?

'Are you alright?'

'I'm just a little tired, Sir.'

He frowned. A flake of dandruff floated down from his receding hair. Two years since, he'd read that poem about sex and souls. Now, the youthful Mel was growing old.

'One more question then. Young Curran. Say, is he a friend of yours?'

I blinked. 'He's in my House, Sir.'

'Yes?'

'I mean, I see him round the place.'

'And he's a friend?'

'I don't know what you mean.'

Mel looked a trifle shifty. 'Look, the lad is talented. And clever. But remember, people in this place have strong ideas. One or two would like to put an end to drama altogether.'

'Like the Puritans?'

'Yes, in a way. The Puritans thought actors were as bad as prostitutes. Later on, they had the theatres closed. I won't exaggerate, but there are people here who'd do the same. Be careful. What you do and how you carry on affects us all.'

'Yes, Sir.'

'There's a line. Don't cross it. Else we'll all go up in smoke.'

By lunch, it felt as if the world was made of cotton wool. I could not hear distinctly, as I climbed the stairs to Surgery, where Matron fed her ancient Pekinese. The air was rank with warm wet fur and slowly cooking dog meat.

'Take an aspirin. You'll live,' she murmured.

'But there's rugby practice. Should I go?'

'My boy, that's up to you.'

'Old Boy's Match tomorrow,' Merriman had told me after lunch. 'By Golly, you look rotten. But for God's sake, don't go sick, old man. I'll see you on the Upper, half-past two'

In a corner of our study stood an old chaise longue, a hand-me-down from every Head of House to his successor. Though the springs were coming through, we'd covered it in rugs and cushions. Merriman and I competed for the chance to lounge along it. That was when I spotted Curran, curled up with a book and leaning back upon a mothy cushion.

Curly, as I said, had grown accustomed to our study as a refuge for an idle afternoon. Merriman and I regarded him as a domestic pet, but he was entertaining too and had a witty repartee. His imitation of the beaks drew gales of laughter from his chums, but he was sharper than his years and full of penetrating insights picked up from a donnish dinner table. He often made our earnest talk sound gauche and ill informed.

We had been too easy-going to allow him passageway, to come and go where others feared to tread. Casual banter can rebound and Curly had a waspish tongue. I sensed that he'd begun to treat the study as his own.

In collared tie and uniform, with stains of food around the pocket, Curly looked a different species to the night before. A scruffy, rather bolshy lad confronted me in my own den.

'Bill's been after you,' he muttered without looking up.

'What's he want?'

'I've no idea. He scowled and scuttled off again.'

'What is that you're reading?'

'Keats's poems. In the drawer.' He waved the leather tome.

'Look Curly, this is not your study. Just remember – '

'Never mind, it's not your book. There's an inscription on the flyleaf. Your name isn't Christopher, I'm sure.'

'Just give the book to me.'

'I don't think all that much of Keats, do you? His early stuff is limp, but then the Odes are quite magnificent – and then *Hyperion* – '

'Curly, don't take liberties – '

He glared at me. 'Excuse me, Wallace. Who's been taking liberties?'

'I thought we'd dealt with that last night. I told you, I was sorry. Look, I spoke with Mel. I've settled things. But you shouldn't be here at all, especially in the afternoon. You're junior, you should be with your friends.'

'Aren't you my friend?' He put the book down. 'Wallace, I've been wondering. I meant to ask you something. Are you queer?'

'I beg your pardon?'

'Are you queer?'

'Of course, I'm not, you idiot.'

'There's nothing wrong with being queer. My father's colleagues – plenty of them are. But then of course it's Oxford.'

'Curly, I am warning you.'

'I mean, look at Shakespeare. He wrote sonnets to the fair young man. I'm sure you must have read them.'

Curly started to declaim ' *'A Woman's face with Nature's own hand painted'* – sonnet after sonnet. Shakespeare must have fancied somebody. Or else why write the stuff?'

'You think I'm queer?'

'I didn't say. I only asked. I wondered. After what you did last night – '

'Look Curly, I'll be straight with you – I *honestly* don't fancy you. I'm very, very tired. And last night – if you want to know – there was a girl, I rather fancied and – ' I trailed off. 'I can't explain.'

'A girl?'

'You wouldn't know her. It was long ago. Give me that book. And then for goodness sake get out of here.'

'OK. I will. But let me finish off *The Nightingale*. It's Keats's best. Just let me finish. This is proper stuff.' He lay back and declaimed again ' *'Now more than ever seems it rich to die'* You know what dying is, of course? It's slang for orgasm.'

I didn't know.

'Poor Keats, he poured it all into his verse. You know what he wrote at the end, about his girlfriend Fanny Brawne? *'I should have had her.'* That is what he wrote. *'I should have had her.'* That was it. Before he coughed his lungs out on the Spanish Steps.'

He grinned. 'Look Wallace, you've been kind and so has Merriman. Just give me one more minute and I'll trot off like an angel.'

Matron's aspirin was having no effect at all. The surging sea that filled my ears was growing ever stormier.

'Get out now before I hit you.'

Curly hung onto the book – *'Still wouldst thou sing, and I have ears in vain— To thy high requiem become a sod.'*

'For God's sake, don't be such an ass?'

I made a grab. He leapt onto the chaise. 'I've nearly finished.'

'Give it back, you fool.'

I grabbed his arm. We wrestled to and fro, till Curly lost his balance, toppled down onto the floor. I tried to grab the book again. 'Let go of it!' I yelled.

'Still wouldst thou sing and I have tears in vain.'

I had my hands on him and we were tugging at the book. Then with a sickening wrench, the binding fell apart and pages scattered like confetti on the floor. The door swung open. Bill stood there.

'Wallace! Curran! What is going on?'

Two lads scuffling for a book and paper strewn across the floor. Curly's shirt was open and his collar all adrift. I had one arm around his neck, as if about to throttle him. Bill looked terrified, as if a nightmare had come true.

'Wallace, see me in my study. Curran, go downstairs at once.' He closed the door.

'So, thank-you, Curly. Perfect way to start the afternoon.'

'Well, you have let us down with a bump. I feared as much,' said Bill. He stood in front of the mantelpiece, decked with trappings of a sporting life. 'Now I must demote you. You will cease to be a prefect. I forbid you to have any dealings with that boy. As for this play acting, well, I knew where it would lead. I gather you disgraced yourself last night. In public too. I must write and let your parents know.'

I was aghast. 'To tell them what, Sir?'

'What? You have no understanding? You have acted – inappropriately.'

'Excuse me, Sir. What does that mean?'

'I think you know precisely.'

'Look, Sir – we were arguing and Curran had a book of mine. He wouldn't give it back.'

Bill gave an icy glare. 'Wallace, you embraced a boy on stage. In front of everyone last night. That is disgrace enough – and then I find you in your study playing with that very boy, who is two years your junior.'

'Sir, it's a big mistake.'

'How many more mistakes do you intend to make, I wonder? I knew we were in for trouble when that fellow Mountjoy picked you up.'

'He didn't pick me up, Sir.'

'Do not contradict me, boy,' he bellowed. 'Let me make it clear that Mountjoy brought a stench into this House. You understand?' His eyes were wet and staring. 'Wallace, listen. Do you understand?'

'I'm sorry, Sir, but – '

'Sorry. That will do. You'd better say no more. The Chief will hear about it, but with luck you won't be sacked. It's better for the other boy that nothing more is said. Go now. And just remember this will be your final warning.'

I waited. 'Well?'

'About the play, Sir. May I carry on tonight?'

It was the final straw. He crashed a fist down on the mantelpiece. 'To hell with it!' he stormed. 'To hell with you. Yes, carry on with all your dressing up and fancy work. Can't you see where that has got you? You'll be finished. Now get out before you do more harm.'

Stunned, I wandered through the panelled dining room and in my ears, the ever roaring sea.

The study was deserted. Two halves of the broken book lay on the desk. Beside them was a scrap of paper with a note in pencil. 'Shakespeare, Sonnet 20 – Sorry about Keats.'

I picked the flysheet off the floor and read the childlike inscription, '*Christopher with love from Isobel*.' Poor Keats, I thought, destroyed before his time by murderous consumption, dying on the Spanish Steps, a thousand miles from home.

'*I should have had her*,' he had written.

Well, I'd beaten Jonny Keats, for all his wild imagination. Better get my rugby kit. I mustn't miss the practice.

Chapter Seventeen

I left School in July with a sense of disappointment. It had not proved the pinnacle of early hopes and dreams. Demotion to the ranks had proved both painful and unnerving but, like the Fox in Aesop, I believed the struggle was not worth the grind. Velvet waistcoats, golden caps were Emperor's New Clothes, which, as a child, I'd fondly thought were real.

National Service followed somewhere out on Salisbury Plain, where lack of privacy, square bashing to the shrieks of sergeant majors came as no surprise. It seemed that we were back in Day Room, busy filing locker pegs. Horrors of a bayonet charge, the hours of spit and polishing felt oddly reminiscent of so many dawn parades.

Oxford proved a consolation prize of cobbled passageways, ancient courtyards, evensongs and bike rides through the countryside, a world of medieval streets and punting through the summer Parks, days in dim-lit libraries and crowded lecture halls.

The magic led you to a door on which your name was drawn. At first, it seemed a piece of *deja-vu*. A college scout to make your bed, a college servant in the Hall, porters armed with bowler hats and rowing on the Isis. Closed within this fellowship and treated as a Blood again, I briefly fell in love with it and signed up for the carnival.

There was a girl from Somerville, with something in her deep blue eyes and in the way she held her chin. We used to meet in cafes or take long walks up the river, tracking through Port Meadow to the Trout. I held her hand from time to time and kissed her when we said goodbye. But that was just as far as any well-bred girl would go.

The boys were loud and confident, the larkish lads who thought the world a toy box for their plunder. Dangerous, seductive men, with flashing eyes and gleaming teeth and wild nights out on the town, I recognised their casual charm and canting wit and repartee.

174

Meanwhile, austerity was gone, a fresh young monarch had been crowned and far and wide the ramparts of the Empire were crumbling. But for young men of my type, it felt too much like public school.

From time to time, I'd sneak away to London for the theatre, skulking secretively back on board the early train. Climbing into College in the early hours required finesse, for Bulldogs walked the streets and fined absconding miscreants. Theatre had not featured in my parents' DNA. My ignorance of what to see was many fathoms deep. Once or twice, we'd sallied off to Portsmouth for a touring show, (*'We'll Gather Lilacs'* wearing out the needle on our gramophone), but I knew little modern drama, least of all the *Avant Garde.*

During my second year, a friend announced that he had tickets for a new ground-breaking play.

'D'you want to come?' he asked. 'It may not be your cup of tea.'

Ken was an unusual type, who hailed from Bolton Grammar School. Black sweatered and bespectacled, with ankle boots and charcoal jeans, he introduced me to a range of books beyond the modernists, with sections of Jack Kerouac and Ginsberg.

'This play is full of tramps,' he said.

'Tramps?'

'Or vagrants. Down and outs.'

'Unusual,' I said.

'You want to go?'

Late one winter's afternoon, we took the train to Marylebone and then by underground to Leicester Square.

The Theatre in Great Newport Street did not look promising. A small and shabby foyer led towards an auditorium, resembling a seedy club where men in macs saw women shed their clothes. Nor did the clientele resemble those I'd seen on expeditions to watch *Salad Days* or *Lilac Time*. Many dressed in sombre black, the girls in clinging turtlenecks, smoking pungent cigarettes. I felt remote and out of place in my cravat and tweeds.

The show began. Two tramps appeared before a sort of tree. They greeted one another and removed their hobnailed boots, ate a carrot, sat and waited for what seemed like hours. Nothing happened; it was duller than a Sunday afternoon. There were no French windows and no servants on the telephone – no views to the garden or the tennis courts of Sunningdale.

When the interval arrived, I looked at Ken. 'It's great,' he said. 'It's life.'

175

I said I thought that real life was more amusing.

'Is it? Don't you realise what happens every day?'

'Eating carrots? Taking off your boots?'

'Well, it's a metaphor. You wait until the second half,' he grinned

'Does something happen?'

'No.'

'But what's the point?'

'Exactly, that's the point.'

Stupefied, I gazed around the busy, black clad gang, puffing smoke and clearly thrilled by this departure from the norm, when suddenly my eye was caught by a familiar face. Surely not? It could not be. That flaming hair, the page boy trim, the eager, crooked smile.

'Millie!'

You looked shocked, surprised. 'It's Charlie, don't you recognise me?'

'Charlie?' You looked mystified. And then – 'Oh yes, the lad who sang. Weren't you a friend of Christopher?'

I blushed. The group had turned to look.

'How are you, Millie?'

'Can't complain.'

I'd seen her belching up the waters, deathly pale, a ghostly wraith. She was transformed into a proper Beatnik, slim and sexy, with the sallow, sleepless gaze of one at home within her skin.

'Fancy seeing you, a mate of Christopher's in London.'

'I'm at Oxford.'

'Oh?'

A blank. I might as well have said 'The moon.'

'Touring, me,' said Millie. 'I'm an ASM. Stage manager.'

'So, what about the horses?'

'Mum does them. But hey, this isn't quite your scene?'

I shrugged. 'But Millie, tell me now, is everything OK?'

'You mean what happened at the Hall?' She frowned. 'Those people settled it. They hushed it up. They sent me to a clinic, had it terminated. Terminated. That's the word they used. They terminated me. When I got home, the lad was gone – he'd joined the army, disappeared. I haven't heard a dicky bird from him or Lady Madeleine.'

'Millie, I'm so glad that you're OK.'

176

'Yes – I'm OK.'

'And now you're working.'

'Pleasant turn of phrase you have – but yes, I am.'

The bells were ringing for the second half and we were ushered in. The last thing that she said to me was 'If you see that bastard, tell him that I'll punch his lights out. If you know what's good for you, you'll steer well clear of all of them. That family means trouble. They'll kick you out and walk away.'

The second act was even worse. Nothing happened once again. Characters came on and off. 'We wait,' said one.' 'We're bored to death.' There was a scatter of applause. Many seats had been abandoned in the interval.

Stunned by two hours' tedium, I looked for Millie in the foyer. She had disappeared. I wondered what else Connaught had kicked over, besides Millie's heart. Ken was nudging me.

'Come on, my lad. We'll miss the train.'

That evening at the Arts had been a shock. But it was prescient, a warning that the world was on the change. The windows in the drawing rooms were rattling and hobnail boots would soon be crunching through the hall and out across the flower beds. Part of me was looking for a way back to the garden; other voices whispered that the garden was a sham. Walking through the city, past the battlements of colleges, I wondered what it would be like when all the walls came down, when lawns and lakes gave way to flats and parking lots and summer roses trampled by the boots and chicken bones.

I was both insurgent and besieged. I waited for the axe to fall upon the cherry tree. But as for Millie, she had made a proper go of things, in spite of everything that fortune threw in her direction. Curious how fate throws up these meetings and these separations, winding through the rail tracks of life.

My father had retired and he and Mother moved to Chichester. He settled down to write his memoirs in the shade of the Cathedral. He'd visit fellow officers and talk about the old days. It felt odd meeting him again, a man who had commanded ships and seen the world and faced the enemy. He'd stood upon the bridge and met the wild Atlantic gales and visited exotic shores where foreign spices filled the air.

I had not seen the world, except in books or in the theatre and now this stranger had appeared, to claim my mother, root her up and place her in a shadowy front room. She smiled and volunteered to work at the Cathedral book stall and offered help to visitors in search of the Crusader Tombs. I felt a stranger in this oak beamed cottage, with its polished wood and ancient dressers, diamond windows and a silence punctured by the hours.

'So welcome home, young man. It's good to know you've done your bit,' he said. 'A shame you didn't choose the Senior Service. Might have fixed you up with something much more entertaining.'

'Thanks. But anyway, that's over. And you're looking well.'

'I can't complain. Your mother misses Alverstoke. That's no surprise. But we shall settle down.'

I waited. There was something more.

'So, now you've done with Oxford – yes, I envy you, with life spread out and everything to play for. Tell me what you have in mind.'

I paused, uncertain what to say. The wireless chimes of six o'clock were threading through the hall.

'I'm twenty-three,' I said. 'I've spent my life in institutions. Now I need a break.'

'What sort of break?' he barked.

'I want to breathe, expand, do things I love, go and explore.'

Shadowed by the window of the low beamed room, whose panelled walls shot streaks of light, he seemed like some rough destiny.

'You want a break. I understand. Perhaps you ought to see the world. A spell abroad? Australia? Or maybe Africa would suit you. A year in the Transvaal perhaps? We'll find you some employment.'

'No-no, I'm after something different.'

'Different? To what? I thought you said you want to breathe.'

'I want to do the things I love.'

'I don't quite understand.'

'I want to act.'

'I beg your pardon?'

'Act. As in the Theatre.'

'Good God! Are you completely mad?'

'I wouldn't put it quite like that.'

'You've a degree. Don't throw it up. It gives you Open Sesame to anything you choose. Other men would give their eye teeth for the opportunity. Charles, you mustn't disappoint me.'

'Look, I know it's not what you'd expect.'

'Acting! It's a grubby life. Footloose, feckless, mostly jobless. Throw this chance away and you'll regret it in the years to come. Find yourself a proper job and then we'll speak again.'

'Sorry, but I'm serious,' I said.

'And so am I.'

Like rutting stags, we faced each other in the shadowed room. Father, well used to command and quite unused to opposition, now repeated 'Listen, if you're serious, then so am I. Take your course with this adventure. But remember – you'll be your own. There will be no support in any shape or form. The finance and the planning for this enterprise is yours. I wash my hands of anything you do.'

The figure by the window was implacable as fate. He gazed across the fading Close, as no doubt he had gazed across the wild North Sea when in pursuit of battleships like *Bismark* or *Prinz Eugen.*

Mother drifted in to say that dinner would be served.

College friends had scattered and my correspondence with the few from School was intermittent. Merriman was studying at Edinburgh Infirmary, Hardcastle had graduated with a first in PPE. Ken had vanished back to Bolton, leaving no address. And Laura, with whom I had spent so many earnest afternoons, was on a Law conversion course and studying for bar exams. Our meetings grew less frequent and we drifted silently apart. Later, came the news of her engagement to a star in Chancery.

Meanwhile, the fledgling who had flown back to the nest was tolerated. Though not fully formed, he was imprisoned, as they saw it, by his own perversity.

I wandered along Westgate on a sunny morning in September, when a poster caught my eye, a figure in a jester's hat and bells – '*Chichester Players proudly present Shakespeare's 'As You Like It.'*

Connaught Hall, the perfume of azaleas and new mown grass, rose like a phantom from the mud. And Isobel. For all I knew, she might have children now, comfortably housed in Wokingham, the spouse of Timmy Mountjoy, heir to Cooper & Mountjoy, 'Shoemakers to Royalty'.

I hurried home. This one connection to the theatre was a spring, a muddy spring perhaps, but it remained my only chance.

'Dear Lady Mountjoy,' I began, *''I doubt if you remember me. I was a friend of Christopher and stayed at Connaught Hall....'*

I finished by saying how sorry I was for the loss of the Brigadier and with the hope that Christopher and Isobel were thriving. I slipped out of the house and placed the letter in a scarlet box.

Cast your bread upon the waters. One week later, a familiar envelope appeared, written in green ink and with an armoured hand upon the crest.

'Dear Christopher,

'I read your letter with delight and some surprise. We thought that you were gone for good after the tragedy. Of course, we all remember you and how extremely well you sang.

'Much has changed at Connaught, but the House remains the same. You will have heard the news about our Summer Festival. This year has seen record crowds. I was afraid they'd wreck the lawn.

'I read about your plans and think it best you pay a visit, so that we can talk about the future.

'Kind regards to all your family,

'Madeleine Mountjoy.'

I took the train to Connaught with a further sense of *déjà vu,* as if a former self was ghosting through the grubby panes. From the station, I was borne through Surrey woods and drystone walls, along the banks of rhododendron, through the iron gateway. Glossy boards proclaimed

The Connaught Festival presents 'Richard III' by William Shakespeare

Up the winding gravel drive with bamboo rustling either side and round the bend to park before the Hall. The windows were unchanged, the roses and the lush green lawns, the gable ends and chimney pots, the sighing reeds along the lake. I felt fifteen again, a strained and anxious visitor, fearful I would be refused a passport to a foreign land.

Lady Mountjoy is expecting you,' the maid assured me. 'She's waiting in the Ballroom. Come this way.' I walked beside the trophies and the giant sprawling tiger skin, into the Hall of Mirrors, where reflections of the past cavorted in their tarnished frames. There, in a medieval throne, perhaps a prop from *Richard*, sat Madeleine in two-piece tweed. She had not changed by one iota since that summer's afternoon when I had sung the ballad of the '*The Foggy, Foggy Dew*.'

She seemed oblivious at first and occupied with correspondence. Then, placing the pen on a silver tray, she sat up straight and gazed at me.

'Christopher Wallace! Welcome back.'

'Thank-you for inviting me.'

'Well, well. Sit down. You'd like some tea?'

I sat down on a hardwood chair, like any hopeful candidate attending an audition, while silver service jugs and tongs and teapots clattered round. Beyond the balustrade, the roses glittered in the sun.

'You wish to act?' I nodded. 'Well, if you'll take my advice, it's just as Noel Coward said, 'Don't – if you have any sense at all.''

'But Lady Mountjoy – '

'Yes, I know. At seventeen, my head was turned. I don't regret it. Christopher might well have done the same. Happily, his father wouldn't countenance the notion. Yes, of course, I had a ball. But it's a rotten way of life. Queuing up with thirty other hopefuls for a part, waiting for the telephone to ring. Wondering and waiting, as your life begins to drain away. Arthur saved me from all that, the disappointment and despair.'

'So,' I said, 'you wouldn't go through everything again?'

The chain from which her glasses hung rattled noisily.

'Go through it all? Of course, I would. A hundred times again.'

She broke into a smile. 'The thrill of it. To know that you've accomplished something wonderful. There's nothing in the whole wide world to beat it. Change yourself, become another character entirely, make that audience believe, transport them for an hour or two – to Belmont, Cyprus, Dunsinane. Yes, I was young – and so are you, for all your twenty something years. But you were friends with Christopher. And so, though you are foolish, I will help you if I can.'

'Christopher was very kind. We really thought the world of him.'

'He has that kind of charm,' she said. 'It's dangerous to be so gifted. And it leads you into trouble. As it did for Christopher.'

'Is he well? Where is he now?'

'Always in and out of scrapes. It broke his father's heart, you know. And now, he's left the army. Says he couldn't get a proper foothold.'

She did not elaborate and went on pouring tea. 'All the same, the Festival is a success, as you must know. After the fire and Arthur's death, Geoffrey took the whole thing on. He made it more professional and hired a wonderful producer; put the programme on a sound financial footing too. Now you see us, eight years on, we're on the map and in the pink.'

'I'm very glad to hear it.'

'That was a baptism of fire. With Arthur's death. And then the other fire. And Isobel.'

I waited. 'Isobel?'

'Oh yes, indeed. But that is over.' She paused to flick a crumb from the white doily on the trolley. 'Yes – oh, I remember now. We also heard some gossip about Isobel and you. Someone, I forget, who said that Isobel had formed a crush on one of our young actors. Nonsense, really. Still, after the fire – ' She trailed away.

A question hung suspended in the air.

'So, Isobel is well?'

'As well as anyone could wish.'

It was satisfactory in a way. Within an hour, I was dismissed and bound again for home. Madeleine had promised to send contacts of her theatre friends, though whether they would help me, who could say? All the same, a doubt remained. She'd told me almost nothing about Isobel and little more of Christopher, while Geoffrey, who had loitered in the boudoir, apparently had taken centre stage.

She came to the porch to say goodbye. 'Charlie, it's been such a pleasure. I'll shall certainly tell Christopher. He used to call you 'Little Charlie.' 'Charlie knows a thing or two,' was what he used to say. I must say that you *looked* a bit like Christopher when he was young. Something in the way you walked and how you cut your hair. Someone even asked me once if you two could be brothers. But then, you were so very young and there was so much going on.'

Chapter Eighteen

Madeleine proved as good as her word – and so began a life of grease paint, wandering the country as a rogue and vagabond. It was not the dream I'd hoped for, but it had its consolations.

Madeleine's connections were no longer smart or radical. Her old acquaintance, Ivor Banks, had topped the bill before the War. By 1958, his stock had shrunk; his company had dwindled into minor tours to Suffolk and East Anglia.

A cold brisk wind was buffeting the few remaining leaves around the dingy hall where I was summoned to appear. Routemasters roared along the road to Elephant and Castle. My impression of the actor manager was of thinning hair and dyed moustaches. Clearly, Ivor had seen better days.

'Charlie? Ah, your letter, yes? And how is darling Madeleine?'

'She's well.'

'So glad to hear it. Haven't seen her since the War. I think we have a vacancy. I'm looking for an acting ASM. We start on Monday. Sheringham. Eight pounds a week before deductions for your bed and board.'

Acting ASM. 'Shall I give you my audition piece?'

'I don't think that is necessary. Madeleine speaks well of you. Says you've had experience.'

'Well, not exactly – '

'Excellent. We'll see you Monday – Sheringham at ten.'

I could not believe my luck. To start with eight whole pounds a week. Small rivulets must lead to floods. Where better than to start with this old chum of Madeleine? A good deal, as I found out when the train to Sheringham pulled in.

Ivor Banks had been a star some forty years ago when, with his wife Irene, they had trod the boards of famous Reps. A gilt framed poster featuring 'The Second Mrs Tanqueray', followed them from hall to hall, a ghostly figure of the past. The ripple of applause that wafted from the circle stalls when they appeared at Windsor or at Leatherhead was gone. But Irene had a hide of steel and carried on as if the Brave New Post-War World had never dawned.

Wrapped in fox furs on the platform, they made an incongruous pair, flotsam from an age of top hats, buttoned gloves and morning coats. The company consisted of the young and desperate, like me, and others surely past their best, still hanging by their fingertips to a profession that had given small rewards for years of toil.

'Charles.' A hand was offered, as if I were meeting royalty. 'Let me introduce the company. This is Mr Wrench' – a balding, weathered country lawyer – 'Mrs Topsham' – large and bonny, might have been a district nurse. 'Mr Vine' – a sneering chap, with thin lips and a scowl – 'Miss Backhouse' – whey faced, straw blond hair, with large and staring eyes.

'As for the company manager, you'll meet her in the bus outside.'

A blue and rusting char-a-banc lay parked beside the pavement. I recognised the driver straightaway.

'Millie! What on earth brings you here?'

'Why, it's that posh boy again. Welcome to the crowd.'

Sheringham Town Hall was both a theatre and a picture house. It stood at the end of Station Road between two buildings and a pub, A fraying poster advertised '*The Lady and the Tramp*', together with flier for a show entitled '*Girls and Girls*'.

We started to unload the set. 'Do everything I say,' said Millie. 'It's my guess that you know nothing about acting ASM. Steady on, don't drop the flat or we'll be in the soup.'

'What brings you to Sheringham? I thought you'd gone up north,' I said.

'Sodding Madeleine,' she murmured, blowing out the Woodbine smoke.

'Madeleine? I thought you warned me off that family.'

'Needs must when the devil drives. And they owe me a trick or two.'

So began our friendship, our 'professional association'. Our job was to mount and fit the threadbare scenery. The repertory of well-known plays was taken from a stock that dated more than thirty years ago – '*Rookery Nook*' and Hamilton's '*Rope*', along with a version of '*Then, There Were None*', known by a racier, more racist title of the day.

We ran through the technical, marking out where people stood, testing doors that might be jammed, cueing lights and sound. I soon grew used to lighting failures, blackouts, fuses, walkouts and relentless ticking deadlines. Next, we'd man the box office and disappear to call 'Act One,' while actors huddled, making up in tiny cupboards, toilets and the gaps behind the scenery. Finally, we'd ring the curtain back to show the living room of Rookery Nook, with Mrs Topsham marching on complete with pail and mop.

Raising laughter from a paltry house in Sheringham took courage. One sensed that the cast were often going through the motions, uttering their lines as if the whole thing might disintegrate.

Rookery Nook was new to me. A hoary piece of misadventure and misplaced identity. The plot depends on the arrival of a soaking wet young girl who enters barefoot, in pyjamas. This was played by Millie, transformed into something rich and strange. Millie's character was 'Rhoda Marley', thrown out of her home by a Prussian stepfather called Putz. (A German; laughable in 1927 and, incredibly, still laughable in Norfolk).

The sight of Millie in pyjamas, head doused in a bowl of water caused a ripple through the scattered throng. Watching from the wings, it caused a ripple through the ASM. Millie, whom I'd thought of as a wannabe tomboy, a puckish maid of all work, more at home when mucking out a barn or fixing fuses, Millie was transformed.

Standing in a pair of pink pyjamas, she looked vulnerable as a sparrow in a storm. I'd never seen her wearing make-up or without a pair of slacks. Now the tykish manner softened, I could see a girl, who'd struggled all her life against her lot. This girl who enchanted Christopher ten years ago, was older now and wiser, but as winsome and alluring as when the roguish squire took her innocence away. On stage, Donald Vine, the sneery, narrow eyed lothario, a chap whom I disliked intensely, offered Millie dry pyjamas and a dressing gown.

She could act. The years of watching from the wings had taught her something. On that night in Sheringham, I fell for her, as Christopher had done. I felt a throb of hot desire, watching Millie in pyjamas.

Theatre digs have always been a byword for discomfort, with arctic rooms and leaking roofs and beds as hard as concrete; mice that lurk in skirting boards and blankets thin as blotting paper, bacon thick with grease and tea with the consistency of treacle. I became acquainted with them on our journeys out from Lowestoft and Lavenham. We had our tormented moments, like all troupes before us. Rafters creaking in the gales, howling wind through gaping floorboards, ice in dirty toilet bowls, blue fingers, numb extremities. Little of my eight-pound pay survived these luxuries. But still, I was an ASM, a pro. I played the walk-on parts – an Admiral, a party guest, the victim of a murder plot. As we struck the sets in small town theatres with creaking boards and church halls with their fraying curtains, I felt I could tread the air. Besides, I was in love.

Millie kept the company afloat. She drove the rusty bus, discovered all the quickest routes, and had the knack of finding influential figures in the town. She argued with the landladies and kept the Box Office accounts. She wielded spanners, handled wrenches, heaved the stage weights to and fro and wore her pink pyjamas like a dream.

The rest were children, bribed and bullied, prized from pubs at closing time. Even Ivor was bewitched by Millie's dynamism. With the other members, Ivor wore the mask of royalty; with Millie, he was putty, like a small boy at a fair, fretting that his mother might not stay beside the swings.

Winter turned to spring, with crocuses along the villages greens and sunlight warming Suffolk spires and lighting up the pasture. I was happier than I had been for many years. I felt a closeness to this girl whom nothing fazed, but who could then transform herself to something ravishing.

Whether Millie noticed my devotion was a mystery. Offstage, she maintained the ballsy manner of a docker's mate, while melting into Audrey Hepburn underneath the limelight. Now, she swore less often, seemed less confrontational. Now and then, she tossed a rare half compliment in my direction, after I had rigged a flat or hung a tricky lighting bar. In the months we worked together, loading up in lashing rain or freezing fog, we grew to trust each other. We were good companions, busy making notes backstage or greeting punters at the door or seated side by side along the benches of a pub. There was an unstated fellowship, a growing intimacy. We became what people call 'an item'.

No doubt there was jealousy. Thin lipped Donald Vine attacked me over tea and porridge.

'Way out of your depth, you are,' he growled.

'I'm sorry?'

'Cool it, kid. That girl is off your radar.'

'Do you think so? Maybe, it's because you wish she fancied you?'

Donald was no fighter. As he flicked a crumb of toast away, he mumbled 'Don't say that I didn't warn you.'

Later, as we packed the bus, Irene Banks came sauntering by, dressed in ragged fox fur.

'Charles, my darling, just a tiny word. Forgive me if I'm wrong, but I suspect you may be growing fond of Millicent. This will not go down well with the company, you know. Pleasure and Business never mix. You really should be careful.'

Millie was immune to any sniping innuendo, knowing that if Ivor sacked her, he would be without a driver.

Then one morning, Millie seized my hand and dragged me to an alley, where to my amazement she flung both her arms around my neck and kissed me on the lips. Dazed and thrilled, I countered just as any fellow would and pressed my tongue into her mouth. She smelt of cigarettes and engine oil.

Just as suddenly, she pulled away and went on packing, as if nothing had occurred.

Later on, that week, she kissed me, as we climbed aboard the bus. No-one spoke, but Ivor gasped and cleared his tonsils. 'Brazen hussy,' Irene hissed. The rest climbed on in silence.

I guessed she was using me to test Ivor's authority, playing 'take or leave me and to hell with anyone's objections.' Like a child who plays with fire, Millie pushed her luck to breaking point.

That night Millie took me too. In pink pyjamas, in the raftered garret of our lodgings, while the wind was whistling its variations on the gutter. My door creaked; a slim dark outline climbed into my narrow bed. Her body, lithe and bony, smelling faintly of the engine oil, acted as a powerful current. Half awake, I answered slowly, then with anxious eagerness. Millie knelt and played the game to her own satisfaction, leading in a careful, measured way. She sat astride and pressed her powerful thighs around my hips – then rolled off like an acrobat to let me take the lead. I finished, gasping, as she placed a hand across my mouth and whispered – 'Shh! – you'll wake the house'. Then, like a cat, she slipped away.

In the dark, erect and stunned, I did not sleep for hours. Millie, Christopher's old flame, his lover of the hayloft. Was this what he'd taught her, how to rouse a tumult of excitement, then to vanish, leaving me alone? Was I her revenge – a sort of payback for the Mountjoys? Or was I an idle toy, with which to taunt the company?

Was this Millie's trick, to take me and then to abandon me – as Christopher abandoned her before?

There was something else, beside the overwhelming ecstasy of Millie's lithe, elastic body moving in the dark. I felt a flash of memory – a ruined mattress in a hut, the silken touch of pale thighs, a neck of porcelain. Millie, did you take revenge on everything that went before – did you long for resolution, somebody to heel the hurt and wash the mud away?

As for consequences, well, I had not used protection – this was all so unexpected. Was I to be next in line for shame and retribution?

As we drove to Southwold and unpacked the bus, she gave no hint of what had passed the night before. But as the final costume trunk landed on the empty stage, Millie turned. 'I'm shattered. Fancy half an hour? Let's go and have a gander at the sea.'

'I'd better tell you,' Millie said, as we passed neatly painted huts, dog walkers and early season bathers trotting through the sand. 'You're safe. Don't worry, Charlie. There's no babies any more. That's what they said when he – ' she hesitated, 'when that bastard – ' She turned her eyes towards the pier.

That bastard, Christopher.

'The doctor said 'There's something more, beside the termination. There's something more.' I'd ruptured it, the womb. It wouldn't work no more. I couldn't have a baby now, not even if I wanted one.'

She sat down on the sand. A Labrador was barking, chasing pebbles.

I put an arm around her and we sat and watched the waves.

'Charlie, no-one knows this. Mother knows, of course, but no-one else.'

A heavy weight fell from my shoulders. Consequences, there would be no consequence for me. Millie lay back, with her legs spread wide across the sand.

'Just so you don't fret about it.'

'Millie, I am really sorry.'

'Don't be sorry. It's all over, done with.'

'Not for me. I think you may have guessed it, Millie. I'm in love with you.'

'Don't be silly Charlie. I've been through all that before – people loving one another. No – it's just the sex they're after. Rutting animals, you men – they'll say anything you want. It's biological – they want to bonk you, bang you – in the club. Well, that was settled long ago. I won't be in the club no more.'

In spite of the warm April sun, her hands felt cold and clammy.

'Look,' I said, 'I don't believe you. There are things, I know about. I know you've not forgotten him. You're still in love with Christopher.'

Millie's body stiffened. 'You are still in love with Christopher. I know that you can't let him go and that is why you say you hate him.'

She was on her feet. I felt a stinging slap across my face.

'Bastard! Say I love that fucking dickhead! Charlie, you're an asshole!'

She began to run along the beach. I sprinted after her. 'It's true. You know it's true. You can't forget him, Christopher. Yes, Christopher. And I know what it's like. I love them too. I wish that I could wash the whole damn family away. I can't. I've tried – they're poison, Millie, in my blood. I hate them too. That's why I want you, Millie. You can help me wash it all away. Forget them. I can help you too.'

She stopped and stood there, panting. We were glaring at each other, wet with sand across our slacks and shoes.

'Millie, will you marry me? We'll bury it, forget about them, start again. I love you. Marry me.'

She glared at me for one long minute, then began to cry. She lay down on the sand and cried in wails of despair. I held her hand and sat beside her, gazing out to sea.

The Labrador was barking and the bathers larking in the waves.

'We can make a go of it.'

I offered her my handkerchief.

We were married in Sudbury Registry Office, a tall Victorian mansion, close to where the artist Thomas Gainsborough was born. Witnesses were Mrs Topsham and the ageing Timmy Wrench, who looked as if he might conduct the whole event himself. The rest of the company stayed away – Donald in a fit of pique, the Bankses miffed but powerless to put an end to our affair. There was barely time for a pint of mild at the Black Boy pub next door, before the journey to Long Melford to perform *'Ten Little N – '*

I hugged myself all afternoon whenever Millie came in view. Dressed in best blue wedding slacks, her bouquet in a china jug, she rigged the set, and told our hosts to paper the house tonight.

'Sod the guarantees,' she said. 'Either way, you're going to lose. Better fill the place up anyhow.

'Ten Little N – ' or *'Then There were None'*, as it is known today, opens with eight strangers on an island west of Cornwall, summoned by a hidden host, who speaks through a haunting gramophone. Scene by scene, each character is

murdered in a gruesome way. My part, as a minor player was to be the first to go, choking on a glass of poisoned scotch.

Dressed in elegant DJ, with Brylcreemed hair and polished toecaps, I glanced at my features in a misted shaving mirror. Not bad for a newly wed, I thought, a handsome dog. I went to ring the curtain back and take my place upon the stage. Whether they had paid or not, there seemed to be a decent crowd.

Just before I went onstage, Millie squeezed my hand. But when I turned to kiss her, she drew back and made a sour face.

'What's the matter Millie?'

'Nothing – just a spook across my grave. Charlie, for a second, I imagined you were – '

'Christopher?'

My cup of happiness was dashed. In my ear, a sighing started, like a cowrie shell, or breakers on a distant shore. Ivor Banks was mumbling and then Irene mumbled too. I found I could not hear the words of anyone on stage. Petrified I'd miss a cue, I tried to lip read, gazing round, incapable of following the plot. I grabbed the glass of tea that posed as whiskey for the poisoning. Convulsions of my death throes were a welcome consolation. I writhed across the floor in seas of perspiration and relief.

'Touch over the top, old man,' mouthed Timmy as he dragged me off. 'Mustn't overdo these things. Ivor's quick to take offence.'

I shuddered at the awful revelation.

God! I thought, I'm going deaf.'

Chapter Nineteen

'It may get worse,' the doctor said. 'Things settle down – or else they don't.'

He prodded me with steel rods and turned away, dissatisfied. A neat young Indian, with perfect English and a small moustache, he ran his hands beneath a tap. 'There's very little you can do but wait and see how things develop.'

Disinfectant wafted round the tiny surgery.

'You mean I could be permanently deaf?'

'It's hard to say. But time will tell. There's damage to the cochlea. It sometimes happens after an explosion or a sudden bang. Can you remember anything that might have brought it on?'

'Tell me what to do about it.'

'You could try a hearing aid.'

'A hearing aid?'

'They're very simple. Hard to recognise.'

An actor with a hearing aid. Or worse, a world of soft white silence, exiled from bird song and the sound of violins.

'But you can hear me now?'

I nodded.

'So, it could be years before – ' He broke off suddenly and shook my hand. 'Just do your best to keep away from noise.'

We squatted in a bedsit in Stoke Newington. No honeymoon, no presents, we could barely pay the rent. The Irish family below regarded us with some disdain when we enquired about hot water or complained about the cooker. No doubt there are better ways to start a married life. Often, we'd go hungry and with hunger, came the arguments. Minor tiffs and squalls, but quite enough to rock our shaky bark.

'Millie, would you mind not leaving washing in the sink?'

'Charlie, that's my towel.'

'I wish you wouldn't smoke at breakfast.'

Steady nagging of a brief liaison after hasty courtship.

Millie was unflinching,

'Why is there no bread for tea?'

'Sorry, Love, I've eaten it.'

'And jam? You think we're made of money? We'll be eating cat food next.'

But there was sex and plenty of it. Marriage seemed a licence for it – and in Millie's case without the fear of consequences. Millie's lithe and agile body, coupled with those bold bright eyes, made our troubles disappear – or so I fondly thought. When the springs across the iron bed began to rasp and groan, a frail peace broke out. The family below endured the racket with contempt.

After the shenanigans of Suffolk, I was unemployed. Ivor was engaging actors, but we were not welcome. So began the weary round of queuing for auditions. I had known, or thought I'd known the tedium of being on the dole. We shuffled in a line on Wednesday morning, signing on for work.

'Resting?'

'Yes – and so am I.'

'I'm certain something will turn up.'

The genteel unemployed, who keep the wolf behind the door with empty promises of better times. But playwrights wanted sterner stuff, men, who worked in factories and swore and lived in basement flats.

Tramps. I was no good at tramps, not even tramps in bowler hats. But tramps were all the rage with the Late Fifties *avant garde*. Suddenly, there came a call for tramps of all varieties, gooseberry pickers, stevedores, deck chair attendants, newsvendors, Geordies, gypsies, toilet cleaners.

'Lad, you haven't got the face,' a smooth director told me. Nor the accent or the style. Heaven knows, a real actor can be almost anything. But there was no demand for footmen decked in golden livery.

This was progress in those 'Never Had It So Good' days – when broken chimneys, bomb sites, ruined churches, all were swept away. Instead of which, came vacuum cleaners, black and white TV and Omo ads for high rise flats and brand new garden cities. There was no more queuing in the rain; there was a Wind of Change. The Empire blew away and it was down with Rattigan and Wilde and up with tramps and Angry Men. Laurence 'Lord' Olivier portrayed a stand-up comic, holding up a crumbling music hall.

There was no call for stuffed shirts from the world of Ivor Banks. Posh accented schoolboys must reinvent themselves, show that they could also play the vagabond and labourer. I wore rough clothes and dressed the part and spoke the speech of working men, but all to no avail.

Cooped up in our bedsit, we could feel a growing restlessness. Like a colt who sniffs the air, Millie missed the open road, pining for the buzz of touring, heaving lighting boxes out, one hand on the map of England and the other on the cash box. There was work in Shaftesbury Avenue and in the Strand, casual labour, always in demand. But her heart was never in it and the former pin-up girl of Ivor's circus saw it as a drudge. She'd return at midnight, with a cigarette between her teeth, saying nothing of the night or of the company she kept.

Meanwhile, I was doing what I could to tackle agents, bussing off to Covent Garden, knocking on a thousand doors; turning up for casting in some dreadful Hoxton hall, to find it crammed with hopefuls all pursuing the same part; starting an audition piece and brusquely being interrupted – 'Thank-you. Next. We'll ring you'; letters, writing endless begging letters, wasting hard earned cash. We could not pay for photographs. I had no c.v., no record of my former triumphs – and I could not ask again for Madeleine's assistance, now my bride was Christopher's old flame.

Nor could I admit that, like the Prodigal, I'd blown it or confess to parents of our plight. Better the indignities of counting every penny, as if every coin were hoarded gold.

One morning, in Long Acre, I spotted a familiar figure.

'Ashcroft!'

'Wallace!'

'What brings you to London?'

'Pleasure, Wallace, pleasure.'

'Seriously?'

'I'm visiting my agent.'

Ashcroft had been out of Town, acting up in Sunderland.

'Rumour has it that you're getting on,' I said.

He gave a smirk.

Ashcroft had matured since the lanky days of *Hamlet*, when I nearly sliced his cheek in two. Now, he wore the restless look of men who rarely sleep at night, with darting eyes and bloodless, pallid features, like the Dane. We were never friends, but like a mariner becalmed, any passing figure was a blessing.

'Had a spot of fortune. I was understudy at the Rep and, would you believe it, they were staging *Hamlet*. Chap who played Laertes broke his arm during the sword fight. I was given two hours' notice. Thought of you. Remember when you came back on the train and scared the hell out of us when you looked so bloody vengeful?'

'You've played *Hamlet*? In a theatre?'

'Sunderland. They loved it.'

'How long were you on for?'

'Well, at least a week or two.'

'And now you've got an agent?'

I could not contain my jealousy. Ashcroft grinned 'I'm on my way there now. You want to come and meet him?'

Ashcroft's agent lived in Seven Dials in a sort of cupboard, paper everywhere and barely any room to stand. I found a tiny, balding man called Mr Lipfriend in a chequered tie and double-breasted suit.

'Pal of Ronny Ashcroft, eh? You're resting, by the look of things?'

Fingering his lower jaw, he scrutinised me critically. 'Take your chances where you find them. Look at Ronny here – walk-on in the summer. Now he's doing Shakespeare. All the rage. Good, nice educated boy – trust my word, but Ronny's on the way to greater things.'

'Charlie's a terrific guy,' said Ashcroft. 'He was in our *Hamlet*. Charlie here was riveting.'

Mr Lipfriend looked surprised – 'You were in this Shakespeare too? Ah, forgive me. I supposed you was another rookie, all wide eyed and wet behind the ears.' His golden fillings grinned. 'A friend of Ronny Ashcroft is a friend of mine. There's nothing I can lay my hands on, but a pal of mine in Kent is looking for a young 'un. Think it might be worth a try?'

He grabbed a dusty 'phone and dialled a number, drummed his fingers, barked a rapid conversation and then scribbled an address. Within minutes I was out of Lipfriend's airing cupboard, on a bus to Oxford Street and hurtling to Soho.

I was engaged in weekly rep in Margate, starting mid-July. Lady Luck had handed me the break. I rode back to Clissold Park and thundered up the threadbare stairs.

'Millie, look, I've got a job.'

The love nest was untenanted. Cups and plates from breakfast lay abandoned in the sink. The unmade bed was empty and the pillows all awry. The lino needed sweeping, there were cobwebs on the window panes and Millie, dearest Millie, you were gone.

A scribbled note lay on the bed.

Charlie, love, I've got to go. It isn't working any more. Too much baggage, as I guess you realize, old thing. Maybe I'm not posh enough, as Christopher would say.

Good fun while it lasted. But I've got a job in Manchester.

Keep in touch. Perhaps, we'll meet some day.

My eight-week bride had proved a bolter. Millie vanished like the dew. Ashcroft played Laertes at The Empire, up in Sunderland and I must play the cuckold here at home.

Millie, were you feigning when you swore to love and cherish me, simply playing make-believe, as other people do? Would you find another fool to straddle in an attic bed, telling him that there would be no consequences afterwards? Christopher had put a stop to any hope of consequences, when he took you to the hayloft on that April day.

Then a dark suspicion sidled up along the skirting board. Was I just a substitute, a counterweight for Christopher? Was I just the understudy, posing for the man?

There on Southwold beach, she'd told me 'There's a touch of Christopher in you' and she mistook me on that fatal night in Melford. But Christopher was rash as fire, false as any Cressida. Did you then abandon me, as Christopher abandoned you? Did you play the hypocrite as well?

That brief time with Millie was a fairy tale, another life. Now a limb was torn away and grey reality returned. Dregs of happiness were drifting like the tea leaves in the sink. Millie had removed the last few pound notes from the coffee jar. Pigeons crooned above me, as I prised the final shillings out, settled with the landlord and set out to board the Margate train.

******

Five years followed as an actor, five years in and out of work, hoping any streak of luck would last. In *The Seven Ages* there is one consistent character, the shape shifter, the actor who appears in every scene. I was now that character; I played the prince and layabout, anything that offered payment and the chance of bed and board. I had learnt to act. I learnt from watching others from the wings just as you did Millie and so many did before. Learning how to find the meaning, feel the substance of a word, live through every syllable out there upon the stage.

Life in Weekly Rep is now a long forgotten memory. Then, there was a crazy pleasure riding on that roundabout. One play in rehearsal and another one on show. First nights, every Monday, followed by a sheaf of notes from the director. Next day saw a read through, after which we'd block a second play – then get ready to present the second night's performance. Wednesdays, we would run the new Act One and block the new Act Two before the matinee and evening shows; Thursday, we'd combine two Acts with blocking out Act Three; on Friday, we would run Act Three, then put the whole new play together. We would be word perfect now and ready for the technical. On Saturday, we'd run the new show, then perform a matinee. After that, came Sunday and a breather, while the set was struck and new sets rapidly erected and the lighting rearranged. Monday saw a morning run, a Dress throughout the afternoon, notes galore and then the big first night. Next day, we'd begin the whole bang shooting match again.

It was a breathless way to live and called for boundless energy. You felt as if you trod the air and if you stopped, you'd disappear. Austerity had faded out of other people's working lives, but theatres for grade three tours remained in poor repair. Gilt paint in the galleries was chipped and wafer thin; velvet seats were rough and worn; springs protruded from the lining. Mice invaded dressing rooms and radiators thumped and banged. From Burslem down to Broadstairs, the balconies and crimson curtains, where great actors had performed, had all seen better days. Yet we stood where they had stood – Fay Compton, Rawlings, Byam Shaw – ranged in dusty frames along the flaking corridors. Treading those same boards remained a thrill.

Millie, did you ever see me acting on those stages?

Sea sounds in the ears had now withdrawn and almost disappeared. Sometimes I forgot about my earlier affliction. But as the years went by, I found the world was growing slowly fainter. More and more, I lip read as the bird song and the traffic and the sounds of dripping water slowly faded from the ear. Then at night, I'd sit up in a sweat and listen out for something – anything. I needed help. But like the Dane before me, I delayed.

Wiltshire, 1963. I played a wandering merchant soldier, '*bearded like the 'pard*' in Whiting's play, *A Penny for a Song*. Performances were popular amongst provincial audiences. Set two hundred years ago, with England threatened by invasion, it is a nostalgic piece of gentle English comedy. A far cry from the cutting edge of tramps and stevedores, it bore uncanny memories of lakes and lawns and bright-eyed girls; an Englishman's Arcadia, with good in everything.

The 'Rep' was a converted church, into whose wings the actors squeezed like cattle in a pen. Sets and furniture were brought in from a garage down the road. Still, the stage suggested that idyllic, painted countryside, where soldiers, home from bloody fields describe the suffering of war. A canon ball rolls slowly on – a rustic calmly shuts the gate. There seemed to be no serpent in this garden.

It was a very noisy show, with crashing canon, rifle shots and brassy bugle calls. And one hot afternoon, the crisis came.

Suppose a weary actor feeds a cue that skips a page or two, or doubles back into another scene. Others find themselves repeating lines already spoken and suddenly, the play begins to loop round like an acrobat. Or suppose a train should jump the tracks and go the other way. That summer afternoon saw something similar to this, when Mel, my former teacher, surfaced like a genie from the past.

Pleased with how the first act ran, we gathered in the makeshift Green Room, sipping mugs of water and cold tea – it was a thirsty day. Then something struck me from behind – a piece of scenery, a rake? I tried to stand as dizzy clouds revolved. I felt a strange sensation, as if floating underwater. Lips were moving, but there was no noise.

'Give me time,' I said. 'I'll be OK.'

'Act Two beginners.' Did I hear them gather, as the curtain rose? There was no doubt about it; I was deaf – or would be very soon.

Even now, the heart goes out to any actor visited by nightmares such as these Sweating like a trooper, I rode down on every cue, wandering in foggy silence, till at last the curtain fell.

Backstage, was a note.

'Good effort, Wallace. Beta-plus.
Why not meet for tea at Annie's?
Best wishes,
David Melvin'

Mel had changed. The few remains of wispy thatch had turned to grey. Swallows swooped and dived among the gates of the Cathedral Close, as we sat in Annie's Tea Shop; choirboys hurried by, a clergyman in bands, while in some distant echo chamber, bells were tolling Evensong.

Mel had ordered tea and crumpets.

'You need feeding up, young Charlie.'

First name terms? We talked of School.

'Things have moved on. Did you know that Bill has finally retired?'

Bill? I thought that Bill must be immortal, like a tortoise.

'Who's in charge of Abbey House these days?'

Mel spoke slowly. 'Well – it's me.'

'Goodness, that'll make a change.'

'Just moved in. I start next term.'

That heavy curtained study and the photos on the mantelpiece seemed a melancholic memory. Did one's life boil down to this – after all the years of youth? Would Mel be another Bill, a watery eyed veteran, fretting about beastliness and boys?

Some wag told me Mel was queer, living with a one-bar fire out across the other side of town. But that evening when he'd talked of flowered banks and souls, you realised how much he longed for that immortal moment. Could there be a Mrs Mel to answer those desires? Were there lots of little Mels? One knew nothing of the private lives of any beak.

'Have you heard from Ashcroft, Charlie? People say he's doing well. I hear he's been cast in one of those old classics on TV.'

When a friend succeeds, I thought, a little something in me dies....

'Yes – he got me started. Very generous and kind.'

'Tait has been ordained, you know, and Hardcastle's a barrister – that's another branch of your profession. Only, better paid. I enjoyed the show,' said Mel. 'It was – entertaining.'

'Not exactly *avant-garde*.'

'A good piece all the same. People need to be amused. They don't need shaking up and down every time they see a play. Just feed them a crumb or two to chew on as they wander home. There's a place for entertainment, even in the provinces. People want to be amused. So, tell me, how's the acting life?'

'Great. I love it.'

'Getting work?'

'It's on and off.'

'It must be. Look,' said Mel, 'I did like your performance. Most intense – almost too much so. Hm, I thought, this fellow's doing more than just performing lines. He's genuinely anxious. That's a trick you must have learnt, how to make an audience believe that what you say is real.'

'Thanks,' I said, embarrassed.

'And to tell the truth,' said Mel. 'I'd never thought you'd make it – never really saw you as an actor. What I mean to say – is that you *still* look anxious now. Or maybe you're preparing for the show?'

I fiddled with the butter knife. 'I'm fine, but yes, a little anxious.'

Mel drank tea, he didn't speak.

Then in a rush I told him of the nightmare – how it kept me in the small hours of the morning; how the thought of losing all I'd worked for, closing off the world, of missing all the sounds of laughter, all the easy conversation, was a terrifying prospect. It came in a flood, confessing how the fear gripped me.

Sullen shadows crept across the Close. I told him everything. I felt relieved and yet ashamed. I told him I had failed.

When I finished, Mel said nothing. It was growing dark outside. A car drove slowly by, a dog was barking somewhere up the street. These, I heard distinctly.

Then he said, 'How old are you?'

'I'm twenty-nine.'

'And do you think that there's a future in the theatre?'

'Hardly. No – not any longer.'

'Go then, see a doctor. You're still young. It's not impossible to save your hearing now. You can buy the smallest hearing aids. It's not the end for you.'

'How can I act?'

'You can't. You would be mad to carry on.'

'Well, it's a mad profession.'

'It will make you very wretched.'

'Not if I succeed.'

'You won't, you've said you won't. Face up to it.'

'Thanks.'

I needed someone else to say the words.

'What do you suggest?'

He paused and glanced towards the leaded windows where the massive gate stood with its medieval carvings. 'There is a way out, although I'm not sure you'd approve. Why not be a teacher? Then you'd always have an audience.'

I laughed. 'That is the last thing I would do.'

'You hold us in contempt?'

'I didn't mean that.'

'Charlie, listen. Right now, there's a vacancy. A colleague is in hospital. A chap called Fitz; I don't know if you ever came across him. Not a scholar, but a worker. Anyway, he won't be well till Christmas or beyond. Why not give the place a try? You'd do us all a favour. You'd be paid. It's just a term. Besides, you've got a good degree – and teaching's very much like acting.'

'Mel, I couldn't.'

'Think about it, Charlie. Seriously.'

Time was pressing and I had to hurry for the evening show. We shook hands. 'Oh, by the way,' he said, 'I take it you're not married?'

'No, I'm not.'

'Good. It makes accommodation easier to find.'

He was gone. I set off for the theatre with a single thought. 'Mel, I'm scared of ending up like you.'

Chapter Twenty

Sunday morning, bright September. Abbey bells were chiming. Mist hung on the Slopes above the town. I peered along the avenue where plain trees spread their yellow leaves and autumn sunlight spilt across the floor. The room was sparsely furnished with an iron bed, a wooden table, upright chairs and one electric fire.

I knew this room. I'd sat upon those creaking chairs and heard some verses written many centuries ago. Now I sat where Mel had sat and gazed out at the turning leaves and wondered, was this everything that life had left to offer?

Fate had stretched its tentacles and dragged me back towards a road I'd never thought to see again. The train had jumped the tracks and I was coasting slowly backwards.

The hearing aid, a pinkish piece of plastic lay beside me. 'The nerve cells in the cochlea are damaged. Caused by some explosion...'

Skeletons of trees; the sudden noise – the nerves were shot away.

Start of the September Term, how odd and how familiar. Timetables distributed and House lists. Did I have a gown?

'And this will be your classroom.' Down that dusty corridor, across the gravel Courtyard, where the wooden benches, line by line, are carved with grimy signatures.

Books to be collected from the Book Pound, mark books, books on grammar; well worn, canvas classics, many dog eared and defaced; new books from the Abbey Bookshop, neatly packaged by the score; chalk and dusters, wads of foolscap, folders, rulers, exercises – all the pedagogic preparation for the term.

A pleasant chap, who said he was the head of my department, met me in the Common Room that overlooked the High Street.

'Here's a form list,' he explained. 'The Boarding House is where they live. The letter in a bracket signifies which one it is. But then of course, you know all that. Good luck and let me know if there is anything you need.'

I eyed the neatly printed list of new boys in '3C'. 'Appleton, Atkins, Blomfield, Butcher' – fresh faced lads from country prep schools, no doubt packing trunks with mothers sewing Cash's name tapes on, wondering if all the stories about public school were true. 'Harrison, Horton, Kennedy, Kenning' – surnames with the neat initials for the names they kept at home.

One name leapt across the page, as if in neon capitals. This was not a trick, if it were not a printer's error. There it stood, as plain as day, staring blankly back at me.

'Mountjoy J.M.G.' and then in brackets '(*b*)', the boarding house. Mountjoy J.M.G. was due to join The Abbey House next term.

Mountjoy C. could only be the son of Christopher. Christopher, who must have left some fourteen years ago. Now, a son and heir, a twig, a scion of the clan was stepping in the footsteps of his father.

Did that mean that Christopher would visit? Parents rarely did. But Christopher, his casual gaze and cheerful greeting of a novice, sent me reeling back towards a young probationer, with tie askew, beside the Day Room door. How would Christopher respond? What would I make of Christopher?

Surely, he'd have changed – and yet, how swiftly he'd become a dad. Leaving Millie spewing water right across the drawing room, within a month, a little month, he had left home and joined the army, found a bride and wedded her. So, there had been a brace of weddings, hot on one another's heels, Christopher and Isobel, twinned in marriage, like the comic ending of a Shakespeare play. Mountjoy was returning to the fold.

As for the Abbey House, it had not changed, as I discovered later when invited by the Mels for tea. The panelled hall, the honours boards, the stone paved corridor, the Day Room, ranged with benches, looked as if the very clock had stopped and everything had slept for a decade. Iron stairways, ancient studies, creaking doorway to the yard. The ancient 'lats' still open to the winds.

'Work in progress,' Mel assured me. 'So much has to go. I'll meet the Head and then the Bursar. Not a lot will change this year.'

I spotted him at once, two rows back and chatting to a pale lad who looked as if he hadn't slept. A line of nervous faces gazed in stunned obedience, collars starched and all adrift or climbing round a savage haircut, charcoal suits, a size too big in wonder and surprise.

I climbed onto the wooden dais and enacted lines I half remembered other beaks reciting long ago. Costumed in a greenish gown, whose seams were stained with chalk, I was affected and severe as I called out the register.

'Appleton, Atkins, Blomfield, Butcher' – each name followed by a cough and 'Sir! Sir!' from a strangled throat.

'Mountjoy?'

'Sum.'

'I beg your pardon?'

'Sum. It's Latin, Sir. It means 'I'm here.''

'Indeed?'

'That's what you're meant to say. In House – '

'Yes, thank-you, Mountjoy. 'Sir' will do. Now – Munsey? Peterson?

He grinned – so early on that morning, looking utterly at home, perched on a wooden bench with autumn sunlight creeping in. I recognised the cowlick hair, a chip off the old block, indeed.

I cleared my throat. 'Let us begin. We'll start with something easy. Dickens – '*Oliver Twist.*' No doubt you've read it. Hands up.' Half a dozen hands. 'Good. Butcher, you begin.'

They stumbled through the opening pages, mumbling in treble tones or croaking frogs of voices on the break.

Enough! I seized the text and, in a voice of ham-Dickensian, declaimed the death of Oliver's mama. '*She placed her cold lips on his forehead; passed her hands over her face; gazed wildly round; shuddered; fell back – and died.*'

I paused a second longer than I should have done. But no-one moved.

'*The surgeon leaned over the body and raised the left hand. 'The old story,' he said: 'no wedding ring, I see.*'

'No wedding ring'?' I said again.

A hand shot up. 'No husband, Sir.'

'Correct. So, Oliver is –

'Illegitimate.'

'Sir, he's a bastard.' Muffled giggles round the classroom. Mountjoy, testing me again? Working out how far this novice teacher was prepared to go?

'Thank-you, Mountjoy. I must ask you to refrain from calling out. One hand up is quite enough.'

I spoke of illegitimacy in the nineteenth century, the stigma of unmarried mothers and its repercussions. It was over the heads of a flock whose thoughts were probably on fagging, locker pegs and collar studs. Did they know the facts of life? Did I at their age?

The bell rang for the lesson's end. The class trooped out in single file. Mountjoy loitered in the rear.

'Yes, what is it?'

'I just want to say I'm sorry, Sir.'

'Sorry?'

'For that word.'

'What word?'

'You know, the 'bastard' one. It's not polite.'

Despite the likeness and the old familiar swagger, Mountjoy's eyes were milky blue, not brown, as Christopher's had been. And there was a wistfulness I'd never seen in Christopher.

'Thank-you, Mountjoy. Better cut along or you'll be late.'

He flashed a smile, a blaze of light. Christopher at thirteen must have played this card a dozen times.

Mel invited me to lunch.

'You will find the food is better,' he assured me. 'Roast today.'

Bill's old team consisted of two colleagues. One a breezy teacher by the name of Jolyon, who burst with outdoor confidence. He strode around the school pursued by an enormous wolf hound. Jolyon's dog lay at his feet in class, emitting weary growls. At weekends, Jolyon shot pheasant, aided by the wolf hound.

The other was an ancient seer, a bald and hunched old monk, called Frank, who looked as if he'd seen it all. I knew Frank well, old Mr Vaughan, who had been teaching since the Ark and said he'd taught the fathers of a good half of his pupils. Frank's classroom was the mausoleum of ancient school mementoes, photos from last century of stern be-whiskered beaks and haughty athletes, holding leather balls. He greeted me with a sarcastic nod.

'I thought you might turn up again, young Wallace. No, you haven't changed.'

Later, he would ask me, as we watched the Firsts one afternoon, 'Do you find much changed since you were here?'

'Not a lot.'

'Things rarely do. *Pueri non mutant.* Boys do not change. It's only you and I grow old.'

Mel approached me after lunch. 'Charlie, I'm a tutor short. I wonder if you'd help me out?'

'Tutoring?'

'There's not a lot to do. An evening's duty in a week – and maybe some fortnightly orders.'

'I'm not sure.'

'Well, think about it. Join the team. You will enjoy it.'

Frank was right – the life of school was filtered, like a negative. Where I had sat, now others sat, with inattentive faces, judging the performance with a silence or a rustled note. I watched the dark clad cavalcades processing through the Courtyards, early morning gatherings or setting off for games. The Abbey clock had struck and, Sleeping Beauty like, the same routine had frozen for another century. Boys wore boaters, with embroidered waistcoats for the Bloods; beaks in mortar boards, the Tuck Shop and the CCF parades. I watched those many younger selves as through a wall of polished glass – new boys skittering like colts before the adolescent swagger; satisfied Sixth Formers before whom the world lay like a map. I longed to reach out and say, 'Be careful how you go.'

Down the Avenue I pedalled, brief case crammed with midnight marking; then I sat through morning Chapel, where the blue winged angel hung. Crowds along the duckboards on those misty afternoons, cheering warriors in gold and blue.

My first evening duty was a curious experience – waiting in the study for the monitor to knock. Later, I'd be summoned for a tour of the dormitories, climbing up the stairways I had thundered down a thousand times, hearing music from a doorway, drifting gaily down the stairs. Mersey beat – '*She loves you, yeah, yeah, yeah*' – in hopeful antidote to lines of iron beds and boys who stood like sentinels before you.

A fortnight into term, I was transformed as any butterfly – if ever time reversed and butterflies returned to chrysalids. From time to time, I thought of Millie, wondered what became of her. Was she driving buses, heaving scenery and stringing lights? Had she found a better bed than mine?

Came the last day of the fortnight, known as 'New Boy's Grace'. As ill luck would have it, Mel was out and I was substitute; a novice beak and wet behind the ears.

Sitting in the study, crammed with photographs of family, (there was indeed a Mrs Mel, a country girl from Shaftesbury – and to my surprise a line of tiny little Mels; a teddy bear was nestling underneath the patterned sofa), I heard what I took to be a flock of starlings. It was autumn and the birds had perched along the tiled roofs. I was not expected to be anywhere about the House. At prep time, all was silent. Bill had rarely ventured past the door – except for mealtimes and evening rounds. But the shriek of starlings seemed unnaturally persistent. Then it dropped an octave and became a kind of roar.

Something quite dramatic must be happening out there. I ran downstairs, towards the corridor. By now the noise was deafening. The Day Room door was closed. I threw it open to a scene of Bedlam.

Instead of sober heads, bent over books and pens and foolscap pads, a frozen bacchanal appeared, like statues in a children's game. Boys stood on the tables, arms aloft in celebration; paper scattered everywhere and pools of ink ran on the floor. Some had ties around their foreheads, others hung from windowsills like peasants at an execution, caught, as in a photograph, mouths agape in all the thrill of acting out a play.

In the corner, by the Box, two burly lads in shirt sleeves were struggling with a smaller boy. The jacket, torn across one shoulder, shot a glimpse of pale blue; the face, a blend of fear and fury, flickered. Blood was trickling across his nose and cheek.

I waited, counted twenty-five, then spoke as softly as I could.

'OK. Put him gently down. Then go back to your places. You there – ' pointing to an older boy who had not moved, 'Go and find the Head of House and tell him to report at once. And you and you – pick up the trash.'

They settled back onto the benches, as the Head of House appeared. He looked concerned, but not at all surprised.

'There's been a riot. I require the names of all the ring leaders. No doubt, some of you will think that this is part of House tradition, trampling another boy. You think it's a kind of game? Morgan, please arrange a Hall Keeper to keep some order.

Banalities trip off the tongue. I glanced at Mountjoy CJM, caked with sweat and smeared with dust, the tear upon his shoulder flashing violent electric blue. Then I noticed that his mouth was twitching in a grin.

It was not until I reached the study and had closed the door that I began to shake, as thoughts of Harvey and the other boys screaming at Trelawney came to mind. Trelawney scrabbling at the narrow flap below the wooden box. A figure, barely human, muck and filth around his face.

'Grovel, scum. Let's see you grovel.'

Frank was right. Boys never change. Inhumanity was carved in letters on the Day Room wall.

House Prayers was an odd affair, a stiffly formal non-event. I tried to keep a steady voice, aware of being scrutinised. But when the study door was closed again, there came another knock.

'Ah, Morgan, yes?'

The Head of House, a dark-haired beanpole, with the manner of a young staff officer.

'Thank-you, Sir. I'm sorry you were made to feel uncomfortable. I've sorted everything and rest assured, the ring leaders are dealt with.'

Morgan stopped and waited.

'Is that all?'

'Yes, Sir. And I'd be grateful if you'd leave the rest to me. House Discipline's a matter for the prefects. That's our job, you know. Housemasters only interfere when matters get more serious.'

'So, this matter wasn't all that serious?' I said.

He shrugged. 'Well, it was rather noisy. High spirits at the end of New Boys' Grace. But nothing more.'

'Crushing a boy in a wooden box?'

'That's House tradition, Sir. We all went through it. Look at us. We've always Boxed the bolshy ones. That way they can learn respect. If you don't teach them early, they think they can get away with murder. So, we aim to teach them young. Besides, Sir – '

'Yes?'

'He had it coming.'

'Mountjoy?'

'Yes. He's quite a tyke. Lippy too – he'll have to learn if he is going to survive.'

'You let the Boxing Party loose to riot during prep?'

'It's an exception, Sir – it's just the evening after New Boys' Grace. After that, it's back to normal. Honestly, you'll see. And everything's in order now. The dormitories are silent. After all, they've had their fun. You needn't bother coming round.'

I gripped the highbacked chair, my nails dug into the wooden surface.

'Thank-you, Morgan. Just one question. Do you use the cane?'

'Always have, Sir. For the Day Room.'

'And the other boys?'

'We leave that to Mr Melvin.'

'Does he cane a lot?'

'He's new, Sir. But I don't think that he's caned a boy so far.'

Mel was slugging whiskey. 'Stupid, stupid. Don't they realise that bullying makes bullies of them all?'

'Do you let this Boxing of the younger boys go on?'

'Didn't know it still existed. Who's the boy involved?'

'Lad called Mountjoy.'

'Yes,' he said and pondered. 'Yes, it would be Mountjoy.'

'Why?'

'Between us, Charlie, Mountjoy's just too full of Mountjoy.'

'That's his fault?'

'It certainly annoys the other boys. He's familiar; treats the Seniors as bosom friends. His grandfather was here, you know, as well as half his family.'

'His father was in Abbey House.'

'Was he? No-one mentioned it.'

'Yes, his father left under a cloud.'

Mel sighed a little wearily. The first weeks of the term had been a struggle. In the lamplight, he looked green. 'Let's hope that Mountjoy doesn't go the same way as his father. I'd be grateful if you'd keep an eye on him for me. After all, we're in 'loco parentis' for these boys.'

Chapter Twenty-One

1963. The world had changed to rainbow hues, Carnaby Street and the Mersey beat; yet in the shires and provinces, the change was imperceptible. The Summer of Love was five years off, prosperity was on the wing, but formal suits and country tweeds remained the order of the day.

Closed in that provincial world, life had much to offer – just as frogs in lukewarm water do not look for an escape. On those autumn afternoons, when sunshine played upon the furrows, lighting up the yellow leaves, the future was a blank. Voices echoed up and down the ancient corridors. Anthems drifted from the Abbey, where the monks had prayed. Routine wraps a net around perception, days and weeks go by and only looking back, you realise what you've become.

I had become a school master, the solitary bachelor – the sort of chap we used to laugh about when we were young. The costume fitted better now and each performance felt more real – the flapping gown, the restless walk to launch into the day.

By half term, Mel informed me that FitzHugh would not return and would I stay until the summer? Without thinking, I agreed.

Christmas passed and winter settled in, with lanes impassable and snow banked hedgerows high up on the hills. Lakes and rivers turned to ice and teaching in half heated rooms became a daily exercise to keep frostbite at bay.

'Keep an eye on Mountjoy.' Mel had said. It was an easy task. Mountjoy stood out from the crowd of nervous country lads. Undaunted by the pressure to conform, there was a *joie de vivre,* a half-supressed delight in everything he chose to do. Prefects, colleagues, older boys were baffled; was it mockery? Mockery was somewhere, but the confidence seemed natural. Prefects less endowed with charm, waited for his guard to drop. Scuffed shoes or neglected duties, smirking, lateness into bed – martinets would set their traps, but failed to dent the mask.

I kept a careful eye on him, after that evening in the House; '*in loco parentis*' – literally, 'in place of parents' – as indeed I might have been a parent in a different world, had things turned out differently or had the planets been aligned.

Mountjoy's work was neat, but one suspected that he might do better if he felt the challenge to be worth an extra mile. He settled for a middle ranker, happy not to seem pretentious, as he crossed the Courtyards with a pile of books beneath his arm. Yes, a mini-Christopher, the cowlick hair, the upright stance – but Christopher was darker and his progeny was fair.

'That fellow, Mountjoy – quite unruly,' Frank declared one day. 'Wasn't one of them expelled?'

'His father, Frank. You must have taught him.' I thought everyone remembered Mountjoy. 'He was quite a sportsman. Captain of the Seconds.'

'Ah, that chap. A tearaway.' He made a face. 'I heard a rumour that he'd been cashiered. Some misdemeanour when the army was deployed in Cyprus. Hadn't heard that he was married. Didn't seem the type.'

Children's faces are like changing weather in their moods. Mountjoy's mood perplexed me; it was cloudless as a summer's day. Boarding school could never be a life of endless pleasure, bursting, as it was, with strange demands and arcane rituals. Rarely, though, was there a hint of trouble or anxiety. Was this Mountjoy too good to be true?

As the sun began to climb, plans were once more underway for celebrations at Commem. Word got round that I had been in theatre. I was asked to help a chap called Bainbridge who had been entrusted with the annual show.

Tom was an historian, with little knowledge of the drama, but he set about the task with energy and vim. *Spring 1600* was the play, a well-known piece by Emlyn Williams. Tom explained that it involved not only William Shakespeare, Richard Burbidge, Queen Elizabeth, but quantities of old Shakespearian gags.

'Perfect choice,' he said. 'We'll cast before the end of term. We need a bustling figure to play Burbidge and a junior for Beeston.'

'Beeston who?' I asked.

'His name, supposedly, is Jack. He is a country lad who's keen to join a band of players.'

'Jack is a boy player then?'

'I think you'd better read the play. I don't suppose you've come across a fellow who could act the part?''

Emlyn Williams is a half-forgotten figure nowadays. In his pomp, he was revered for pieces like *The Corn is Green*. *Spring 1600* sees the 'lad' called Jack set out for London. But Jack is actually a girl throughout the opening scene. Threatened with the prospect of a suffocating marriage, she escapes in a disguise, like Viola and Rosalind and joins a troupe of players led by famous Richard Burbidge.

Ann – or Jack – auditions for a play penned by the secretive, and mostly absent, William Shakespeare. 'He' is cast as Viola, who's shipwrecked in Illyria, and then disguised as yet another boy.

Ah! The girl, who plays the boy; the boy who plays the girl who plays the boy. How many times have we been there? And what skill possessed these lads for Shakespeare to endow them with such memorable poetry?

Squeaking Cleopatra and the queen of devilish Macbeth were played by other boys before Nell Gwynn dispatched them from the stage. But in those early days, the boys were Galateas and Ganymedes, who trod the boards until their voices broke.

Ann – or Jack – disguised in breeches, falls for Richard Burbidge, when Burbidge plays Orsino – or Orlando in the other plays. Does he know this Tomboy is a girl? We never know. Meanwhile, we would cast a boy to play the heroine, who plays a boy, just as those other players did of old.

Back in the Burbidge household, Shoreditch, all is hurly burly. Men rehearse and argue, learn their lines and criticise each other, hustle, bustle, fight and make it up. But in the final scene, the Queen appears in silhouette, to watch a dress rehearsal that begins with music and the words *'If music be the food of love, play on.'*

'Who can play the part of Ann?' said Tom. 'Have you found anyone?'

My class was full of hearties, who could play a meanish rugby half and might well prove acceptable at any regimental board. Sensitivity was not their game.

'Is there nobody?' said Tom.

'There's no-one I can think of.'

'What about that fellow Mountjoy?'

'Possibly. He's rather young.'

I had not mentioned Mountjoy. I would rather he were less exposed, for all the actor's blood within his veins. Anyone who played a girl would be a butt for mockery. Mountjoy was a sprite and I'd been told to keep an eye on him.

Some days later, Tom announced 'I've had a word with Mel. Mountjoy should be up to it. He seems resilient enough. Besides, they say his grandmother was famous in her time.'

A cast list in italic script was posted in the Undercroft. The Head of School was cast as Burbidge. Others featured further down, with 'Ann, daughter of William Byrd: Mountjoy CJM'.

Rehearsals started, although my attendance was irregular. For afternoons, I'd been assigned to cricket nets or umpiring. A new arrival could not bend priorities where Sport was King.

'Won't you come and help?' said Tom, a fortnight into term. 'Come this Sunday, two o'clock and tell me what you think of it.'

Duly then, I rolled up to the back of Big School Hall. A scene was underway where Ann – disguised as 'Jack', the country boy – meets Richard Burbidge and auditions for the Shakespeare play.

Rough boys from the riverbanks have been called to read the part; all receive short shrift from Burbidge. Then of course, Jack wins the part.

Dwarfed by the boisterous Head of School, a chap called Haringey, Mountjoy looked remarkably at ease. A ragged script in hand, he read the lines of the supposed ploughboy,

'I have a high voice, Sir, I think. The farm boys called me girlish.'

Murmurs from offstage, but Tom put paid to any hint of mirth.

At this point, 'Jack' is called upon to sing a madrigal. Here, Mountjoy stopped.

'I'm sorry, Sir, I haven't got this far.'

'What's that?'

'We've never practised any madrigal.'

'Well, cut that bit for now.'

'I could sing something, if you like, if that would set the mood.'

Tom shrugged. 'OK. just give us something and we'll carry on from there.'

Mountjoy hummed a note or two and started off uncertainly, but then with growing confidence, his voice rose to the rafters.

As the bustle of the afternoon subsided in the hall, lads rehearsing lines or standing idly by the stage, stopped what they were doing and sat quietly to listen. Mountjoy's voice had yet to break, but what he lacked in strength and pitch was made up in bravado. Standing on that stage, surrounded by a group of older actors, he began an ancient ballad, full of romance and regret.

'Oh, I am a bachelor, I live with my son
And I work on the weaver's trade.'

Memories of Jonny Tait, of Christopher and Madeleine drifted past the portraits, as the music died away.

No-one clapped. The play began, with fumbled lines and missed directions. Tom would stop the scene abruptly and then start it off again.

'Where did you learn that song?' he asked. 'It's not exactly William Byrd.'

Mountjoy grinned. 'I don't remember. Probably from home.'

'You have a voice, at least. We'll find a proper madrigal – and hope you never come a cropper like that fellow in the song.'

He settled on a piano stool and hummed the final, winsome words,

'to shield her from the foggy, foggy dew....'

Days began to lengthen. Early birdsong broke the silence. Chestnut trees along the Avenue were dressed in emerald. Boys with cricket bags would race from lessons, clutching bats and pads. I avoided cricket now, cloistered in the shadowy Big School, where blinds blocked out the light.

'Thanks,' Tom said. 'It's heavy going on your own. Let's stir them up.'

The two of us were working side by side. Mountjoy found encouragement in everything and everyone. You understood how Rosalind had once upon a time been played, full of buoyant swagger, like the Christopher of old.

Christopher. I often wondered if he'd come to watch his son. Would he be the same old feckless friend whom we admired? I had transformed into a beak, half deaf into the bargain. If Christopher was coming, it was better that we did not meet.

'Good work, lads. You're on the way.'

Tom was giving breathless notes. Boys sat on the stage or lounged on metal chairs in Sunday shirtsleeves, looking satisfied.

'Mountjoy, think about projection. Don't forget the gallery. People need to hear the words. Now everyone, the final moments – build the tension – after all, the Queen of England's coming up on stage.'

After he had finished, Tom said 'Mountjoy, look, you're doing well. But your voice is light and this place feels like a barn. You must give it everything.'

'Thank-you, Sir.' A sudden grin. 'It's much more fun than cricket.'

'Well, I hope your parents will be coming. I should like to meet them.'

'Mother's here on Friday. Father's coming down on Saturday.'

'Then perhaps we'll bump into each other on the Upper Field.'

So, Commem began with all the buzz, when every smart hotel was filled and there were CCF parades and gym displays.

'Home Team, I rely on you to make these parents welcome,' Mel addressed us when we met in break. 'It's about the only time we ever let the drawbridge down. Put your best foot forward, wear a smile and don your Sunday best. Drinks are in the Rose Garden from six. Let's hope it doesn't rain.'

Walled in honey coloured stone, the Rose Garden across the street had been Bill's sanctuary, a quiet retreat from cares and irritations of the day. Cloudy skies and thoughts about the future weighed less heavily while pruning clematis and climbing roses.

Mel was not a gardener and the weeds had had a field day. Paving stones were full of moss, the lawn was patched with yellow leaves and beds were home to bugs and viruses of every kind. But with a week to go, the trailers of dead leaves were bundled off and in a final sprint, the last few dead heads were removed. The lawn was rolled, the borders neat, the roses clipped and trimmed.

I biked up to my digs, to smarten up for Mel's reception. Gazing at the tiny mirror, dabbing Brylcreem on my hair, I looked healthier than I had been for many years. I pushed a lock of hair back, flashed a grin at my reflection, half recognised the features of a chap I'd known some years before, then carefully I tucked the plastic hearing aid behind the ear. I wiped a speck from off the suit and buckled on my cycle clips.

I was early for the party, but I pushed the metal gate and stepped in through the narrow arch. Maids, who cleaned the private side were waiting, trays in hand, with cold white wine in shallow glasses. They looked oddly out of place in black and white beside the brilliant colours of the roses.

Mel stood in a thick tweed suit in earnest conversation with a parent in a pillbox hat, whose back was turned towards me. Frank was waiting, bald and hunched, clutching a glass between both hands. Jolyon and lurcher wandered down the pathways, sniffing roses, while above the swallows swooped and dived. Light began to fade; a scent of honeysuckle wafted by.

In a clearing to my left, Melissa Melvin chatted to another group, an aged couple, perched on shooting sticks. Melissa had an eye for wallflowers and the shy, uncertain types. Her no-nonsense welcome put the waverers at ease and made even the stiffest feel that they were among friends.

'Charlie! Why, you must have met the Willoughbys.'

A chalk white hand was stretched in my direction. We had never met, but I knew Willoughby, their son, one of those easy-going lads, who leave no trace of any kind. No memories of sporting triumphs or disgraces mark their paths or etch their names in gold upon the boards. The waters close upon their leaving, as if they had never been – until years later, they return with old school ties, reminiscing, dewy-eyed about their youthful escapades.

'Mr Wallace. Yes, I think we've heard of you from Benjamin. You are new, like Mr Melvin. Benjamin has told us that the House has undergone a change,' he said, 'not always for the best.'

Gradually, the garden filled with couples in their cocktail dresses, tweedy fathers grumbling about the chance of rain. A happy murmur drifted round the walls. I made polite enquiries, observations on the day's parade and said I thought Commemoration brought the best out of the school. I chatted to a colonel on the prospects for the next election and a pleasant clergyman who claimed to know Profumo.

Then a tap upon my shoulder. 'Charlie – let me introduce you to the Mountjoys. Mrs Mountjoy, this is Mr Wallace, our new tutor. I've asked him to keep an eye on your young reprobate. Jonny's done extremely well – a credit to the family. We were saying, weren't we, that the Town could do with decent rooms. Times like this are hard on parents. Mrs Mountjoy's been obliged to stay at the Three Tuns, which, as you know is just a pub, albeit quite convenient.'

Clad in a black cocktail dress that fell to just above the knee, she wore a little pillbox hat.

'It's good to meet you, Mr Wallace.'

Then she raised her eyes and we were gazing straight at one another. Clear blue eyes, whose irises were flecked with dots of green; hair that still looked burnished – and the subtle angle of the chin. Neither of us spoke.

'Right,' said Mel, 'if I may leave you? Charlie, would you just bring Mrs Mountjoy up to date about her son?'

He turned to join the party, leaving Isobel and me alone, beside a wall of climbing roses.

215

Isobel was first to speak. 'I saw your name on last term's list. I wondered if it might be you. Jonny says you're helping with the play.'

'Indeed, I am.'

'Well, that's splendid.'

Short staccato words, as if to keep the sky from falling through the cracks of our surprise.

'I didn't realise,' I said. 'But yes – I'm glad to see you.'

That Madonna face had barely changed in all the years; the glitter of the eyes, the way she moved her head from side to side.

'Well, it's good to meet you. Jonny says, 'Be early for the play', because there's bound to be a crush.'

Before I found an answer, she was gone.

Seven-thirty. Half an hour before the play began. Rattling down the narrow street, towards the old Three Tuns, I passed a group of diners who were finishing their meal. I rang the bell at the wooden booth that acted as reception and waited while the heavy publican hove into view.

'Note for Mrs Mountjoy. I believe she's staying here.'

Grabbing a stub of pencil, I wrote hastily 'I'll meet you in the snug after the show' and signed it 'Charles' – then crossed it out and simply scribbled 'Charlie'.

Perched high in the gallery, I noticed how unlike his mother Mountjoy seemed to be. Her son? It had not crossed my mind. In that brief opening scene when 'Ann' objects to the approaching marriage, Mountjoy strutted in a dress that looked more like an eiderdown. There was nothing ladylike about his whole performance. Confronted by an audience, it was as if he wished to prove himself a real lad, 'boying' all the greatness of the part. Nothing in his posture or delivery was delicate. He slouched and bellowed in a high-pitched tone that bounced along the walls. We must have made a great mistake in casting.

Line by line, things settled down. The role switched from reluctant bride to that old trick of Shakespeare's when young Ann declares

'My father's clothes are in the closet. We will ride away, change clothes, cut hair and come to London.'

Now the stage fills out with actors in the Burbidge entourage – Will Kempe, Henry Condell and a host of famous characters, to land us back in Shoreditch and the cut-out world of Merrie England.

After that, it was a breeze. He played the part of Ganymede in multiple disguises with such zest, while I remembered Isobel once more – that moment on the Oxford train when Jonny Tait had brought the news of her impending marriage. '*Engaged to T.G. Mountjoy of The Manor, Wokingham.*' Mountjoy, Jonny Mountjoy, was her son.

As for Timmy, Toadish Timmy, 'My Intended', he had called her, as if speaking of a plot of land; the marriage must have followed fast upon her father's funeral. The past came tumbling out again, like china from a tray.

Jonny did not in the least resemble Cousin Timothy. Timothy was lumpen; Jonny was a mini-Mountjoy – but not the son of Christopher. The genes were those of Isobel.

Loud applause – the interval. I slipped downstairs to hunt for Tom, who seemed elated by success.

'Cracking show,' he murmured, as a cat who's got the cream. 'Charlie boy, is something up?'

I shook my head. 'I'm sorry, Tom. I have to get away.'

'What's up?'

'I honestly can't tell you. In the morning, possibly…'

He nodded. 'Well, I'm sad you can't enjoy the big hurrah.'

Avoiding colleagues in the hall, I backed across a lane behind and through the kissing gate to where the Abbey Close was bathed in light, past the little alley that led on into the marketplace. The Conduit stood in shadows, hooded, skeletal and cold. All the time, a knot of cold excitement in the stomach. What if the impossible had really come to pass? *In loco parentis* – what if I were *not* 'in loco'? What if it had come to pass – and there were real consequences, real human consequences of that meeting long ago?

Beyond the bar, a snug was lit with ancient carriage lights. The odour of warm beer and cigarettes was overpowering, but there was a high-backed settle, perfect for a *rendez-vous*. I bought a pint and found a seat. Of course, I was too early. Anyway, I doubted she would come.

Half past ten and not a sign. Last Orders given – and then 'Time!' I drained my glass, counted the coins and moved towards the bar. A blurred face flickered through the window and the door swung open. She was there.

'I never expected to see you again.'

'I didn't think you'd come.'

She looked distracted, twisting cotton gloves between her fingers. In the dim light of the lamps, she looked both strained and weary.

'Thank-you for coming, anyway. Did you enjoy the show?'

She nodded, uncommitted.

'He's a good lad and you must be proud.'

'Yes,' she said. 'Of course. I think I am.'

'I didn't realise. And when I saw the name of Mountjoy, I somehow thought of Christopher. But Jonny Tait – remember him? – he told me you were married.'

Still, her mind was far away.

'How is Timmy?'

'Who?' She turned.

'Timmy who?'

'Timothy Mountjoy.'

'Oh, my cousin. Never see him. Busy with the firm.'

'Your husband – '

'Gwilym?'

'Wait a bit. So, Gwilym is your husband now?'

'Gwilym? Yes, he always has been.'

Gwilym? And not Timothy. So, no 'Intended' after all. That must have been a shock for him. Cousin Gwilym won the prize. I rather liked him. He was kind and helpful in those Connaught days.

'Goodness me. I bet you're happy.'

Gwilym, sitting at the piano, teaching me 'The lusty horn,' he must have thought me so naïve. With dancing eyes and boyish grin, he was a Mountjoy, though he never had the others' looks. He was small and wiry, unlike Christopher and Isobel.

'So, you married that November, soon after the fire.'

'Yes – he was my knight in armour. Gwilym saw to everything. Dealt with the disaster. We were close – as cousins often are. Gwilym stood beside me and he never let me down. Told Mama that we would be a proper Mountjoy family.'

I wondered what a proper Mountjoy family involved.

'So, you married Gwilym,' I repeated rather pointlessly. 'I bet he made you happy.'

There was silence for a while.

Then suddenly she said 'You understand? I always thought you did. I thought we'd never meet again, that you had disappeared and gone to live an actor's life.

Mother mentioned it one day – she said she'd helped to fix you up. That was the only time that she referred to you by name, since – well, since that business with Christopher and Josh. It never crossed my mind that you would surface like a cork.'

'I never meant to, but for this.' I tapped the plastic hearing aid. 'So how did Gwilym save you?'

'Don't you really understand? It was what Elizabeth would call a 'shot gun' marriage. There was lots of gossip. Mother couldn't stand the word. There'd been far too many shotguns breaking up the family.'

'You and Gwilym? Honestly?'

She looked at me, incredulous. 'I was four months gone – sixteen weeks, the doctor said.

'You mean that you were pregnant in the summer?'

'In July.'

'Four months gone and far too late for any termination. Anyway, when Millie…. Mother wouldn't hear of it – again. Gwilym had been keen on me since childhood. He was up for it. Gwilym was as loyal as his word.'

'But then it wasn't Gwilym's child?'

'Charlie, think about what happened. Jonny Mountjoy – Jonny Mountjoy – '

' – is my son?'

Had I guessed it? Jonny Mountjoy! Was that really what she meant – had I known it all along? – and blocked the very thought of it, pretended not to recognise those puckish features that were mine? It was not imagination! It had happened after all. Real things have consequences; so-called memories were true. People said that Christopher and I could have been brothers. Jonny looked like Christopher – but Jonny was a real son?

I had been a boy. My sixteenth birthday in September – barely two years older than Jonny would be now. Was it really possible? I stared at Isobel in silence, as the memories came flooding in.

'I don't want you tied up in this,' Christopher had said. 'It might be tricky for us all.'

I was tied to everything, cabined and confined – though like Christopher, I'd tried to wash my hands of the affair.

From the other bar, we heard the sound of regulars departing. 'Good night. Till tomorrow. Just be careful how you go.' Swing and snap of bar room doors and someone lifting tables. Clink of glasses, deep in soapsuds, murmur of a sleepy barman.

Isobel was silent, as the memories revolved.

Walking through the orchard, strewn with yellow leaves and fallen fruit, stooping now and then to pick a plum.

'How could we carry on?' she said. 'By post? By secret meetings?'
On revient toujours à ses premières amours.

'So, Jonny – '

'Yes,' she murmured and I swallowed hard.

'You never said. You never told me anything.'

'We never told a single soul. Mother never guessed.'

'You bottled up the secret. Only Gwilym…?'

'Of course, Gwilym knew. Yes – I lied to Mother of a drunken party back at school. A one-night stand. The man had gone away. I didn't mention names.'

'You never wrote.'

'You were fifteen, you were so very young. What sort of letter could I write? You were at school and miles away. We kept you in the clear. There were detectives everywhere, asking questions about Josh. What was he up to? Who were his friends? Christopher was packed away to National Service in a trice. Everyone was stunned. And Gwilym simply took control. He put some order into things. Then there was Father's inquest. People said he'd dropped the gun and accidentally shot himself. Those months were like some ghastly dream. You think that you'll wake up, but it goes on. Gwilym was a rock.'

I sat in silence, drinking in a past that I'd seen nothing of – the chaos of the Hall, adrift and no-one steadying the ship, except for Gwilym, saintly Gwilym overseeing everything.

'Thanks,' I said. 'What happens now? I'll put things right with you and Jonny.'

'What?' She looked surprised.

'I'll put things right.'

'Charlie – don't you understand that Gwilym is his father?'

'But you said – '

'He is the father. Has been from the very first.'

'What about the truth? – the hut, the mattress. What we did that day? Scored into my memory. And don't pretend you don't remember.'

Isobel looked shocked and frightened.

'Yes, I know you wanted it – '

'But what about the truth?

'The truth! You think that something happened on that evening there, inside the hut – do you think *you* had sired a child? You were fifteen – a boy. And I know – full of fantasy. You think that we –?'

'You know we did.'

'That day? That evening on the mattress?'

'Yes, we did it!'

'No! Forget it, Charlie. In your dreams.'

'We did it. I remember it! Remember every second. You and me together! And your – '

'Charlie, this is not a play. What we did was nothing. Nothing! A mistake – a little teenage fumble in the hay. What went on with Gwilym was more serious and it was real. Yes – *we* did it, him and me. We did it in the Nursery.'

'The Nursery! I don't believe you.'

'Nobody suspected us. Those little secret *rendez-vous.* Not even Elizabeth – until I found I had a child.'

A sealed door had opened for a glimmer of what might have been.

'You ran away that morning and you knew how much it hurt.'

'What could I do? I didn't want to hurt you anymore. You were very, very young.'

'Then you married Gwilym. People say it's boys who walk away. You shut me out and threw away the key.'

'Don't be so hysterical.'

'They call it calf love, silly names like that. I loved you, Isobel. If there's a better word, I'd say it. Love! What else is there to call it. I know just what happened and it's locked inside my memory. My memory! We had it there – right down on that dirty mattress. Don't you dare deny – you know it's true!'

Sheltered in the corner of the snug, I felt her draw away.

'I love you.'

'Charlie, stop it. They might hear you.'

'Let them.'

'Stop it now.'

The barman put his head around the door. 'Excuse me, closing time.'

'We're going' she said, rising. Then she turned and stared at me. 'Charlie, you must let it go. I know it's hard. You have to try. You can't go on pretending to remember what was never there.'

But I knew it, knew the truth, locked within the very marrow. Isobel could not deny the fixative of memory.

I couldn't let her go like that – as if the curtain fell, as if the past could melt away like ice cubes in the water. We were so close I felt her breath, my leg brushing against her knee. A thin blue vein ran down her neck. I had to know the how and why and details of it all.

'Isobel, don't disappear.'

'Come,' I heard her whisper, as she slid along the narrow bench, smoothing a crease at the back of her dress, as with one hand she led me to the door and up the narrow stairs. Touching the cold handle of a bedroom door, we moved inside. A single bed lay in the dark. I smothered her with kisses and she clung and muttered 'Charlie,' flung the coverlet aside and pushed the silken cocktail dress above her thighs. I fumbled with a shirt and shoes and tumbled on the counterpane.

And there we lay, our two hearts beating steadily in time. I wrapped myself around her like the petals of a rose.

'I loved you from the first, my darling love.'

We travelled through those long, lost years, as night gave way to birdsong and we were back at Connaught with the pink azaleas and strips of sunlight on the lake. Time had turned, the wheel revolved and we lay wrapped together in a past we could not wash away.

Night's candles were burnt out and jocund day stood tiptoe on the mountain top.

'Wilt thou be gone?' she said. 'It is not yet near day.'

A knocking on the bedroom door, a quietly insistent tap. Torn from drowsy sleep, I gazed towards the window frame. A pigeon at the pane was pecking at its own reflection. Pages of a book beside my iron bed were fluttering. '*To Christopher from Isobel*' the torn inscription read. The bedroom felt familiar – the basin and a single chair. Fled was that music. High above me hung a sky of deepest blue.

222

Downstairs in the narrow hall, I found a letter on the mat. It had been re-directed many times.

Charlie,
Hope this reaches you. Just to say, I'm coming home.
Tell me where and when to find you.
Ever fondest,
Millie

Chapter Twenty-Two

I met her at the railway station with the chipped green roof. Clouds of steam belched from the train and swallows swooped above the roofs.

One small figure limping down the platform with a battered case, pale, exhausted, with her shoulders bowed. She'd put on weight.

'Millie – am I glad to see you.'

Out of breath, we sat upon the bench by the Memorial Gardens.

'I'm surprised you bothered to reply.' She seemed *distrait* and gazed towards the gleaming Close. 'A pretty place you've got. Not like our usual stamping ground.'

'Come.' I took her suitcase and I led her to the Luckpenny. We ordered tea and scones.

'How are you then?'

'I'm on and off. But mostly off, of late. That's why I'm here, as no doubt you'd have guessed. I'm crippled Charlie. I'm a worn out nag.'

'Your foot?'

'A stage weight. Twenty feet it dropped. Last summer, up at Morcambe. Crushed the bones. For weeks, I couldn't walk. They paid some compensation, but it didn't come too much. I didn't wear those studded boots with toecaps, like they said you should. I couldn't work. What good's a stagehand who can barely walk? And there was I, with nobody to turn to.'

'What about your Mum?'

'Died last year. We sold the stables, but it was knee deep in debt. Just enough to pay the creditors. So, we were left with tuppence. Dad's War Pension barely pays the rent. And then I thought, there's just a chance – an actor fellow that I knew. He won't leave me abandoned, like some others I could mention.'

'Millie, you're my wife. We lived together, till you went away. I'm glad to see you back again.'

'For better or for worse' eh, Charlie? There's no sign of any better. Poorer? Yes – I'm penniless.'

'I'm not exactly rich.'

She looked around. 'Posh School, you're at. I bet it costs a bomb. Don't say they don't pay you good.'

'It's OK, but I'm leaving.'

'Why?'

'I have to.'

'Charlie, you're as bonkers as could be. What are you going to do?'

I took her hand and pressed it. Millie looked as if she'd dragged herself a thousand miles across the world. Her face was lined, the vigour vanished and the vital spark blown out. But on her head the fiery hair was still ablaze with life.

'Resign! You must be mad.' Mel leant against the captain's chair.

'Something's come up, Mel. I can't explain.'

'Charlie, this is serious. Don't chuck it all away. You're on the cusp of a career. That play last week – a triumph. Bainbridge thinks the world of you. He says you turned the whole thing round. He's asking if you'll do the show next year. You've dipped your toe; you've learnt to swim. You'll make a splendid beak.'

'I'm sorry, Mel. You saved me and I'd love to stay, but now I can't.'

He paused. 'Are you in trouble, Charlie?'

'Trouble?'

'With that girl? The one who's blown out of the blue. I saw her in the High Street. Looks a rum old customer to me.'

'Millie is a friend. I'm not in trouble, not with her.'

'So, what's she turning up for, like some character from Hardy? That's what brought it on, I guess. Charlie, am I getting warm? Who's this woman anyway? I hope she isn't threatening you.'

That put him off the scent. 'She wouldn't threaten me,' I said.

'So that's it. I suspected it. That girl's entrapped you, hasn't she? It's not too late to sort this out.'

'Believe me, Mel, she is a friend.'

'You're lying, Charlie.'

'Mel, I'm not. There's other reasons, which are private. Millie doesn't understand. In fact, she said she'd rather stay.'

I lied. I hadn't told a soul that Millie was my wife, richer, poorer, limping in my wake. But Millie was no albatross. In time, she proved a consolation from the wreckage of the past.

Millie joined me in the bedsit, despite protests from my colleagues. Settled in that narrow space, we might have been in Finsbury Park. Once, I found her sitting on the iron bed, beside the window, Keats's poems on her lap, laced with yellow sellotape. She had read *Hyperion,* along with all the Odes.

'Did you like them?'

'Yes and no. He's such a *boy,* a dippy boy. He always wants to fly away. Life is a bitch, but hey, it's all we've got.'

'Well, he'd had a rotten time. Lost both parents to consumption, then he had to watch his brother coughing up his lungs.'

'Worse things happen.'

'Still, for Keats, the dream world was a draw. Dreams were far more real than the misery of living.'

She was unconvinced. 'Look, Charlie, love, I know what life's about, people cheating you. But there's no pot of gold to find. Carry on with what you've got. That's my motto anyway.'

'People dream about a better life. It stands to reason – '

'People dream when they want something they will never get. Once, my dream was Christopher. I'm finished with that now. Keats is like a long, wet dream, as if he's aching to get laid.'

'I'm sure he was.'

'You mean he didn't ever…?'

'No. He didn't ever – '

'Poor wee sod.'

'He died a virgin.'

Millie paused to take this in.

'Well, at least we had it, you and me. When I'm fit – and when I'm better – we can do it all again. I won't make you rich, but you won't have to wet dream any more.'

Millie's body was familiar with that scent of engine oil. She had put on weight – but lying there beside her was a comfort. Millie was no dream of shadows; she was warm and comforting.

'This is Christopher's?' she said, examining the flyleaf.

'Yes, it was.'

'He gave it to you?'

'When he left.'

'A present, was it? Then he must have liked you.'

'We were friends.'

I taught my final classes, marked the essays, set the homework and, as luck would have it, 1 encountered Jonny every day. He was ribbed about the play, but it had put him on the map. Mountjoy was a name about the school.

Days before the end of term, I climbed the stairway to my classroom, to collect a few remaining books. The Williams play was missing and I went to look for it backstage.

Big School was deserted. There were cricket finals on the Upper. Dust motes played around the portraits of the ancient Heads. I clattered down towards the Green Room, where the smell of sweat and Leichner still hung in the air.

A pair of tights was strewn across the floor, a safety pin; the buckle from a shoe appeared and glistened in the dark. No sign of a play book. I was starting back again when from above, there came a sound. Somebody was singing.

The bachelor, the sighing maid, the dew and all its consequences. Jonny was the singer and the consequence of everything.

He finished, bowed towards the portraits, then he turned to me.

'Mr Wallace.'

'Hello, Mountjoy.'

'Hello, Sir. You're leaving us?'

'I am.'

''I'm sorry, Sir. I liked your lessons. And of course, the play.'

He flicked his hair and switched the beam of an electric smile.

'Yes, Mountjoy, I enjoyed them too. And it was good to meet your mother. Do please let her know how very glad I was to see her.'

'It's a shame you didn't meet my father. You'd have liked him too.'

'I'm sure I would. Please send him my regards. You'll do well, if you don't slip up. You could become an actor.'

'I should like that very much. My grandmother, she was an actor. Now she runs a Festival. You ought to come and see her plays. I'm told they're really good.'

'Thanks – I'll see about it.'

'Well, goodbye, Sir. I'll be off for tea.'

We stood a moment longer. Jonny was about to speak; he started, drew a breath – then stopped and vanished down the narrow stairs.

I sat on a metal chair and wept.

Chapter Twenty-Three

20—

I remember, I remember…. Those are pearls that were his eyes….

Millie has no passion to be ghosting down to Connaught. Far too many wraiths along the way.

'Don't go, Charles. It will just upset you. Don't be such a fool.'

Filling cans of water, dropping dahlias in the bin.

'Everyone you thought you knew is dead and rotten now. Look at you, you're crumbling at the seams.'

Eighty-six years old. She's right; with aching knees that scarcely bend and well into the Seventh Age, I'm breathless even climbing up the stairs. Would I ever get there, if I set off on my own, stumbling off a train without a minder or a friend? Death has many thousand exits. Yet, if it be now, 'tis not to come.

We had moved to Shropshire, to a crumbling mansion, curtained by wisteria and neatly trimmed with box trees. There, for many years, I taught the rudiments of classics, cricket and the poets, shadowed by the Blue Remembered Hills.

Millie never quite recovered from her injuries, but gamely took an interest in the boys and taught them how to ride a melancholy cob we'd bought one afternoon in Ludlow Market. Thursdays, she would read the *Daily Star* and in the 1980s travel down to Greenham Common to protest about the bombers.

I had come to love her for her stern unflinching gaze, her honesty and absence of illusion. The bindweed and the honeysuckle twisted round about each other, neither of us rich or poor, united in our sickness and our health.

Once or twice, I heard from Mel that boys were growing restless. 'You would hardly recognise the place,' he wrote. 'No fagging now and all the prefects' privileges gone. CCF is voluntary. There's a move to outlaw uniform.'

After which he added 'Mountjoy's scraped his way to Cambridge. All he really wants to do is act.'

Some years after Mel retired, our correspondence ceased.

Scanning *The Telegraph*, I found that Madeleine had died. A brief obituary referred to her success before the War and then paid tribute to her founding of the Connaught Festival.

We both missed the theatre, although for different reasons. Millie liked the edgy Fringe, while I preferred romantic fare.

'Always trying to escape,' she said. 'This is the only world we've got.'

Since we retired, the days have followed without question or reproach – or with little more reproach than any ancient couple shares, hobbling hand in hand towards to the grave.

Now, this autumn morning, I re-read the invitation

'We warmly invite you to join us in a Gala performance.... The Cast will feature well-known actors and a special guest...'

'Don't go,' Millie urges me. But how can I resist?

In late July of the following year, I travel down to Haslemere; then by taxi through the pinewoods, where the sunlight sparkles – out along the drystone walls and banks of rhododendron, through the iron gateway, plastered with those garish hoardings – *'Welcome to the Connaught Festival!'* Up the steeply winding drive and there before us lies the Hall, gables gleaming like the ace of spades. The great Renaissance portico is open wide to welcome us.

Other cars have been diverted to the picnic area. Guests with hampers, rugs and sunhats drift towards the Rose Garden. Somewhere, by the lake, a peacock screams.

A dark blue limousine is also parked by the front door. A frail figure now emerges, gazes warily around, adjusts the silken summer dress. Cobwebs hang about her cheeks; those cornflower eyes have lost their lustre. Age has withered all of us, but something of the charm remains. She gazes slowly round at these familiar surroundings, throwing a short-sighted glance at an old stager on the lawn.

Now, her silver haired companion, younger, *soigné* and distinguished, waits, immaculately dressed in linen suit and panama. Note that easy confidence, the dazzling smile, the casual sweep across a lock of hair. Anyone would recognise that face from all the gossip columns and the Sunday supplements.

I've followed his career, with cupboards full of cuttings and reviews and mentions in the press. After that first break, a TV Trollope, a detective film, he played romantic leads and soon became a household name, before he moved away to Montreal with a Canadian.

This of course is Jonny Mountjoy, making his return to Connaught Hall. A porter in brocaded uniform appears to greet him and the lady, who looks back towards the stooping fellow on the lawn.

Jonny turns towards him too. Baffled recollection struggles, as his mother totters through the door.

Now he steps across the driveway, full of resolution, a glow of recognition in his eyes.